*A
Harlequin
Romance*

OTHER
Harlequin Romances
by ESSIE SUMMERS

Many of these titles are available at your local bookseller,
or through the Harlequin Reader Service.

For a free catalogue listing all available Harlequin Romances,
send your name and address to:

HARLEQUIN READER SERVICE,
M.P.O. Box 707, Niago a Falls, N.Y. 14302
Canadian address: Stra-ford, Ontario, Canada.

or use order coupon at back of book.

ANNA OF STRATHALLAN

by

ESSIE SUMMERS

HARLEQUIN BOOKS   TORONTO
WINNIPEG

Harlequin edition published October 1975

SBN 373-01917-3

Original hard cover edition published in 1975
by Mills & Boon Limited.

Printed in Canada

1917

To all the readers of my books in lieu of answers to your letters this book is affectionately dedicated.

When an Australian reader realized that an extra book a year could be produced in the time I spent answering readers' mail, she suggested this dedication, saying: 'I'd opt for another book any time.' So here it is with many thanks for your appreciative and inspirational letters.

Essie Summers

CHAPTER ONE

ANNA had thought the coming week was to be one of a strange poignancy, in which she would say farewell to Fiji and hail to New Zealand; when, as far as blood relations were concerned, she would be on her own in a strange city and a new country, even if that same country had been her birthplace. But Fiji was home.

But now, thanks to the letter she had thrust deep into the swinging satin reticule she had carried at her mother's wedding that very day, it seemed she had kin in New Zealand, a grandmother and a grandfather. She wasn't sure it was going to be a good thing, despite that very nice letter. What if they were no more admirable than their son who had ruined – no, *almost* ruined her mother's life?

Mother had been so fine a character it hadn't been possible for anyone to ruin her life. She had been wounded, disillusioned, finally deserted by Alex Drummond, but she had picked up the pieces and carried on, making a wonderful home life for her only child. Now she was reaping the reward of it all. From the moment Doctor Magnus Randal had come to the guest-house for the term of his association with the hospital, Lois Drummond had known a happiness beyond description. It had been something delightful to witness. Anna knew that, and though naturally she hated the thought of parting with her mother for a whole year, she had refused the offer Magnus made for her to accompany them to the Hong Kong hospital where her stepfather was to study certain tropical diseases as a follow-up to his session in Suva.

She wanted her mother to shed all worries, to have no anxieties as to what to do with an only daughter in a foreign city. It would be the first time since her disastrous marriage over twenty-five years ago that Lois would know freedom from all care, family responsibilities, financial worry, emotional deprivation.

Her mother's best friends, the Sylvesters, had offered Anna a home in Auckland. It was only a courtesy relationship, but Aunt Edna and Uncle Alan couldn't have been

7

dearer had they indeed been true family. They were here now, for the wedding, and as was natural with such warm-hearted people, had been responsible for everything Anna couldn't have coped with on her own.

Her mother and stepfather would be returning to Auckland and during that year Anna hoped she might have found a niche for herself, perhaps as a receptionist in some tourist hotel, the only business world she knew. She was flying back with the Sylvesters next week, when she had formally handed over the guest-house to the new owners. Would she now continue with those plans, seek a position? Or would she go down to her father's people?

A stirring of Anna's pulses betokened excitement, a sense of adventure, but she had said nothing to anyone. No shadow must be allowed to fall upon this day for Magnus and Lois. They must go off on their idyllic honeymoon to Singapore, then to Hong Kong, all unknowing that a voice from an unknown past had reached out and called Anna.

She hadn't known a lot about her father, just that he'd been a ne'er-do-well, weak, charming, completely unreliable. She could only faintly remember him. Her mother had told her that when this uncle in Fiji had left her, his only relation, his guest-house, it had seemed like a miracle. She had been able to sweep her husband away from Auckland, from his old associates, from the gambling, the drinking, the unjustified spending, his inability to either stick at a job or keep it.

Somehow Lois had made the old, rundown guest-house pay. It had meant she could have Anna with her while she worked; the life had satisfied Alex for a while ... it hadn't seemed like work at first, running the launch, taking visitors round the coral reefs, or organizing outdoor entertainments, mixing constantly with tourists from all over the world ... moneyed people mostly. Lois had known a breathing-space of renewed hope, of more security. Then the novelty had worn off. As the business extended the work became heavier.

Lois had no one to turn to. Her uncle had been her sole surviving relation, and Alex had vowed he had neither kith nor kin when she had met him. He'd seemed friendless enough, apart from those undesirable cronies, and at first she had been idealistic about providing a family life for

8

someone even more alone than herself. He told a good story . . . he had been knocked about from pillar to post – oh, he'd traded on that, she had excused him much on the grounds that a harsh and cruel childhood had been no basis for a mature adult life. Pity he hadn't turned that imagination to good account . . . what a writer of thrillers he would have made!

Anna had still been very small when Alex had disappeared from Fiji, taking with him the contents of the guest-house safe, and every single treasure that could be turned into ready cash, including Lois's engagement ring. From then on Lois had known a more peaceful existence, if never happiness, because at least now he could not undermine her small daughter's character by his regrettable standards.

Many years later she had been granted a divorce on grounds of desertion and a little over two years ago news of Alex's death had been reported in New Zealand newspapers. He had died quite heroically after saving many miners from an accident in South America. A year later Magnus had come into her life, and Anna had been glad, fiercely glad, even though it meant the disruption of her own life, that for evermore Lois's happiness would be in Magnus Randal's safe keeping and that never again would she know want, fear, disillusionment. There were some things you just knew. Magnus was the same calibre as Lois herself, steel-true, blade-straight. His steadfast eyes, his compassionate mouth, his firm chin all spelled integrity.

Thank goodness Anna had picked up the mail herself this morning, that there had been so much of it, belated letters of good wishes, of farewell to her mother, who had certainly made a niche for herself in the community, last-minute business letters, cards, gifts. She had looked at this one curiously. It was postmarked Roxburgh, New Zealand, and was addressed to herself.

She'd turned it over. Yes, the sender's name was on a sticker at the back: Mrs. Gilbert Drummond, Strathallan, Crannog, via Roxburgh, Central Otago, New Zealand.

Auntie Ed had sometimes talked of Central Otago holidays, where the lakes, snow-fed, were brilliantly blue, and great mountains cradled them; a place of extremes, with very cold winters, very hot summers. A huge, fruit-growing area that was a mecca for tourists at all seasons, with skating, curling and skiing in the winter. That was all she knew.

Even so, the names revived in an extraordinary way, a flash of memory. Gilbert? Strathallan? Of course! Anna and her mother had taken a trip to Britain two years ago, mainly, Anna had guessed, to take her mother's mind off the shock of reading about Alex's death in a New Zealand newspaper.

They had spent some time in Scotland, particularly Perthshire, whence Lois's forebears, the Murrays, had come. One week-end when Lois had gone off to stay with an elderly couple who'd visited Suva, Anna had investigated her paternal side's territory.

She had learned that the Drummonds probably came from Drymen, that a very early forebear had been Gilbert de Dromond, and an Annabella Drummond had married King Robert the Third and had been the mother of James the First of Scotland. Her mother had said long ago that the only time her father had ever mentioned his family, he'd said he believed Anna was a family name, and he would like his daughter to be called that. Anna remembered now that in her probings she had discovered that a Stuart king, mindful of the fact the Drummonds had shared the misfortunes of that Royal House, had created one of them Viscount Strathallan. It had given Anna some feeling of having roots on her paternal side.

So it had been true, that feeling. Here was an estate in the South Island of New Zealand, a place predominantly settled by the Scots, bearing the name of Strathallan!

But there was no time for dwelling on that strange, exciting letter now. This was the time for farewelling. Mother looked wonderful, just like a girl . . . the palest green dress, filmy and slim-fitting, a colour that looked like the translucent spray upflung from the Fijian surf, with the sun shining through; she had a floppy crinoline hat of the same shade, her green eyes like stars, flakes of pink in her cheeks, love in her eyes . . . now the hat was being flung on her bed and she was fluffing up her hair . . . a quick, laughing look at her reflection, Magnus coming to stand in the doorway, every inch the impatient bridegroom, 'Lois, my love, I'll take you as you are . . . no more titivating, come on!'

A frantic last check of bags and suitcases, then out to

where a beaming Fijian driver in his draped *sulu* waited beside his taxi. They all knew and loved Mother. Scores of people were piling into their cars, when they were off for the airport. Strange to think that for Anna too this scene would soon be just a memory . . . so much of her life had been spent here . . . coconut palms, hibiscus blooms, sugar-cane, banana trees, coral reefs, canoes, frangipanni blossoms, rich and creamy, a happy, laughing land. But in Auckland there were hibiscus bushes too, and bougainvillea, and heat . . . it wouldn't be too strange, unless, of course, she did go down to that so-different, frighteningly rugged country south of the Waitaki River where her father's parents longed and waited to see their dead, wayward son's only child.

A few days later, with the August sunshine predicting the return of spring to the Southern Hemisphere, she spread out her letter on Aunt Edna's daughter's desk, to investigate and consider this gesture from her father's past. She looked out of the window, with its magnificent view of the Waitemata Harbour, beautifully centred on Rangitoto Island with its symmetrical contours, knowing she was alone in the house and could study it undisturbed.

Her grandmother had written: 'My dear granddaughter, this letter will come as a surprise to you, I believe, just as it was a surprise to me to learn that I had a granddaughter. I think we must all long to be able to leave a little bit of ourselves behind when we have shuffled off this mortal coil, and I'd thought that this would be for ever denied Gilbert and myself.

'I was sad about this, because ever since the first Drummond reached the shores of Otago and founded this estate of Strathallan, there has been an Anna Drummond here, till our generation, but your great-aunt Anna, your grandfather's only sister, died at twenty-one. We tried for so long to trace Alex, my poor wayward son, in the last ten years, but failed. Before that he had always written for money when he needed it. But he always just gave us postal addresses and never told us he had married.

'We had last heard of him in Buenos Aires, then nothing more till we heard about his accidental death in the Argentine. We tried and tried to get word, but this mining village was so remote, so small, that we failed. I think a little bit of me died then. It seemed as if he had never been. And he had been such a dear little affectionate boy – till he grew up.

'When we failed to hear anything about him, his father stopped even speaking about him. Hope was, at last, dead. It aged him more than I like to see. We've been such pals all through our married life, but now I feel he is so scared to have me see how much he is grieving that he has shut off a little of himself. For the first time in my life I feel I cannot comfort him. He needs a new interest to take him out of himself.

'You will wonder how we heard of you. A neighbour of ours – well, she lives over at Corriefeld, which is a few miles away, but she is truly a neighbour in devotion – went with her husband to visit Fiji and stayed at your guest-house. You will remember her, I'm sure, despite the numbers you must meet, because she's Elizabeth Forbes, better known as Elizabeth Goldie, who writes books about gardening and floral art. She and her husband were abolutely intrigued by your resemblance to my husband. He too has that unique combination of fair hair and brown eyes. Only now his hair is almost white. The fact that your name was Drummond set them on the trail, and they made a few discreet inquiries. Please don't hold that against them – they were really discreet. In talk with your mother, who was, they said, the finest person, they found she had come from Auckland – Alex wrote twice from there – and that she had married an Alex Drummond but appeared to think he had no close relatives.

'They flew home via Auckland, and are pretty sure they traced the marriage. Although she worried a little, lest it might upset your mother, Elizabeth felt we had a right to know we had a granddaughter. She was pretty sure your mother had had to take the place of both parents and had suffered much through our son. I was glad, oh, so glad, when she told me that your mother was engaged to a very fine doctor on the island. It seems to me that the Forbes were meant to be in Fiji at this time, and to be told, without having to probe, that when your mother and stepfather leave for Hong Kong, you were coming to New Zealand to live.

'Would you come to see us, Anna? We won't be possessive or press you to stay. We would just like to see you, and if it wouldn't upset your mother in any way, I would like to keep in touch with you. I would also like, when they come back to New Zealand, to meet your mother. Had it not been that you were leaving Fiji, I would have taken a holiday there myself, just to see you. I won't expect an answer till you get settled in Auckland – Elizabeth told me you were going to a friend of your mother's there – but how I pray Gilbert may yet see a descendant of his. Elizabeth told me that although you are young you have great strength of character, and that the friendship between you and your mother is just beautiful to behold; that despite the fact it meant you must part from her, you seemed unreservedly glad that she is at last to have a second chance of happiness.

'Coming from Elizabeth that means a great deal. She herself had a ne'er-do-well husband, then found her true love in Rossiter Forbes. The last few years have compensated her greatly. I was afraid to tell Gilbert at first about you, in case you wanted nothing to do with us, but we've had very few secrets from each other in a long married life and he sensed that something was disturbing me.

'If you do not wish to come, I shall try to understand. I think women bear these disappointments better than men, but for your grandfather's sake, please come, dear child. He has not seen this letter. I have told him only that I was going to write you, not that I was asking you to come to us. Come and look us over, then return to Auckland if you must. We'll ask no more.

> Lovingly,
> Grandmother.'

Anna's eyes were full of tears just as they had been when she had read it first. It had a strange sound to one who, till now, hadn't known of a relation in the world, save her mother.

'We'll ask no more.' The pathos in that was almost unbearable. She picked a ballpoint up from the desk, began to write. She told her grandmother she had brought her mother's car across from Fiji, that she would drive down the North Island, cross Cook Strait on the car ferry, and come down the South Island so she could see the whole country, almost, as she came. So she couldn't give a definite date for her arrival as she didn't know the distances involved, but would ring Strathallan as she neared Central Otago.

Thus far, good, all right for a preliminary, but how to phrase the rest of her letter? What was the clan motto of the Drummonds? ... *Gang warily.* Well, she *would* go carefully. They sounded all a girl might hope for in grandparents, but you never knew. There might have been some reason for her father's instability of character, his waywardness. She mustn't hurt her mother by becoming too deeply involved too soon. This letter read all right, but the proof of the pudding was in the eating, in this case, in the quality of life as lived at Strathallan. But even while she knew she must proceed with caution, she couldn't help responding to the loneliness that was inherent in that letter. But she would make no rash promises about staying on ... yet.

She wrote: 'Your letter has moved me, of course. I thought my mother and myself were quite alone in the world. That's why I was so glad when my stepfather came into her life. I've not told her about your letter yet, which may sound strange, but it arrived on her wedding-day, and I thought that that day belonged to the present and the future, not to the past.

'I'm so sorry for all you must have suffered through the years and am only sorry we didn't know about you sooner, but hope that now, in some way, we may all find compensation for this lack. More I can't say. It may not be easy for you, having someone of my age projected into your ordered lives, but I'll try not to disrupt them. I think it was sweet of Elizabeth Forbes. We took a great fancy to her and had read her books for years, even though she wasn't writing about gardening in Fiji! We sensed that in later years she'd come into a time of greater happiness, when she wrote of the delightful garden she had created when she married again and left Lavender Hill for Pukerangi, which she said so truly meant The Hill of Heaven. I'm looking forward to meeting her again. It was a kind thought of hers, perhaps sensing I'd be a little lonely when Mother and Magnus took off for Hong Kong. I won't start looking for a job in Auckland till I've seen you. Once I get a position it might be some time before I got leave.

'Please understand if this letter doesn't flow very well.

14

It's not easy to write. Until I arrive, my love to you and Grandfather,

Anna.'

She stared at it a long time. 'Love to you and Grand-father.' Words she had thought she would never be able to pen. It had been completely out of her ken.

What was it Magnus had said, kissing her good-bye? 'God bless you, little one. May many a glad surprise be just around the corner for you as it was for me. This time last year I didn't even know my ideal woman really existed.'

He'd meant, of course, that marriage might be ahead of her, too, but *this* was what had been around the corner. Kinsfolk of her own. Well, the die would be cast when she posted her letter. Butterflies fluttered uneasily in her stomach. New relations could be such unknown quantities. She supposed it was like meeting future in-laws for the first time. They might be kindred spirits, they might not.

She heard a door open and close. She would go down and tell Auntie Ed and Uncle Alan now. They'd be glad for her, perhaps a little apprehensive, and would assure her that their home was always open to her if she didn't want to stay in the south. She would ask them not to tell Mother and Magnus yet. Time enough for that. She'd write herself and just say she was off exploring New Zealand before settling down.

It was more than a week later. What an extraordinarily varied country New Zealand was. It ranged from a semi-tropical North to an extremely Scottish-type Far South, not only in the history of the pioneer settlers and the number of Macs in the telephone directories, but in the landscape too, except that there was no heather, but higher mountains.

Now she had left Dunedin behind, journeyed thirty-five miles south to Milton and had headed west beyond there. This was like the Border country, rolling hills just such as she had loved in Scotland, the land of her forebears, hills cropped close and sheep-dotted, whin-hedged ... or did they call it gorse here?

Beyond and above were hills with here and there snowy shoulders, streams sang loudly, clouds like giant soap bubbles scattered and amassed, restless and beautiful, larks soared in the sky, magpies swooped. So many English birds were here, many new to her. She must get a book on birds, be able to recognize them all, the natives and the exotic ones. She loved the New Zealand custom – a relatively new custom, she'd been told – of putting over bird-calls as signals on the radio just before the news. They were native bird-calls, with enchanting notes that chuckled and twanged and suggested cool forests, mossy-green underfoot, dappled with leaf-shadows.

She had meant to ring Crannog from Dunedin, to announce the time of her arrival to her grandparents, but with her fingers in the toll slot, panic had seized her and she had stopped. What if her first sight of Strathallan daunted her? What if it was like that near-derelict house on the main road she had passed yesterday, long unpainted, with a rusting tin roof, cracked window-panes, a verandah lolling lopsidedly under its overgrown vines because the posts had rotted through? What if – well, she'd changed her mind?

She had told her grandmother it might be ten days before she reached Dunedin because she was going to sight-see all the way. So she would put up, unannounced, at the Crannog pub listed in the directory, no doubt a relic of the gold-mining days, because it was called The Pan and Shovel, go out the next morning to drive past Strathallan, inspect it, drive back and ring her grandparents from the pub. If she found it too unattractive, she'd tell them, on the phone, that she could stay only a few days this time, that she had to be back in Auckland for a job. How odd that only now, nearing journey's end, she should feel this reluctance!

She had little more than a hundred miles to go, so she hadn't left Dunedin early. Crannog was just past Roxburgh. She dawdled, taking a keen interest in every miners' monument among the hills and minor gorges on the way, stopping at small-town museums where, because it was a little early for many tourists yet, those in charge delayed her each time, warming to her evident interest.

It was a pity, then, that just before she got to Miller's Flat, a truck with a load of stuff from some demolition job on board passed her, dropped a piece of four-by-two with some enormous nails in it and Anna ran over them with both offside tyres.

Despite the fact there had been quite a lot of traffic passing till now, she had to wait nearly half an hour before someone came along and offered to send out a mechanic from the Flat, and even then it was an age before he arrived, jacked up her car, and took the tyres into the township to repair. He explained that they had had an incredible number of urgent jobs in, and he had had to finish one before coming out to her.

'You'd better come in with me. You're going to get pretty cold waiting here at this time of day. No one'll pinch your car with two tyres off. Lock it up, though.'

Now she did wish she had set off sooner and had not been decoyed into stopping. The early spring night was closing in fast and the hills to the west would soon shut off the sun that was already dropping low.

By the time the mechanic returned her, and attached the tyres, the sky had a leaden look. He asked, 'How far are you going tonight? Not too far, I hope, that's a snowy sky.'

'Is it?' She sounded surprised. She'd just taken it for the grey of twilight. Of course she'd never seen snow fall and had assumed it would be all over. 'I'm going to Crannog. It won't fall for some time, will it?'

'Probably not, but waste no time. If your home's there you'll want to make it. But if you're just touring, I'd say put up at Roxburgh – but even if you go on to Crannog, at least you won't be going through the gorges. They're on beyond Alexandra, the Cromwell Gorge and the Kawarau Gorge.'

She thanked him and was away. She was glad she'd had some coffee from her flask when waiting for a motorist to show up, because the temperature was falling rapidly. She switched the heater on.

She turned a corner sharply a few miles further west and met swirling snow in a white-out sort of skiff. It was most alarming by its very strangeness and lack of visibility but lasted only a few moments. The light came through again, wanly, but reassuringly.

The moment she could see again, she was enchanted . . . it lay like a filmy veil over everything. Nevertheless, she kept to a crawl. Common sense, if not experience, dictated that. A hundred yards or so and the road was clear again, though the wind-driven snow lay in flakes against the dry grass tufts of the verge, the dead stalks of last autumn above the sweet green of the new season's grass.

Well, it wasn't far to Roxburgh now. She might make it before any more snow fell. She'd stop there. It was larger, so she could get a good choice of accommodation. She was beginning to feel hungry.

Around the next corner snow was sheeting the road thinly. The car skidded a little. What an alarming feeling! Your hands were on the wheel, but there was no control. Conditions like these were right out of her ken. This road was so winding. The enormous Clutha River must be on her right – she couldn't see it – she just hoped it didn't swirl near the road on any of these bends. Visibility was getting nil and in this half-light one's lights were of little use. You needed full dark for contrast. She wished she had asked more about any hazards to expect. But then locals never recognized hazards unless they were really startling ones. Custom dulled the edge of danger.

The darkness deepened and now her headlights showed up fruit orchards and a lighted window or two. If the snow came on really heavily, she might have to knock someone up and ask a bed for the night. How ghastly! You wouldn't know who might answer your knock. It was a terrifying thought. Even apart from fears, it could be vastly embarrassing. No one would relish having to put a stranger up. You could get a busy mother, already harassed by many things, or an elderly, frail wife, put out by this descent upon her by a feckless, ignorant stranger. Anna pressed on, the wiper only just coping with the sleety snow driving against the windscreen, but still giving her a fan of clearish glass through which to peer.

Her lights were good, but the whitening of the landscape was somehow diluting their strength now, rendering the terrain almost featureless. She hoped she was still driving to the left side of the white line that had long since disappeared, yet not too far to the left, or she might tilt off the verge into a ditch. She set her teeth and ground on, tense with anxiety.

She carefully steered round a left-bearing corner of the hillside and then, with ghastly suddenness, into her vision loomed a horrible sight – a man, staggering from side to side, with his face covered with blood. Anna turned left instinctively and stopped dead as he lurched almost unseeingly towards the right of her. He put out a hand as if to ward off the obstacle and fell across the bonnet.

She got out on the passenger side as less risky and was round the car in a jiffy, clutching him. 'What's happened? No, don't tell me. I'm too near the corner. Come on, come on! *Move!* Get into the car, and I'll drive on a bit, then stop, so you can put me in the picture.'

She guided and tugged him to the door, wrenched it open, he half fell in and Anna heaved him the rest of the way. She bent down, lifted his legs, thrust them in, whipped round the front of the car, tried to slide in under the wheel, found he had fallen over into her seat, managed to lever him up, knew her suit would be covered in blood, but that didn't matter, and she got her door shut smartly. Great relief. She'd made it before anything else came round the corner.

She drove on a few yards, peering out anxiously in case another victim was on the road, or their presumably smashed car, saw a wider curve that seemed to snuggle in under some crooked willows and very gingerly eased the car on to the verge.

He hadn't said one word in all this. Heaven send he hadn't passed out on her, because she had to know if there were other people involved, where his car was, what had happened. He might have been stumbling along some time. She snapped on the inside light and had to clap a hand over her mouth to stop her instinctive scream.

No wonder he hadn't seemed to see her car till almost on it . . . his eyes were injured, she thought. She made a grab over the back seat for a white cashmere headscarf she had tossed over there and, very gently, in case she did him further injury, wiped his face from the forehead down, and was immensely relieved to see him open both eyes. There was so much gore she had been prepared for anything. The gash that was causing it ran clear across his forehead.

She said, as matter-of-factly as she could manage, 'That's going to need stitching, but I can stop the bleeding a fair bit. But you must tell me, before you pass out on me, if you're hurt anywhere else – inwardly, say. Ribs broken, or—'

His speech was slurred, but she leaned close to his mouth. 'No . . . don' think so. I walked okay, but—'

'Was anyone in the car with you, and where is it?'

'It's – it's only a coupla chains along from here.' He gave

a strange laugh. 'Can't work it out in the metric system at the moment. Sorry about that. Sure I am.'

'Shut up!' said Anna sharply. She'd just realized something. He reeked of beer. Fool! To mix drink and driving was no less than criminal. '*Was there anyone else in the car?*'

'Sure there is. Barney — friend of mine. Poor ol' Barney. But he's all right, pickled to the ears as usual. You know Barney?'

'I don't! And I've no wish to know him. You're a bright pair. And how would you know if he's all right . . . in *your* condition?'

Again he gave that strange laugh. 'He's soaked like a sponge. Ninety-five per cent alcohol, that's Barney. You can't damage a sponge, lady. It's like punching foam rubber.'

Fear and panic had now given place to rage in Anna. She gave him a little shove away from her even while she went on mopping.

She felt in the pocket for her first-aid tin, brought out a pad of lint, clapped it on the gash with rather less than tenderness, wound on the widest roll of bandaging the kit contained, saw the blood still coming, and tied the by-now-indescribable scarf firmly on top of it.

He seemed to pull himself together. 'Sorry about this . . . road was slippery . . . besides, it was really your fault.'

Good heavens, he certainly *was* drunk! 'Now try to stay conscious long enough to point out where the car is so I can satisfy myself that this Barney creature *is* all right.'

She drove on, peering from side to side. The casualty seemed to pull himself together. 'There it is . . . beyond the culvert. Good job I didn't go broadside into it. It would have blocked the road. Pull well in. It's not a good night for other traffic to see your car.'

It was faintly discernible, tilted on one side with its nose in the ditch. The man managed to get out, to her surprise. She took his arm and guided him over the road. She shone her torch in. Yes, a huge man, comfortably slumped in a corner, seemingly all right and breathing stertorously.

Somehow they got him out. Anna was surprised at her own ferocity. She shook Barney unmercifully. 'You've just got to help yourself out. Do you hear? We can't leave you to get help to shift you. You'll freeze to death. And you're too heavy to lift. Get up! Get up, I say! Out! Up ... come on, you great big lump, up!'

The other victim was hauling madly at his friend, but had gone quiet except for grunts of effort and pain jerked out of him. How he did it, Anna couldn't guess, but he was prising Barney up a little. Suddenly Barney stopped being a dead weight and came to life, helping them. What a relief! His legs buckled under him on the snowy road, though. They hauled him to his feet, got his arms round their shoulders, but intoxication made the man's limbs so flaccid, they lost their grip again and again.

Suddenly the sodden hulk said, 'Pity about your car, Calum. Nice car, that. I thought you were a better driver than that, pal. Very shorry, though.'

The other man said, 'Shut up! Try to get yourself over the road. This girl'll get us to Roxburgh hospital. C'mon, move!'

Somehow they got him over and pushed him into the back seat. Anna wasn't worrying about his comfort, she wanted to get rid of this unsavoury pair as fast as she could. Calum was swaying on his feet.

She got him into the car and buckled the safety belt round him. He protested, she thought. She said in a hard tone, 'I've got to make sure you're secure in case *I* skid off the road. I'm not used to snow. I've never even seen it falling in my whole life till now. Tell me, I'll have to grind along all the way in my lowest gear, won't I?'

'Good lord! Where were you brought up? On a desert island?'

'Exactly,' said Anna tartly, 'on a desert island. Well, a Pacific one. *Is* that what I do?'

'Yes, slow as you can. Shouldn't be too bad from here. 'S' only about three miles.' Then he lost all interest in the proceedings.

It seemed like twenty to Anna. A longing for a soft Fijian night with tropical stars above and a clear, clear sky shook her with an intensity that surprised her. This, for her, was an alien element, and frightening. Just imagine ... some men climbed mountains for sport!

Suddenly the road was clearer ... there were lights, and cars proceeding carefully but not as slowly as Anna ... she saw footpaths. Then a man walking along one came into view. She braked, sprang out, rushed up to him, said, 'Look, I'm a stranger to New Zealand, and don't know Roxburgh. I came upon an accident a few miles back. I've got a badly gashed man in the front seat and one hopelessly drunk in the back. Can you direct me to the hospital? The injured one seems to have passed out.'

He gave an exclamation. 'Well, you sure struck it unlucky for a tourist! Lady, I'll come with you. Any idea who they are?'

'Well, the one in the back is called Barney. He's not hurt, but he's had a skinful. The other man said you can't hurt a sponge. He's called Calum. But—'

'Yes, I know. But we're wasting time, you mean. It'd have to be Barney and Calum, of course.'

They must be well-known soaks, Anna thought.

The man opened the back door, 'Shove over, mate,' he said to Barney, and to Anna, 'Drive straight on down the main street . . . hospital is on the left, with trees in front and a stone wall. I'll tell you when to stop. They were pretty lucky they got someone like you – you've managed to bandage Calum up. You'll be okay here. The traffic's kept the road pretty clear.'

Anna felt a little better. Soon this would be just a memory. She'd hunt for a bed at some hotel. She'd ask this man to go with her, perhaps, because any receptionist would rear back when confronted by the sight she must present . . . covered with gore, her shoes plastered with slush, to say nothing of reeking of beer from Barney's close embrace when he'd staggered and nearly fallen.

'My name's Rod Staikes. We'll get Calum in first. They can get some orderlies to get Barney out. He won't know what's happening anyway.'

The man called Calum opened his eyes as she stopped, said, 'You made it! Remind me to put in for a medal for you, girl,' and lapsed again. Rod Staikes went inside, reappeared with a couple of men, and they got Calum out. The fresh air revived him and he straightened up, said, 'I can make it under my own steam, I think. You two get Barney in. He might be hurt, though I doubt it.'

It took the three men, eventually, to carry Barney in. He was enormous. Calum staggered. Anna said, 'Better lean on me. If you crash you'll start the bleeding again.'

He grinned, 'The luck's all mine, not Barney's. Sure I'll lean on you . . . very nice too.'

Anna said vindictively, '*You* may enjoy it. *I* won't.' She thought to herself that an amorous drunk was twice as bad as just a drunk!

Calum said mournfully, 'I thought you were an angel of light. That's just not nice.'

They got inside and suddenly, thankfully, it was all cleanliness, warmth, efficiency. Her responsibility was almost over. Rod Staikes explained succinctly what had happened. They all seemed to know each other. The Sister was cool, brisk, quick without bustling.

They put Barney into a chair and left him to snore on happily. The doctor arrived presently. The Sister had started to mop up Calum's face and head once she'd got Anna's bandaging off. It was far from a nice sight and began to bleed again, but not profusely. Anna considered it was less serious than she'd thought.

A good thing about smaller hospitals was that you weren't banished. Anna felt she'd like to see this thing through. The doctor greeted Calum as a friend, and set to work. He said to Anna, 'Are you squeamish? I hardly think so, because Sister says it was quite expertly bandaged, but you can retire if you want to.'

She said, 'I've worked as a nurse-aide. When you're done perhaps you'd advise me on my choice of a hotel for the night. I'd meant to go on further, but first the snow, then this, held me up. I think I'll need some explaining. Any respectable hotel could have doubts.'

Calum looked across at her. He was focusing better now. 'I'll have to buy you a new outfit. You can put up at our place for the night.' He said to the doctor, 'Kitty'll want to thank her.'

The doctor said, 'Think you're going home, do you? I think we'd better keep you here overnight. We'll alert the police about your car, though this young lady told Rod it was well off the road.'

Calum said, 'Rolf, I must go home. The children can get a bit much for Kitty on her own.'

'Bunkum. I'd back Kitty to cope with anything. Though I daresay you could go . . . this isn't as deep as I'd thought.

23

We'll have to get transport for you, though. And it'll be a problem. Every taxi will be engaged for the Hydro Ball.'

Calum groaned. 'Kitty'll fear the worst if I'm kept here.' He looked across at his rescuer. 'Most of the pubs will be full tonight. And you need cleaning up.' He seemed to be sobering up fast. 'Kitty will want to meet you, to thank you for all you've done. You managed that difficult drive pretty well, yet you must have been all shook up. How about it? It'll get me home, and we can put you up. Much nicer than a pub, our place. Rolf, she deserves a medal. She made a damned good stop when I loomed up in front of her car. I was weaving, I'm afraid. And even if at first I cursed her for a hit-and-run driver, at least she had second thoughts and came back.'

Anna was struck dumb, but only for a moment. 'Hit-and-run? What on earth do you mean? How could I possibly have hit you? Turned *back*? I was on my way *to* Roxburgh when you appeared like a ghost in my headlights. Look, you're too drunk to have the faintest idea of what you're saying! I certainly *won't* spend the night at your place. I'm pretty fussy where I stay, it's a hotel for me!'

To her immense surprise he did not humble himself and apologize for his unjust accusation. Instead he glared at her as fiercely as she had glared at him. '*Drunk?* have you gone mad? I'm not the one who was drunk, it was Barney. You darned well know that. Let me tell you I've never been drunk in my life!'

The doctor put a restraining hand on his arm. 'Now, don't get excited, Calum. You're in no shape for losing your temper. It looks to me as if you're both addled. She's just as entitled to be as flaming mad as you are. More, in fact. She acted as your rescuer and you've blamed her for tipping you off the road. And though you mightn't realize it, you're positively reeking of beer. I can only suspect that Barney, as usual, had a kitful of bottles.'

'He did. This gash wasn't the windscreen – it was a bottle.' His face changed completely. He looked at Anna ruefully. 'I'm sorry – you'd better put it down to shock. Naturally you'd think I was tight. I saw old Barney collapse into the gutter as I came into Roxburgh and thought I'd better get him to his shack and into bed.'

'You would,' said the doctor. 'Too tender-hearted by far.

24

And look what a mess it's got you into. The police would have picked him up and a night in the cell would have sobered him up properly. I dare not risk that now – in case he's got some injury we can't get him to tell about, so *we'll* have to put up with him. The staff are going to love that!'

All of a sudden Sister Grey and Rod Staikes collapsed into laughter. Anna gazed at them almost exasperatedly for a moment, then succumbed too. The doctor said hastily, 'Now, Calum, don't join in – you're wrinkling up your forehead. Wait till I'm done.' He turned to Rod, 'I thought you told me yesterday you were taking Jenny to the Ball?'

'I am. I'd better ring her and explain what kept me. She asked me to run over to a friend's and lend her a silver evening bag for the same affair and said not to be too long.' He disappeared.

Anna felt she must do something to compensate for her too-swift judgment of this Calum. She said, 'The snow seems to have stopped falling. I *could* take him home if he really *must* go, and come back. That is, if it's not too far. I've already come over that road and it's not too bad, negotiated with care. I wouldn't attempt it if it was still snowing.'

'It's not that way,' said the doctor. 'It's the other side of Roxburgh, but not a great distance. But, Calum, I'd rather you stayed here. Kitty'll be all right.'

He shook his head. 'I'd like to offer this girl a bed for the night. Kitty'd never forgive me if I did less. Would you take me home?'

Anna nodded. 'You can guide me. It was more scaring before. I had you flaking out every now and then. That's why I thought you were intoxicated.'

By the time Sister had finished the bandaging, and sponged his face some more, the dark-avised Calum looked a different man. The orderlies had removed Barney to some bed for the night. Calum smiled, then winced. 'Gosh, this is a bit restricting. Did you really have to put on an enormous cap of bandaging like this, Sister darling? I feel like a Sultan.'

Sister grinned back. 'I did. And mind, no taking any of it off for sleeping in. I think you're quite mad. Kitty'd far rather think you were under our eye. It's ridiculous to think she can't manage three children for a short time. She's not on her own, as—'

Calum interrupted. 'It's not that. She's always game to take over in any emergency, and made Ian go up with Betty when her mother took so ill, but she's in an absolute flap about this girl coming down. You'll have heard . . . the long-lost granddaughter. *If* that's what she is. The Forbes think they found the marriage entry. Apart from that, it's mostly a likeness.

'She's been flat out. Strathallan has been spring-cleaned from top to toe; never known her fuss like this before. New curtains and quilt for the spare room, new blankets, sheets all sprinkled with yellow roses and what-have-you, every book on the shelves taken out and dusted. As for the kitchen cupboards! I said to her: "Kit, are you really expecting her to peer into every one?" and she answered quite seriously, "It's just I'll feel easier in my bones if I know everything's in apple-pie order. She'll be used to servants in the guest-house." I'll never forgive this wretched girl if she comes, makes a big fuss over Kitty and Gilbert, then departs, leaving their lives emptier than before. Or if, as I suspect, she's tarred with the same brush as her father, and thinks she might be on to a good thing. *He* never stopped asking them for money till a dozen or so years ago. This one could bleed them white too.'

Anna froze. She seemed incapable of taking it in. Fortunately, as they all were, it seemed, *au fait* with the situation, and thought of her as a stranger who wouldn't be likely to be interested, they went on talking and didn't look at her.

Sister Grey said, 'Oh, Calum, it may not be anything like that at all. I'd back Elizabeth Forbes's judgment any time, to say nothing of Ross. They're good judges of character and they thought this girl and her mother were just sweet. I think it's because you're so fond of Kitty and Gilbert that you're so afraid for them. Forget it. Let's hope and pray she's all Elizabeth said she was. It could be a new lease of life for old Mr. Drummond. But if Kitty's all het up, you'll be better home. She won't want to be too tired when this girl arrives. Three children with spring mud on their feet could get the old lady fidgety.' At that moment she got her eye on Anna. 'Hullo . . . what have we here? You've gone as white as a sheet. Get your head down.'

26

Anna put her head down and felt the colour come flooding back into her cheeks instantly. 'I'm not swooning – I'm not that sort – just a little tired. And I've had no evening meal.'

The doctor snapped his fingers. 'Coffee . . . let's all have some coffee, and some of those ginger nuts. Sugar in your coffee, my dear, whether you like it or not.'

It was produced with a minimum of fuss and as Anna drank it, strength and purpose flowed back into her. For one ghastly moment she'd felt she could do no more than bawl out this opinionated man and disappear into the murky night, never to turn up at Strathallan – then the memory of her grandmother's letter hit her. It wasn't Kitty Drummond's fault that this man held the ideas he did – a member of the family, perhaps? Well, no matter how blunt he was himself he was going to get a whale of a shock when he found out who she was. But she wouldn't do it here, in front of these people.

As she sipped her coffee she said, 'Who is Kitty? A relation of yours?'

'No, my boss's wife. I work for a chap called Gilbert Drummond as his farm manager. My brother occupies the married couple's house on the estate – a real family affair. But his wife's mother in Dunedin is ill, and Kitty took the three children in. I wanted to send them to friends of ours in Roxburgh, but Mrs. Drummond wouldn't hear of it – thought it would upset them. They're quite young and it would have meant a different school.'

Anna stood up and found her knees would, after all, support her.

She said crisply, 'I'll take him home, and stay the night. He seems clear enough in the head now. Which way do I take?'

The Sister looked at her admiringly. 'Right on through the town, keeping to the main road, past Corriefeld, you'll notice lots of orchards, then on almost to Crannog. It's the first turning to the left before the street lights of Crannog start. It's clearing nicely. I can see the stars through this window. But be careful, there'll be a lot of traffic coming in for the Ball. Why aren't you going?' She'd turned to Calum.

He grinned. 'My lady-love's away. Right. Sister, would you ring Strathallan and warn them? Otherwise, seeing this

27

enormous bandage, they'll think I've been scalped!'

They were escorted to the car. They drove on westward, the road climbing shortly. Anna marvelled at the clarity of the air now. Above them a mountain, Mount Benger, her companion said, was lightly sprinkled with white. A few flakes clung to the rows of fruit trees in the symmetrical orchards that bordered the road.

Calum talked about the accident, chuckling over her thinking he was plastered too; she made herself laugh with him ... imagine him thinking she was the one who'd put him in the ditch! That must have been the only car that had passed her during the snowfall – but she'd been too concerned to even notice the make of the car. She was glad of the small talk. She didn't want to tell him who she was till they were home. *Home?* Would it, could it ever be that, with this antagonistic stranger esconced on the estate? His brother too! Oh, for sure they wouldn't want a Drummond turning up.

She said, 'What a dreadful thing, that car tipping you and going right on. Surely the driver must have known.'

He said, 'I said hit-and-run for want of a better term. To be fair, we didn't touch, but it was a near thing. The car swung out and passed me at a speed quite unsuitable for these conditions. In any case, he began to come back in far too soon, and to make it worse skidded almost across the road and then managed to straighten up. I pulled over to avoid hitting him, and went into a skid myself. I struck the white-and-red warning post for the culvert. It went with a real crack. He must have heard it – or she. But maybe I should give him the benefit of the doubt. I've made one too-hasty stricture tonight, thinking it was you.'

'Well, it was mutual. It'll teach us not to make snap judgments. Or get preconceived ideas about people.'

'Preconceived? What do you mean? Oh, slow up, that's the Crannog school just ahead. It's on the outskirts. There are the lights. Turn left at this corner. Just about a mile to go now.'

He didn't go back to his question. Instead he said suddenly, 'I say, I've got the queerest feeling I've seen you before. Or else I know someone very like you. Have you relations round here? I remember now you said you weren't a New Zealander – you'd never seen snow. Then where—'

She said slowly and deliberately, 'You *do* know someone like me. My grandfather, Gilbert Drummond. I'm Anna!'

She felt very satisfied with the effect on him. He sat bolt upright immediately. She could feel his gaze upon her, trying, she supposed, to see the likeness in the three-quarter darkness. Then he slumped.

'*Anna!*' he said, and sounded winded. 'Anna! Of all the foul luck!'

'Yes,' she agreed icily, 'but for whom? For you? Or for me? Well, perhaps not for me, because at least I know your preconceived ideas about me, Calum-whatever-your-name-is! How would you have met me, I wonder, if that moment of revelation in the hospital hadn't happened? It would be interesting to know. Had you decided on armed neutrality, definite antagonism, or bland and deceptive hypocrisy?'

He didn't answer. He seemed to be as shocked as she had been at his earlier clanger. She didn't care. She hoped he *was* shocked. He deserved it.

She continued, 'You ought to be very grateful to me. I could have showed you up in front of the doctor and Sister, but I've too nice a nature to do such a thing. For my grandparents' sakes I'm not going to say anything to them about this. They would be deeply distressed to know the sort of welcome I'd had from someone I'd played the Good Samaritan to. And I will not upset them like that. It seems my father brought them no joy – at least not from early manhood on. I'm *not* here to feather my own nest, Mr. – whatever-they-call-you. I don't need to. My mother and myself survived some very hard times, especially my mother, but when my father deserted us we made the guest-house pay. Yes, we had Fijian servants, but we worked even harder ourselves. I don't need to look to my grandparents for money. I've a good bank balance and I'll work for my keep as I've always done – worked hard. No forty-hour week for the owners of a guest-house. I came over here to get a job in Auckland. I've just posponed looking for one because my grandparents wanted to see me. I have nothing of my father in me, I hope to God! Is this it? Do I go through these gate-posts? Oh, I see I do, there's the Drummond goshawk on the tops.'

He came to life, said sardonically, 'I can see you've done your homework!'

She said coolly, 'I found out about the family crest long ago, before I knew I had any Drummond relations. Found out in Scotland. Oh, how I wish *I* hadn't been the one to rescue you tonight. I wanted this meeting with my own folks to take place in a natural atmosphere, in one of pure joy. But don't worry, I'll not give you away. But as far as you're concerned, I'll remember the clan motto and gang warily There.' She drew to a neat stop in front of the steps where a welcoming light shone. 'Out you get.'

The door flew open and two people were framed against the light. Anna went round to the passenger door, helped Calum out. He still looked dazed, but perhaps that wasn't solely due to the accident. The two people hurried down the steps, came towards them. Anna almost hated this man for spoiling her moment of homecoming. She said swiftly in response to their cries of thanks and concern, as to a stranger, 'I think he's about all in, delayed shock maybe. I'll be back for my overnight bag when we get him inside.'

She didn't want to appear other than a stranger yet. The old man took Calum's arm. Anna took the other.

Calum said, 'I'm all right, Gilbert. One of Barney's bottles got me. Could have been a lot worse. What's a few stitches? And I was very lucky in my rescuer. She had a good first-aid kit.'

They got into the hall, warm with a night-storage heater, and rosy with a beautiful chandelier. The light fell directly on Anna as she steadied Calum beneath it. She managed to look directly at her grandfather, was aware of his suddenly-riveted attention, and heard a little gasp from her grandmother. She summoned up a gamin grin, looked right at the old masculine face opposite hers and said, 'Like as two peas in a pod, aren't we, Grandfather?' and stepped forward to enclose him in her young, strong arms, holding out a hand very quickly again to include her grandmother in her embrace as well.

'It's true,' she said, 'I'm Anna – oh, my darlings!'

CHAPTER TWO

APART from Anna's chaotic feelings regarding the watching Calum, it was a wonderful moment for three people. They drew apart and regarded each other. Anna put her hands to her eyes in a sweeping-away movement and said, 'Oh, do forgive me, I've got such over-active tear-ducts, but they are tears of joy.'

That made it easier for the older people not to feel they had been betrayed into over-sentimentality, which some young people despised.

Gilbert's voice was only just under control. 'Aye, lassie, but so are mine.' Kitty Drummond took out her handkerchief, mopped her eyes. 'But come away in, beside the fire. I'm afraid it's only the kitchen fire tonight. I couldn't be bothered to light the other.' She laughed. 'We were going to have an early night for once so that if you arrived during the next day or so, we'd be fresh for you. Calum, come away in and let me have a good look at you and when we're satisfied, you can tell us how in the world you managed to pick Anna up.'

He grinned. '*She* picked *me* up, literally. And Barney. I'd found him collapsed in the gutter and was taking him home when I skidded.'

They were horrified. 'Barney? Is he all right? He is? Oh, Anna, what a welcome, dealing with the local drunk!'

Kitty steadied Calum into a deep old chair with wing sides. He burst out laughing, groaned, clutched his head each side, said, 'She thought she was dealing with *two* drunks. I got the contents of his kit-bag all over me, you see.'

Gilbert sniffed. 'No wonder, lad. But it looks as if she still coped.'

'She did, even if she was furiously despising me. I was no help to her, kept flaking out. Somehow she heaved me into the front seat, mopped away the blood so I could see, bandaged me up, found my car where it was ditched, and in some way we managed to shake Barney awake and get him across the road and into the back seat. She picked up Rod

Staikes in the township, and he guided her to the hospital and saw us in. They're keeping Barney. Then I accused her of being the cause of my skid, though I gave her credit for coming back after all. She didn't half chew my ear!'

'I should think so,' cried Anna. 'The car that put him in the ditch was going the other way. So I – er – blasted him for driving when drunk! I mean, what with the fumes of the beer spilt all over him and his slurred speech – due now, I realize, to faintness – I was just furious. Grandmother, I think he should have a hot bath, he was dreadfully cold when I found him. But someone should be in the bathroom all the time, because he might pass out on us again.'

Calum looked so alarmed, Anna's grandfather started to laugh. 'It's all right, lad, I'll supervise, not Anna.'

Anna boggled. 'I'd no intention of doing it. Whatever made you think that?' She gave Calum a sharp look.

He didn't deny he'd thought it. 'Well, you said you'd done nurse-aiding, and from my experience of nurses they're as bossy as they come, and don't spare a chap's feelings.'

Old Gilbert chuckled again. 'It does me good to hear you two talking like this ... sparring ... we're already one family.'

Anna opened her mouth to protest, then closed it again.

Her grandmother, who'd been gazing and gazing at Anna as if she just couldn't believe her eyes, came to herself and said, 'He'd better get into it right away, Gilbert, so do go and run the bath. I'll go upstairs and switch on the electric blankets. Anna's bed is ready. I made it up myself this morning – couldn't resist putting the last touches to her room. We'll have some soup and toast when you come down. Gilbert, make Calum wear some of your pyjamas – they'll be a lot warmer than those daft nylon things he wears.'

The men went off, grinning. Kitty said softly, 'Now, I can look at you, Anna, all on my own. My, but you're bonnie! And how like Gilbert, as he was when I first met him. That broad brow ... under your bit of fringe ... a serene brow, I always thought. It served him in good stead in those years when serenity was hard to come by. I know Gilbert's almost white now, but when he was young his hair was just like yours, fair, with darker gold streaks in layers underneath.'

Anna laughed. 'It would be easier for a man ... nobody would ever come up to him, and say: "Do tell me where you get your hair streaked? It's so natural-looking!" then get huffy when I told them it *was* natural. They thought I just wouldn't share my secret.'

Kitty's eyes were roving still. 'You have the same dark brows, and those warm brown eyes. So unusual with fair hair. And his chin, with its faint cleft in it. Oh, you're just the little daughter I always longed to give him.' Gently she lifted the hair that was barely shoulder-length, back from Anna's ears, her touch as light as thistledown. 'Yes, slightly pointed ears. Oh, how satisfying this is! Alex wasn't like Gilbert at all, except for his ears. He was, I'm sure, a throwback to a forebear of my own, the one whose name was rarely mentioned! But you've been given to Gilbert in his old age. His sister Anna was his twin. There's an oval picture of her in your room, as like you as he is. This house will live again now. It was slowly dying, its day done. William Drummond built it in 1869 when he turned from gold-mining back to sheep.'

Anna's eyes kindled with interest. 'William Drummond . . . named, I suppose, for the first Viscount Strathallan?'

'Aye. Oh, lassie, you know a bit of clan history, then? Oh, how this will please my man. When he knew you were coming he was so feared you might be too modern to care about the things we care about. "With it" they call it these days. Did your father – did Alex tell you these things, then?'

She didn't want to tell her her son had never talked about his childhood, her forebears. She said cautiously, 'I was too young to remember more than a very little about him, Grandmother. Some children have a long memory, but I don't seem to. All I remember is my father bouncing me on his knee and singing old Scots tunes.'

Kitty nodded, pleased. 'Then he did retain some memories of the old songs . . . and he did call you Anna.'

Anna said, 'Just over two years ago Mother and I went for a trip to Britain. Friends of hers managed the guest-house. I looked up some Drummond history, explored the places the clan knew so well. It gave me a feeling of – having roots.'

Kitty nodded. 'Aye, you would miss that. Every child should have a heritage of songs and tales handed down from one generation to the next, especially of their immediate forebears. That's where I think illegitimacy is so cruelly hard on the children. There's so much of it in our permissive society. I think every child has a right to know the stock whence it sprang. But it's denied to so many. I hate that word, illegitimate, as applied to children. It should be applied only to parents. Oh, listen to me, what a subject! Anna, there's a batch of scones under that tea-towel. Would you pop some in the oven on one of the shelves in there? The lower one, in case the men take their time. They'll be nicer warmed up. I'll pull my soup-pot on.' She got up, bustled round, began cutting rounds from a loaf, ready to put in the toaster.

Anna was glad to do something. This little task marked her as one of the family, not a guest. She looked round the large kitchen, said, 'What a glorious room! That lovely blue-and-white enamel stove – it emanates such heat. And that rag mat . . . it makes me feel as if I belonged.'

It was beautifully worked, in a traditional Scots thistle design. It had known the tread of many feet. Kitty said, 'Gilbert's mother worked it not long before she died. It was to replace the one that the first Drummond's wife made more than a century ago. I still have the iron pot she used to dye her rags in. It was beginning to show signs of wear, and the Crannog museum wanted it. So it's preserved for always. I thought that many of my old dear things would have to be bequeathed to that museum, but now . . .' she smiled at Anna, complete happiness in her beautiful blue eyes, 'now you are here, to treasure them.'

Anna was made aware in that instant that the past was reaching out to her, that it would not want to let her go. She didn't know if it was a good thing for her or not. Was it something that might separate her a little from her mother? Because she would never risk that. Would there be rocks ahead? Calum and his brother and brother's wife weren't likely to want her here. She would, above all things, gang warily.

She and her grandmother went out to the car, brought in the cases Anna had with her, then, somewhat to Anna's surprise, Kitty said briskly, 'Plenty of room in the barn for this car, I'll run it round. Easier for me, knowing the place, than for you. Just take in the last lot of stuff, Anna.'

She saw the look on Anna's face, said, 'I can drive most cars. I love all mechanized things.' Off she went with a smooth gear change.

Anna took her bits and pieces in, stacked them on the sewing-machine in the kitchen window alcove, opened the oven door to make sure the scones weren't browning too much and felt already a granddaughter of Strathallan.

Kitty came in, flung an embroidered willow-pattern supper-cloth on the table, put out cups to match. 'They came out with the first William's wife,' she said, seeing Anna's eyes on them.

Anna put out a caressing hand to one. 'How fascinating! It seems to me that everything here will have a story, that one would always be conscious that other hands had served out from these dishes, had dusted those pictures every spring-cleaning.'

Kitty nodded. 'That other eyes had looked out of this kitchen window every morning and seen those same contours, Blue Spur, and Ghost Hill and all of them with a sprinkling of snow like now, and in summer and autumn tussock-gold, emerald green in spring. The only differences would be in the height of the trees. They brought saplings out with them, sticks of willow and poplar, acorns and pine-cones. Year by year they grew and sheltered the homestead and made a garden possible.' Suddenly she laughed and looked ten years younger. 'Oh, what fools Gilbert and I have been! We longed for you to come, but dreaded it too, told ourselves and each other over and over that we must realize you were a different generation, that naturally you'd like modern things best, that you'd think this very old-fashioned. Like Betty, Calum's brother's wife. She's a dear girl, but she can't abide anything that gathers dust. I ken fine she thinks this is downright cluttered. So it is. I wasn't going to worry if you were that way too, but to find you like this, really of the same ilk, not just by blood but by nature, is beyond belief. We hadn't dared hope for it.

'Mind you, I'm not daft about the past to the point of foolishness – only sentimental. I'd never despise the convenience of electric ranges in our hot summers. I love mine, out yonder in the wee kitchen, but I feel it's foolish down there, where snow can bring wires down, to do away with a fuel stove. Not that I've ever liked sooting the flues. I'm always a bit sharp in the temper then, but it's my best friend all the same, that coal range.'

Anna had never seen one before. She gazed at it with the greatest of respect. 'You'll have to tell me how it works. I can't imagine how a tiny fire-box like that can heat an oven away over at one side. I can understand how it would heat the top plate, but how is it that it doesn't burn things all one side?'

Kitty beamed, took a short poker with a bent end off the track, inserted it into a rectangular stove-plate at the right-hand side, hooked it off and said, 'See . . .?'

Anna peered in, saw a soot-covered space under which, apparently, the square box of the oven was housed, and Kitty pulled out a lever at the front of the stove and a bar amongst the soot moved, with a flange at the end, revealing a hole that led into the chimney. Almost immediately the fire roared away, and tongues of flame shot over the top, drawn to the hole with the draught created.

'That brings the fire over the top, then when it's going nicely, you almost close it, and the heat goes steadily right round the oven. The old ranges hadn't a thermometer, of course, but these ones have. So when it reaches the height you want, you put in whatever you're baking.'

'What did you do before? How would you know when it was right for baking?'

'Oh, we used to put a hand in and test it . . . you got quite expert at knowing when it was right, by the feel. If it was very important a pie should be just right, I used to put a scrap of pastry in to make sure the oven was good and hot as it should be for that. But in no time, you could judge without that.'

'That's *real* cooking,' said Anna, with awe. 'I always thought that about some of the more primitive ways of cooking in Fiji, in the villages. It makes it an art, not just a skill.' She was working the lever back and forth. 'This fascinates me. I think it's the most marvellous invention I've ever seen.'

At that moment the men came back, Calum in a tweed dressing-gown, and both looked staggered at this naïve remark and the sight of the women peering into the innards of a sooty stove. 'What's gone wrong with it?' demanded Gilbert.

Kitty burst out laughing. 'Not a thing. It's just that she's never seen one before. Eh, but it does my heart good to hear a young one admiring my Old Warrior!'

Anna straightened up and both men laughed. Gilbert drew out a large handkerchief and held Anna, and carefully removed a very large smut from the end of her nose and some smaller ones from her forehead. 'All I can say, lassie, is I'm glad you came unannounced. Kitty'd have been stiff and unnatural if she'd known the hour of your coming.'

'Aye, that I would. But he's made your face all smudgy. Come awa' to the bathroom with me.'

Anna shook her head. 'No, thank you, Grandmother. I'll be washing it before I go to bed, and I'm ravenous. That soup smells delicious.'

It was, too. They all ate as if famished, Calum possibly because he was weak from loss of blood and needed re-fuelling, and the other three because they were suddenly gloriously lighthearted. Gilbert began telling tales out of school about Kitty's agitated preparations, how she'd even thought of taking up the old-fashioned flowered carpet in Anna's bedroom to replace it with a modern one, and how the weakling lambs had all been banished to the wash-house and a heater turned on for them there, every day, instead of them being in the kitchen.

It wasn't till a clean-faced Anna had been tucked up in a warm nest of a bed, fussed over by both grandparents, and tenderly kissed goodnight, that she suddenly felt a return of anxiety, a dread of the days ahead. Not because of her father's parents, but because of Calum Doig, and that as far as he was concerned this return of the prodigal son's daughter could upset all his hopes for the future. What would his antagonism mean to her? But whatever it meant, she would have to make sure there was no hurt in it for Kitty and Gilbert Drummond. They had suffered enough.

She was so exhausted, she knew nothing till morning and woke not knowing where she was. Noises had wakened her, children's voices, giggling, and the sound of a door opening. Memory came flooding back. Sunlight, surprisingly, was slanting through an opening in the drapes. She looked at the door and two tousled towheads appeared round it, quite disembodied.

Two pairs of blue eyes looked out under fringes, two snub noses seemed to quiver with apprehension. Anna grinned. 'It's all right, I'm awake. Come on in. Wanted to see what I looked like, did you?'

She raised herself up.

Two mouths opened into perfect O's, and she was pretty sure they registered disappointment. But why?

Now sleeping-suited bodies revealed themselves and advanced. Twins for sure. Not quite identical, but twins. They stopped and said, 'Are you really Anna?'

'Yes, I'm Anna. Why not?'

The slightly fairer, slightly taller one said, 'But they said you were from Fiji.' It was an accusation.

Light dawned. 'Oh, I get it. You thought I'd have fuzzy hair. Oh, what a disappointment for you! Never mind, I've got lots of photos with me of my Fijian friends. Some of them have children about your age. You must be cold, hop in.'

They parted, one to each side, and were in before she could change her mind. The other one said quickly, 'If they come, would you please tell them you invited us in?'

'I will. Grown-ups are always afraid children gate-crash, aren't they?'

They beamed on her. This grown-up certainly knew her onions! 'Yes, Maggie's downstairs and Nanna sent her up to tell us you weren't to be disturbed, so we thought we'd just peep. You're to have your breakfast in bed. But as long's you tell them.'

'I sure will. I'll get in first. Now I know who you are . . . the children of Calum's brother. What do they call you?'

'I'm Mac, Malcolm really, and he's Bill.'

Something hit Anna. Those were all Drummond names. Maggie would be Margaret. Margaret Drummond had married King David the Second. Malcolm had supported Bruce at Bannockburn. And of course there had always been Williams. It looked to her as if the Doig family was well entrenched at Strathallan, had been for years. How cunning, in a homestead where there was no one to inherit, to incorporate family names. It was to create an illusion of belonging, she supposed. No wonder Calum Doig hadn't wanted her here!

The twins proceeded to put her in the picture, enjoying no doubt being able to impart to a newcomer and an adult things she didn't know, unhampered by and unchecked by an uncle, an older sister, or the Drummonds.

38

Bill, the slightly shorter one, said confidently, 'She's not really our nanna, of course. Mum's mum and Dad's mum are that. We call Mum's mum Grandma and Dad's mum Granny. But Nanna Drummond likes us calling her that.'

She would, of course, with no descendants of her own till now.

Mac said, 'What'll you like to be called when you're a grandmother?'

Anna blinked. She'd never thought about herself as a possible grandmother. Who would? 'I don't know really. I must start considering it. It's just as well to be ready in plenty of time. *I* call Mrs. Drummond Grandmother, but I expect it'd be a bit of a mouthful for a tiny to manage. I mean, I hadn't met my dad's mother till now, so it's all right. I think she's lovely . . . just like a grandmother in a fairytale, except in present-day clothes.'

Mac nodded sagely. 'Yep, we like her too. She doesn't fuss too much about mud and she knows things. Like where you can find trapdoor spiders and lizards and dotterels' nests and how to fix things. She can make anything go . . . watches and clocks and trucks and things. Our mum's a real duffer at those things and Dad's not always round, but Nanna even got the tractor going when Grandy Drummond couldn't.'

'A toy tractor?' asked Anna.

Bill's tone was scornful. 'Toy nothing! The real tractor. She's very meck-meck-something for a woman.'

'Mechanically-minded?'

'That's it, and she's a wizard with a fretsaw. I'll show you.'

He raced away, came back with a huge wooden tray on which were some wonderful miniature toys, fire-engines, cars, station-wagons, front-end loaders, fork-lifts. They were all beautifully fitted together and painted, with cotton wheels to run on.

Mac said, 'She helped us make them all. You've got to be very careful not to lean on them too hard. We'll let you have a go at running them on the floor afterwards, if you'll promise not to lean on them too hard. After all, they're not made of cast-iron.'

'I'll be very careful,' promised Anna solemnly. She turned to look at Bill, who'd leaned over and picked up a bottle from the dressing-table. 'That's perfume . . . I don't think you'd better take the top off, you might spill – oh!'

She was too late. He had it off, sniffed, gave it a vigorous shake, then decided to dab some on his pyjamas. He hadn't noticed the whole top had come off, and it poured down him in a steady stream.

Anna made a quick swipe with the hanky from under her pillow to prevent it saturating the eiderdown, scooped Bill up, scent and all, and sprang out on the carpet with him. It was a very large bottle and a very strong perfume.

She landed on the floor just as the door was pushed open and Maggie preceded Kitty, who was bearing a tray. They all uttered squeaks of dismay. Kitty whipped off her apron and mopped frantically, saying, 'I don't want it dripping on the carpet, it'll reek for weeks. Nobody could stay in here then.' Maggie said in tragic tones, 'Those boys! Whatever will they do next? You'll catch it when Mum comes back, Bill!'

Anna said hurriedly, 'Oh, it wasn't really his fault. Look, the sprinkler top unscrewed with the cap, anybody could have done it. Bill, it's just as well you did it now. I might have got drenched with scent the first time I used it.' Bill had opened his mouth to yell at the threat from his sister, but closed it again. He had an ally.

A grim voice from the door said, 'Beats me . . . you kids never have the same accident twice running! We never know what to guard against. And what the devil were you doing in Miss Drummond's bed? I heard you being told not to disturb her!' Calum Doig, still heavily bandaged.

The twins sounded virtuous. 'We were asked in . . . so there!'

Anna was laughing helplessly, still mopping with the apron. 'I did ask them in, I was frightened they'd catch cold. Look, very little's gone on the sheets. I'll wash them after breakfast. It would have been disastrous had it soaked the mattress. But I think I'll drop Bill in the bath – it's the only way we'll get rid of the smell. Grandmother, can that gorgeous breakfast be kept hot in that lovely stove? I'll get Bill de-glamorized, then we'll all come down. How about it, Bill? Oh, I'd better get a dressing-gown.'

There was a gleam in the eyes with which Calum surveyed her. He grinned, 'What the dickens are you blushing for, girl? It's downright stupid. You could have gone to the Hydro Ball in that and no one would've been any the wiser!'

How true! It was in deep tangerine, fluffy-surfaced, with a high Empire waist, threaded through with a brown satin ribbon, and had a striped orange and white bodice, with a big collar that was for all the world like a fichu, and puffed sleeves edged with old-fashioned white embroidery. She laughed herself. 'Yes, mad, isn't it? I'd appear before anyone in a bikini, but just because this happens to be a nightgown, I've gone all modest on it. Well, I'll have to take it off – it copped the scent too – Grandmother, my dressing-gown's the flimsy sort suitable for Fiji, could I borrow Grandfather's to come down to the kitchen in?'

Maggie and Kitty had given way to laughter. Calum caught his nephew by the ear as they went through the door. 'But just because Miss Drummond's been sporting about it, don't think you can go on poking and prying into the rest of her belongings. Gosh, what a stink!'

Anna halted. 'I've known worse. Like last night, for instance! At least *he's* not reeking of beer!'

The three children stopped in their tracks, gazed at their uncle. Maggie had a prim expression. She said, 'Uncle Calum? You – you weren't *drunk*, were you? Is *that* why you had the accident? Oh, you won't half cop it from Miss Kirkpatrick! What *will* she say?'

The uncle glared at Anna, flung up his hands in despair. 'Now look what you've done! Children, you've got to get this straight. You're not to go round spreading a tale like that. I only reeked of beer because I picked old Barney up, we skidded off the road and his kit of bottles smashed all over me.'

Anna couldn't have cared less. She departed to the bathroom with Bill. Maggie appeared with his clothes, and Bill submitted with a surprisingly good grace to being bathed and robed by a stranger. Anna had to resist the temptation to cuddle him. Five-year-olds were usually horrified by any attempt to baby them.

She pulled his jersey on, a sturdy Aran knit his mother had made him, he informed her. Then came long overalls made of a warm tartan material. She buttoned up the Huckleberry Finn top and said, 'I'll match you when I get into my trews, they're that tartan.' Again an impact of knowledge. These children were certainly being brought up to regard themselves as family, as Drummonds. But of course it might be chance. The overalls might have been store-made and the only tartan available. Tartan was so popular most people didn't seek their own these days.

She said, 'Were these bought ready-made?'

'No, Mum's got yards of this stuff. The shop ones don't have any hems to speak of, she says, and we grow like beanstalks. She has some trews like this herself, and a skirt. See ... she even makes extra big straps so she can shift the buttons.' Anna saw all right. She was extremely thoughtful as she washed hastily when she'd sent him out, and donned Grandfather's big dressing-gown Maggie had brought in. She doubled back the sleeves, girded it tightly to hitch up the length and ran downstairs.

At the smile Gilbert gave her, Anna knew a lift of the heart and the sheer magic of being here and belonging flooded over her. She bent and kissed his cheek before slipping into her place.

Anna was outwardly correct towards Calum, asked if his head pained him much this morning.

He said dryly, 'I can't afford to have it ache – we're right in the middle of lambing still, and with Ian away we're short-handed. I tried to get an extra casual hand but failed. There's only Philip – you haven't met him yet because he lives at home, quite near here. He's away out round the sheep. I told him we'd probably be a bit later this morning.'

Anna's fault, no doubt. But she said without a trace of resentment, 'Maybe I can help. Do let me know if I can.'

He burst out laughing, but had to put a hand to his head. She thought it served him right. He said derisively, 'I reckon that coming from Fiji, you'd hardly know one end of a ewe from the other.'

Her dimples grooved her cheeks. 'Oh, I don't know ... one end bleats, the other produces the lamb ... quite elementary. And I believe the lambs have to be helped into the world sometimes. Besides, I have seen pigs farrow, in Fiji.'

Her grandfather guffawed. 'Calum, I reckon you've met your match in verbal warfare this time. This one doesn't agree tamely with all you say.'

'No, evidently not, but who wants warfare?'

Gilbert sounded quite serious. 'Well, not the violent clashing kind, but verbal sparring sort of titillates the conversation, you ken. At least *I* ken, and ken full well. Without the occasional skirmish with Kitty, I'd have found our marriage very dull.'

'Oh, marriage,' said Calum, 'But then who was talking of marriage?'

Anna realized Kitty was holding in laughter. One of the twins created a diversion by saying to his brother, 'Blest if I know what they're talking about, do you?'

Anna laughed. 'I don't reckon they know, either, Mac. And I *am* dumb about sheep, except for being able to distinguish one end from the other. I only ever had one New Zealand holiday. I was seven. Mother took me by the Main Trunk Express right down from Auckland to Wellington and vowed she'd never forget my comments. Evidently I squealed at the top of my voice: "Whatever is *that* funny animal?" and everyone in the longcarriage stood up to look right around, expecting to see Wirth's Circus on the move, and all there was in sight was one woolly sheep tethered outside someone's gate to keep down the grass verge! They resumed their seats looking foolish, then a few miles south I saw a haystack and let out another screech. It brought them out of their seats again. By this time they were looking at me with such peculiar expressions, Mother had to explain. It had its advantages. For the rest of the long trip they took charge of me, pointing things out and answering my questions. I've never lost my capacity for asking questions, so you're all going to get pretty tired of me.'

Bill said regretfully, 'Wish it had been Saturday. Fancy having to go to school when we could have been answering questions, not being told to shut up for asking them. I suppose we couldn't—?'

'No, you couldn't,' said his uncle firmly, 'and finish your breakfast, all three of you, off to clean your teeth, pick up your lunches and get your bags ready. And you do your parents an injustice. I've never heard them tell you to shut up. They only say they've finished answering questions for a little time – when you've been hogging the conversation too long.'

Anna was sure Bill muttered 'Same thing,' under his

43

breath, but slid very quickly off his seat as his uncle's eye sparked.

Calum said, 'Waste no more time. We're much later than we ought to be already.'

Anna was evidently to be made to feel the disrupter of the farm routine. She bit her lip.

Evidently Kitty didn't take that meaning. 'Oh, Calum, you worry far too much about their pranks, lad. I never expect bairns to be perfect. The spilt scent didn't take more than a few moments to clear up. The sheets are in the tub and there they'll stay till the morrow. I'm turning a blind eye to the household chores today and coming round the sheep with you. I'd like fine to be with Anna when she first looks over Strathallan. There's nothing quite like the first sight of a place.'

Anna said, 'Oh, I don't know. The differences may strike you more perhaps, because sometimes custom blinds us to either beauty or shabbiness. On the other hand constant use can endear things to us even more.'

She thought the look on Calum's face was a sardonic one. What a cynic he must be! She hoped she wasn't looking for reactions like this, but she didn't think she was being fanciful . . . he had a guarding, watchdog sort of look as if he wanted her to know that he, at least, wasn't taken in. It stung. She had suffered as much as anyone from her father's misdeeds. It had deprived her of a male parent all these years. She hated that anyone should class her with Alex Drummond's instability, always wanting the easy money one didn't have to earn. How horrible to be – in this man's mind – tarred with the same brush.

Gilbert broke in. 'This is an occasion for the homestead of Strathallan. For our granddaughter has come home to her inheritance. She mustn't let anything dim her grandparents' showing her round. Nothing must interfere with that pleasure.'

She sensed the stillness in Calum at the mention of the inheritance. She mustn't let anything dim her grandparents' joy, but she would certainly gang warily.

She said, gently, 'Don't let's talk about an inheritance, my darlings. It's enough to be here, with you, and belonging.'

Calum drained his cup, pushed back his chair. Anna looked at him appraisingly for the first time and hoped he might feel he was also being weighed up. But she said, lightly enough, 'No wonder I found you heavy to manage last night. You do tower, don't you?'

It was true. His height was matched with his breadth and his features were so aquiline that if his chin hadn't been so square, he would have been hatchet-faced. His eyes had very deep-set sockets above high cheekbones and she was suddenly surprised to find those eyes vividly blue. She'd expected dark ones to match the dark hair. But many Highlanders had black hair and blue eyes. Maggie had it too.

He said, quite admiringly, 'I sure hand it to you, Anna from the Islands, that you heaved me round in the most efficient fashion considering your size. I was most confused at first last night and could only surmise I'd had the good fortune to have met up with an Amazon. But perhaps you're a judo expert! It wasn't till you got me out of the car at Roxburgh that I realized you were just a slip of a girl.' He turned to her grandmother. 'Kit, I've got to ring the garage and find out if they got the message from Sister Grey all right, about taking out the breakdown outfit to salvage my car. Do you think you could put something up for our morning tea, and we'll have it in the paddocks instead of coming back here. That'd save some time.'

She nodded and rose. 'Get you away upstairs, lassie, and into the oldest duds you've got.'

Anna had nothing really old in the way of warm clothing. Old things belonged to Fiji and were of the flimsiest. But Auntie Ed had insisted on her buying warm trews and jerseys for Central, and had suggested some cheap ones, knowing farms. She slipped into her Drummond tartan trews, light red, checked heavily in green and orange, pulled a green jersey with a turtle neck over it, slipped a brown belt round it, buckled it tight, and ran down.

She found Kitty buttering a huge basket of ginger gems, made the day before, and a kettle boiling for the flasks clattered its lid impatiently on the stove. She'd stacked the dishes by the sink. Anna went to them, pushed her sleeves up.

Kitty said, 'Oh, leave them be, child, we'll do them when we come back. Lambing comes before all.'

'I won't delay you. I'll just go on till you've finished that.

45

They can drain. I wouldn't keep yon Calum waiting for anything. He'd think I was too much of a new chum to know what's urgent and what's not. I can't see him as a patient man.'

As she spoke she was flicking liquid detergent in, and sloshing cups through at great speed. Kitty laughed, folding a snowy tea-towel over her gems in their basket. 'Och, at the moment his bark's worse than his bite. Something's been bothering him. He's very easy-going as a rule – but of late he's been a bit sharp wi' the womenfolk. No wonder. He likes to know where he's going, and his lady-love won't fix the wedding-day.'

Kitty turned, said, 'Losh, lassie, you've nearly finished those dishes. I've never seen such speed, and I pride myself I don't waste much time. A big wash-up too.'

Anna's laugh was so full of genuine mirth that Calum, coming to winkle them out of the kitchen, stopped and wondered what the joke was. He heard her say, 'Oh, Grandmother, that teeny-wee wash-up! I'm used to a guest-house, remember. Sometimes twenty-five guests and five courses, and for sure that would be the night all the girls wanted to go off to fire-walking or a local hop.'

He had boots in his hand, said, 'You'd better put these on, they're Betty's. The mud, after that light snow thawing, will have to be seen to be believed. They'll probably be too big for you, though. You could always put a pair of farm socks underneath.'

She shook her head. 'I hardly think so. I haven't got very small feet.' She pulled off her brogues, thrust one toe in experimentally.

He knelt suddenly, to help her tug them on over her heels. 'Gumboots are the devil to get into.'

She nodded. 'I used to wear them a lot when I was a kid, paddling round the lagoons in the tropical rain. You can't keep kids in there when it rains. Later when I took a fancy for Regency novels, it made me understand why the men needed their valets to ease them on and take them off.'

He looked up. 'Oh, do you like Georgette Heyer too? We all do, here.'

One little touch of nature makes the whole world kin? For a fleeting instant she felt – perhaps foolishly – that his antagonism need not last.

46

He looked at her. 'Those clothes are too new. Put some old duds on.'

She held his eyes, looked amused. 'My only old clothes are gay printed shifts and shorts. Think how you'd have jeered had I appeared in those during early spring in Central Otago!'

Small creases she hadn't noticed before appeared each side of his mouth. 'Touché! What a fool I am! But it's such a filthy job, lambing. You'd better watch from some distance away.'

She said with spirit, 'I'll keep out of the way if I'm going to be a nuisance, otherwise I'd like to wipe the newness off these . . . it marks me as a novice.'

He laughed outright at that. 'Okay.' He turned to Kitty. 'Would you put this cap over my head, very gently? I feel such a Charlie with this capelline bandage on.'

Kitty said, 'I'm away off upstairs for a moment. Anna will.'

Calum said apprehensively, holding out a striped woollen cap, 'Stretch it well, won't you?'

She nodded. 'Sit down, or I'll have to get a step-ladder.'

He sat. She went round the back of him, pulled it out to its fullest extent, eased it on. He thanked her, rose, said, 'There's an old windcheater on the back door and quite a range of caps. Not glam, but very necessary. In spite of that blinding sunshine there's an icy wind blowing off the tops.'

Definitely more friendly. She allowed a sarcastic note to crisp her voice. 'I believe that you, unlike the snow on the tops, are thawing. Did my dexterity and speed with the dishes surprise you? Had you taken me for a lily of the field?'

He faced her with rugged honesty. 'I had. I thought you'd be used to all manner of servants over there, where labour is cheaper. That possibly you'd be merely the receptionist.'

She chuckled, her brown eyes alight with laughter. 'Oh, even the receptionist worked hard. But it wasn't me. I was the dogsbody, fitting in wherever the need was the greatest. Scrubbing, cooking, waiting on table, taking one of the launches out to the coral reef, doing the laundry, oh, the lot! Well, here's Grandmother. Out we go. If you knew how I was dying to get outside to really see Strathallan. I'd not wanted to see it first in the dark.'

Then she wondered if she'd sounded reproachful. Oh, well, she didn't care. He wasn't above a few digs himself. But she hoped wistfully that the urgency of the paddocks where presumably the lambing ewes would be grouped wouldn't mean he would whisk them away from her first glimpse of her father's home too speedily.

If that had been his intention he hadn't a chance against Gilbert Drummond.

Anna tugged the cap down over streaky dark-blonde hair, zipped up the very ancient windcheater, stepped out on to the back verandah with them into the cool, sweet air of a sunshiny-gold September day. She stood very still, after her first gasp of delight, her hands clasped in front of her, her eyes sweeping from left to right, to take in the ridge of the lavender hills below faraway mountains that were pocketed and peaked with blinding white snows; the silver glint of a stream that threaded through willows as green as English willows, then back to the dearer delights that lay at her feet, in the gifts of the garden.

The bed below the verandah was carpeted with the palest of primroses, and violets made a patch of purple shadow under a silver birch, a young one, just leafing. Under the orchard trees where apricots and peaches were miracles of newly-opened bloom, daffodils spread a living carpet of gold, common double daffodils that cocked a gay defiance at late snow and frost. The sun shone through the coral-rose of an enormous japonica that had grown to unrivalled heights, and pooled rosy shadows on a white concrete path as if it had come through a stained-glass window.

A perfume, borne on the wind, came to her, surely a perfume of summer, not spring? She lifted her face, trying to trace it. 'Can lilies be out already?'

Kitty laughed. 'Well, yes and no. That's the perfume of the cabbage-tree over yonder.'

Anna wrinkled her brow, 'But it looks like a palm-tree.'

'Yes, but it's really a giant lily, the largest in the world. They're funny, tufty old things, and I bless them for shedding their dry flax-like leaves all over my garden, but it wouldn't be spring in my garden without that fragrance.'

Anna said, 'Oh, no wonder Mother longed for spring in New Zealand. She used to say she'd give up all the orchids, the frangipanni, the bougainvillea, for the time of daffodils, the time of roses, the time of golden poplar leaves, the time of snow. No, she didn't say the time of snow, she said the silence and the hush of snow. But I'll admit it scared seven bells out of me last night. Oh, I mustn't linger ... it will hold you up. And there'll be other spring days.'

Her grandfather caught at her hand, said, with a shake in his voice, 'Lassie, there'll also be other springs.'

Anna sensed, rather than saw Calum Doig take a quick glance at her. She turned away a little, saw a light in her grandmother's eyes that made it all worth while. Kitty was looking at her Gilbert as if she, and she alone, had handed him happiness on a platter when she had written to ask his granddaughter to come.

There was a moment of slight embarrassment for them all, except perhaps for Gilbert, because he was quite unashamed of the tears in his eyes.

Calum Doig broke it. 'Well, come on, Anna of the Islands,' he said, 'and show us how you react to lambing.'

Gilbert Drummond had the last word. 'Not Anna of the Islands,' he said proudly, 'but Anna of Strathallan ... where she belongs.'

CHAPTER THREE

THEY piled into the Land-Rover and were away. There were rough metalled tracks leading through the white-painted gates of the paddocks that looked vast to Anna but Gilbert said weren't, in comparison with those of high-country stations.

Anna looked about her, marvelling, at the heights above and beyond. 'Isn't this high-country stuff?'

They all laughed. 'No, lass. Just rolling country. You've got to get back in, nearer the lakes for that, right amongst the mountains. Crannog and Roxburgh are practically low-lands.'

But for the clots of snow dotting the pastures, it was hard to believe that last night's fall had happened, much less frightening Anna so much and putting Calum off the road. They came through another gate, Gilbert opening each one, amazingly agile for his age. It was obvious this was the lambing paddock.

Small lambs, endeavouring to stand on wobbly legs and bearing plain traces of recent birth, were everywhere, anxious ewes butting them with their noses, alarmed bleatings from the mothers of older lambs who were straying, and a tall figure bending over a ewe and a lamb by a willow-tree near the creek. They left the Rover and approached on foot. Philip Sherborne was obviously assisting a second lamb into the world. It was exceedingly primitive and amazingly quick. Anna was fascinated.

Her grandfather, once he'd introduced her to Philip who had already heard from Calum by phone before he left his home that she had arrived – and how – took her off with him to assist him make a reluctant ewe recognize her maternal duties and feed her lamb.

'We don't do a pre-lamb shear here. Some do – they're not so likely to get cast during lambing with the weight of wool off, but we hardly ever get lambing over without a storm, or snow, and we've lost too many through shearing them beforehand. Besides which – as now – it's much easier to hang on to these ewes when they've got a bit of wool on them. Ah . . . got her!' He shook his head over the ways of sheep. 'Some have lambs too weak to feed but do their darndest. Some have insufficient milk or trouble in feeding them, and others perfectly healthy and well endowed for feeding twins or even triplets are sublimely lacking in the maternal instinct — selfish to the core. Like some human parents, I guess.

'See this one's udder . . . full as can be, yet the moment her poor lamb has a go, she's off. Stand away a bit, Anna, or you'll get milk all over you. I'll express it a bit. It flows more easily when it's no' so full. That'll make it easier for the lamb to get a start.'

It was surprising how soon the udder softened. Gilbert said, 'Now, Anna, my darling, bring the lamb up and hold her on. She's hungry and'll soon take it.'

Anna, holding the lamb against her legs, felt the blatant newness of her trews would soon lose their novice freshness thank goodness. She didn't want to be the new chum too long.

Kitty, coming up from helping the others, laughed at the look of her. For a time, as Philip said, it was a case of 'thick and fast they came at last'. Then they had a breather. No other births seemed imminent.

Philip looked at Anna with admiration, both for her looks and what she'd buckled in to do. He was as tall as Calum, more slimly built, but whipcord tough. Extremely handsome, and where Calum's was a ruddy tan, Philip's was a creamy one, showing up against his chestnut hair and hazel eyes.

Kitty said. 'We'll have our coffee while the going's good. Off to the creek.'

Philip guffawed. 'Mrs. Drummond's a tiger for hygiene! We all dance to her bidding. I'll instruct you in the drill, Anna. Though the creek's the least of it.'

The water was icy. They swished their hands in the leaping water with great energy, then sprang back on the turf, shaking them madly to get the circulation going again, and followed Kitty back to the Land-Rover where she produced a flask of hot water, poured it into a red plastic bowl, brought out a cake of soap and motioned to Anna to use it first.

The steaming coffee was glorious and the ginger gems

51

disappeared as if by magic. Anna said, 'I can hardly believe that those lambs frisking round by themselves over there were like those slimy yellow new ones a day or two ago. It's like a miracle.'

'Birth is always a miracle,' said her grandmother. 'You look at your newborn baby, all red, wrinkled, and with puffy eyes, looking more mouth than anything, like a newly-hatched bird ... just one big concentrated yell, knowing only physical needs – and in less than a week you're certain it's smiling back at you and responding to your voice above anyone else's, needing and recognizing love.'

Anna bent swiftly to dislodge a huge clump of mud from the instep of her gumboot. Pity scalded her for her grandmother, who had known that joy of motherhood when a girl younger than she was herself ... planning her son's future, full of hopes and dreams, only to have him so uncaring of her love as to disappear from their ken.

As she straightened up she was struck anew with the sweetness of Kitty's expression and realized something. Her grandmother had triumphed over that long ago. What could have done it? Her Christian faith? Aye, that would be it. Anyway, the sting had gone out of it, the affront to her motherhood. All she would have prayed for in the long years of silence would have been for her son's eventual comfort and happiness and perhaps the reclamation of his selfish soul.

It was a tough morning. Two lambs and one ewe died. Two or three weren't in very good shape and Philip brought the truck and trailer across. The trailer had a hoisting device that lifted the heavy ewes up and into it. They'd be taken to a mothering shed where a close eye could be kept upon them. Anna thought, with distress, that they looked pretty far gone. Calum shook his head. 'I've seen much worse revive. They'll have shelter and ritzy treatment. Not to worry.' She thought his manner to her was a little less antagonistic.

He left her to assist Philip and Gilbert retrieve a ewe that had lambed among some willow roots and was either having trouble getting out from among them, or was about to have a second lamb.

Kitty called her. Another ewe was down. 'Anna, wipe its lamb free of mucous – like you saw us doing before – while I

52

attend to her. There's another to come.'

Anna said swiftly, 'Could I do what you're doing? I saw how last time. Or would I hurt her?'

'No, love, go ahead. You'll never learn younger. Just ease it – she and the lamb'll do the rest. She's just a bit tired with the first effort.' She stooped to free the nostrils of the first lamb.

Anna knew a moment of panic in case she did the wrong thing. Then she found herself talking reassuringly to the grunting ewe who now seemed to be doing her best; Anna got more confidence, and a firmer hold, she and the ewe synchronized, it seemed, and the next moment, to her astonishment, the smaller second lamb was kicking and unfolding on the ground.

'I did it, I did it, I did it!' she exulted, in the tone of a successful Olympic winner, wiped over its face, stood up, still amazed at her achievement, and encountered the grins of the three men standing behind her.

'Good for you,' said Philip.

'And to think,' said Gilbert, 'that only yesterday Kitty was saying: "I do with it wasn't lambing-time. Used to tourist glamour and colour and heat, she'll find this so crude!" But you don't do you, my cushie doo? . . . you were born to this sort of life.'

Anna noticed that Calum and Philip looked swiftly away. Perhaps they were a little embarrassed at the sheer delight in the old man's voice. She realized everybody would be fiercely protective about the Drummonds, fearful no doubt that she might be the new broom that swept cleanly, remembering, possibly, stories of her father who, according to her mother, had known sudden and great enthusiasms that died down as quickly as they had come . . . seeing always a new accomplishment that might offer something different, show quick returns, then having it pall as he realized that this too, like so many other skills, demanded good, honest, constant slogging.

A little chill wind seemed to blow over her spirit. It would take so long to convince Calum she wasn't like that. How many people would be watching her? Then suddenly, hearteningly, she thought of Elizabeth and Rossiter Forbes who had been responsible for her being brought here. They had liked her for herself alone, long before they had known who she was. So at least she had two friends here, not far away. The thought of them made her want to mention them, to remind this dark-visaged man she was not quite a stranger.

'Some day, before too long, but only when you can spare the time, Grandmother, I'd like to go over to Elizabeth and Rossiter's place.'

Kitty nodded. 'Surely, bairn. Oh, even in lambing we're not entirely tied to the place. Neither are they. It would be nice for you to see a familiar face, one that would link you with home.'

A strange feeling quivered over Anna. It was almost physical. Out of it she said with conviction, 'Well, a link with my former life – with Fiji. But when Mother married Magnus, and sold the guest-house, that chapter of my existence was ended.'

'So *this* is your home now,' said Gilbert, with the greatest satisfaction. 'Strathallan. Come on, time for lunch.'

As they reached the vehicles Philip said, 'Like to come back with me, Anna? You could add to your education by helping me into the shed with the animals. Calum ought to go in and have a rest. He said his wound was hurting like hell now.'

Anna saw two things. She saw her grandfather start as if to come in the truck with them, and her grandmother's hand go out to stay him. Why? She took a quick look at Kitty's face. It wore a look often to be seen in women's faces. A matchmaking, pleased look. She was sure that was it. As if an idea had hit Kitty.

Oh dear! Kitty would feel that if her granddaughter were to wed in the district, they'd have her near them, always. Well, thank goodness they weren't matchmaking in Calum's direction.

They certainly moved fast in lambing-time at Strathallan. By the time she and Philip had scrubbed up at the sink on the back verandah, the lunch was on the table. Afterwards the dishes were piled on the bench so they could get back to the paddock.

Kitty broke off mid-afternoon to go down to One-Mile Corner to collect the children from the school bus. Calum said, 'You don't have to, you know. Kit. It's a glorious day now. They could easily walk home. They so often do.'

54

She said, appealingly, wanting his approval of her fussing, 'I'm probably a daft old woman, but I want no harm to come to them while they're under my care.'

He grinned. 'Yes, I understand that. It's a big responsibility. How about taking Anna? She's done well, and must be finding a few muscles she's never known she possessed starting to ache by now. Anna, we're giving you a spell.'

She looked up, her hair blowing all over her head, the Drummond tartan covered with mucous, wool, milk, and worse, and said, 'Oh, *please* don't make me. I don't want to miss a bit of this. It makes me feel less an alien.'

The look on his face was unreadable, yet she wished she hadn't said it. Their glances met, locked, held.

He said, and she could have sworn he said it reluctantly, but felt he must be fair, 'I don't reckon we can count you as alien ... from the very start you got involved, didn't you, when you rescued two local residents and got them to hospital?'

It seemed to put her at a disadvantage, as if she ought to depreciate what she'd done. Then they heard a hail from the gate and swung round. Someone with a shambling gait was coming across the paddock. Anna blinked. The others didn't. They seemed to give a concerted groan, instantly suppressed, then Calum's whisper said, 'Oh, Lord preserve us! It's Barney. He'll be in a state of repentance.'

He was also cold sober. She had to admire the way they received him. He apologized ... 'Because I was hardly myself, last night, causing you great inconvenience, not to say danger and injury, when you so kindly tried to ferry me home. When I think I might have had your death on my conscience, Calum, it's downright remorseful I am. So now I'm feeling less under the weather, I'm here to offer my services with the lambing. They told me at the hospital you were walking wounded and that you'd not got off as lightly as I did.'

Kitty said, 'But how did you get here, Barney? Someone give you a lift?

He waved grandly. 'No, it was pension day, so I took a taxi. I could do no less.'

Calum said, 'Well, it was jolly decent of you. Sure we could do with your help. Kit's just off to collect the children,

55

so we'll be a hand short.'

Barney peered at Anna from under a shock of red hair gone grey. 'You'll be Alex's girl? They told me at the hospital – Sister Grey said Calum had told her this morning when she rang to find out how he was. Well, I'm glad for Kit and Gilbert's sake, they can sure do with someone of their own blood – and by the look of you, pitching in like this on your first day, it's better blood than his anyway. He and work never seemed to get on well together. That was my trouble – though I can manage fine if I keep off the booze. Not that he wasn't a darlin' lad. But like me, he was weak. But you've got a chin like your grandfather's.'

Oh, dear, Barney was a clanger-dropper, but they must be so used to him they didn't turn a hair. And work he certainly did, and took a great fancy to Anna so that he stayed with her all the afternoon. He had a knack with the ewes and they seemed to know it. His hands were gentle, his eyes tender for the pain they bore, even if it was for a surprisingly short time.

He stayed for dinner, and more clangers were dropped, but by Bill and Mac, who informed Barney, with great relish, that Anna had thought Calum was drunk too, because Barney's beer had soused him. He took it all most good-naturedly.

Philip, who usually went home for the evening meal, stayed too. It was his own suggestion. Anna caught the twinkle in her grandmother's eye. Philip said, 'You've all those lambs to feed. I'll give them a round of drinks after you've washed up. I've an idea Anna would enjoy feeding them. I'll show her how.'

Anna wasn't going to encourage this. 'Sorry, perhaps the children would help. I want to get that bandage off Calum's head and re-dress it. It looks anything but comfortable at the moment. He must have dragged that cap off too roughly. The way he's been trying to ease it right through dinner, makes me suspect the lint is catching on the stitches, and pulling on them, and there's nothing more annoying.'

Calum said hastily, 'There's nothing wrong with it. Besides, you mightn't get it back right. I believe there's a real technique involved in capelline bandages. Better leave well alone.'

She said crisply, 'I happen to have that technique. If

56

you'd not been so dopey last night you might've remembered me saying to the doctor I'd done nurse-aiding. That was during one of Mother's spells of being sure I was too tied to the guest-house.'

Maggie said hastily, 'Philip, you can feed the lambs on your own, can't you? We'd like to watch.'

'Oh, no, you don't,' said Anna, getting up. She put a firm hand on Calum's shoulder. 'Into the bathroom where it's private.' Meekly he did as bid.

She sat him on a stool, scrubbed up well, brought out the well-stocked first-aid kit from the cupboard, began unrolling the bandage.

He said, 'Enjoyed making me reverse my opinion of you, as stated in the hospital, didn't you?'

Her laugh had so much amusement in it, and no resentment, that he looked searchingly at her. She pulled a face. 'Of course I did. I'd have been less than human if I hadn't enjoyed setting that preconceived idea right.'

He persisted. 'Ah, but would you have been quite as devoted to your duties ... your new duties ... today, if you hadn't overheard that?'

Now her cheeks did show the flush of anger. 'What a very unpleasant remark! How distrustful you must be, Calum Doig. You think my spurt of energy, my disregard of mud and mucous and manure, was merely actuated by a desire to put you in the wrong?'

He sighed. 'That wasn't why I said it. Ouch!'

'Sorry. Then *why* was it?'

'Just that I hold a watching brief for Kit and Gilbert. They were friends of my own grandparents. What they own they've won by sheer hard work and it had to triumph over heartbreak too. To see them so happy over you fills me with dread in case, if you too let them down, their second state will be even worse than their first. They'd adjusted themselves to knowing they'd never see their son again. As my own mother has always said, you can get used to anything, even to being bludgeoned by fate. But I'd hate to see them take another knock.'

'Such as?'

'Such as being disillusioned again. If you drift into their lives then out again, it will leave their existence more empty than before.'

'So you mean if I don't intend to stay, it would be kinder to vamoose now, before they get too fond of me?'

'I didn't say that.'

'But you implied it.'

'I didn't. I was just warning you not to promise too much, to make yourself indispensable, to allow them to plan for a future that would include you.'

'You mean because I said I might take a job in Auckland?'

'Yes, you did say it, didn't you?'

'I did. But that was in the heat of the moment when you so unjustly accused me of coming for what I may – at some terrible date when Grandmother and Grandfather are no more – inherit. Inheritance doesn't just mean hard cash you know, dollars and cents, it means an inheritance of belonging, of feeling one of a family, of knowing one's family history, treading in the footsteps of generations of kinsfolk. Something *you've* probably known all your life. Something *I've* never known. When my mother's old uncle died she hadn't a relation left in the world – only friends that as a little girl I called Auntie and Uncle so I could feel a little more like other girls when they visited Fiji. God never *meant* the sins of the fathers to be visited on the children, I'm sure, but people see to it that they are! Just because my father was unstable and fickle, you imagine I'm the same. Well, I'm not, and never have been, so get that out of your mind for once and all. Watch it ... don't stand up ... oh, look what you've done! That bandage won't be aseptic any more!'

'Well, use another. There are plenty there.' He caught her hands. 'Anna, I'm sorry. I'd not realized there were two sides to it. I was only desperately anxious, along with all the other members of my family, that people we've known and loved all our lives, mightn't have to suffer any more. Philip's mother adores Kitty and Gilbert, even though – well, that's another story.'

She looked up into the dark blue eyes, felt her own softening, looked quickly away, said, 'It makes me feel horrible to think you'd rather I paid a fleeting visit and went away, than made them fond of me.'

His face was close above hers and very serious. 'No, but I don't want you keeping on promising them you'll stay. It's too soon for a girl of twenty-four to promise such a thing. This is a novelty just now, yes, but other girls Kitty has had in to help have found it too quiet, even girls more accustomed to a rural existence than you – used as you are to the glamour and colour and bustle of tourist life in the Islands. Don't promise too much too soon. After all, what is there here for a girl, apart from the farming and the companionship of a couple two generations ahead of hers?'

Suddenly the anger left Anna, the dimples flashed, and her mouth curved up. 'Oh, I don't know. There are two eligible men right on the property, you and Philip. Isn't that what some girls would like?'

It was sheer teasing, or so she meant it, but he took it seriously. 'Don't be too sure. I'm spoken for and Philip – well, I don't know about Philip.'

She gave another ripple of laughter, said, 'Well, that's all sorted out. Calum, please sit down again and let me take off this last patch of lint very carefully. It's sticking to the wound a little and it's just like I said, the stitches are caught in it. I'll be very gentle.'

She was. He said, when she was finished, 'Thank you, Anna, I'll admit that feels better than it did last night.'

She grinned, 'Oh, I'm not stupid enough to think it better than the hospital job, but it had had some rough treatment today. And I don't think you should be long out of bed tonight.'

'What? It's one of our favourite TV nights. I'll get Philip to take old Barney home if he can get him past the pub, and we'll settle down to being a nice quiet family party.'

So they came downstairs outwardly amicable. But Anna felt he would still carry a watching brief for his employers. As for herself, she felt he would bear watching too. His brother lived in the new house on the estate. Could it be that when Calum married he would want this house, this darling house? That he might persuade her grandparents to retire into Crannog? A fear of what the future might hold rose up in her. She subdued it. She must just take a day at a time. Everything would depend upon what sort of a girl Calum was going to marry, and how much Grandmother liked her.

A memory of what Maggie had said when she'd thought her uncle had been drunk: 'What'll Miss Kirkpatrick say?'

came to her. They were probably engaged, or near-engaged. Maggie didn't call her by her Christian name yet. Miss Kirkpatrick must be strait-laced. Anna frowned at her own thoughts. In a permissive society like today's, it was good sometimes to meet someone a little strait-laced. She wouldn't ask about her. No doubt in time she would meet her.

CHAPTER FOUR

SHE certainly did meet Miss Kirkpatrick very soon, that is, if you could call it a meeting, gazing at the Crannog pulpit on Sunday morning as the Reverend Sophy Kirkpatrick came in, following the beadle with the Scriptures, complete in her Geneva gown. Anna hadn't by then got over the surprise of seeing that name on the church notice-board as she'd come in.

She'd been behind the others, with Maggie, and said, 'Have you got a woman minister? Was that who you meant would have told Calum off if he'd been drunk?'

Maggie was so precise. Anna just loved her. She said, 'Oh, no, Anna. She wouldn't have told him off. She's too fond of him. But she'd have been disappointed in him. And looked sad.'

Therefore Anna had come into church expecting to see a middle-aged woman whom Calum wouldn't want to shock. Now she was gazing at – at a – well, there was no other word for it, at a ravishing red-head! And she wouldn't be a day over thirty, if that. And Calum must be thirty-three.

The Reverend Sophy had a curious blend of serenity coupled with a dynamic personality. Even Anna, whose thoughts were chaotic, could appreciate that. Her voice was delightful, crisp, with an inflection of humour and gaiety, yet you couldn't doubt she was dedicated to her work, and in spite of that dedication you had to recognize that she wasn't a bit other-worldly or too holy. In fact, she was down-to-earth.

Anna was conscious of a mixture of emotions. Perhaps one ought not to feel this way in church. Perhaps one should think only of worship, but – she knew a gladness in her heart not known before, that she was sitting between her grandparents, kin not known before, and who were almost swelling with pleasure in having their son's girl in the pew with them.

The prayer of thanksgiving, when the Reverend Sophy said, 'And for all those secret fulfilments that have come our way, O God, we give Thee thanks . . .' made Anna offer up a prayer of sheer thankfulness that her mother, who had walked a lonely way for so long, in a manless world, now knew a great love and was happed about with the rugged strength of Magnus Randal's devotion.

She must write her this very afternoon, tell her of her in-laws, say that she would just love them even as Anna did. The time would be ripe now. Mother would have had her honeymoon, undisturbed by thoughts of the past and would be settled in to their new quarters. Anna would tell them that she would fly up to Auckland often to see them when they returned next year, and that it would be even more wonderful for them to be on their own.

She was conscious of other things too . . . of the pleasing sound of Calum's baritone from where he sat, strategically placed between the twins. They rose for the hymn before the sermon, Horatius Bonar's hymn of praise. Anna had last heard it sung in a little mission church on one of the more remote islands, with palms waving outside and tropical scents hanging heavily on the hot still air. She loved the second verse, it fitted her changed life. . . .

'Praise in the common words I speak,
    Life's common looks and tones;
In intercourse at hearth or board
    With my beloved ones.
Not in the temple crowd alone,
    Where holy voices chime;
But in the silent paths of earth,
    The quiet rooms of time.'

The Reverend Sophy preached a compelling, warm-hearted sermon. Her turn of phrase was delightful. At times it was sheer poetry. At others she hit hard. And she told a story against herself with twinkling humour.

During the singing of the last hymn Anna was vibrantly aware of the happiness of the two people beside her. No wonder . . . perhaps of everyone in that church, it meant most to them to sing, so joyously, their voices not sounding in the least old,

'Praise, my soul, the King of Heaven;
    . . . Who like thee His praise should sing?'

For a moment the words on the page wavered in front of

Anna's eyes and she almost felt afraid of her grandparents' happiness. It was such a responsibility. She must never let them down. In a sudden revealing and forgiving moment she understood how Calum had felt. She felt cleansed and restored. Animosity was foreign to her nature. From now on she would be on a different footing with him. Time was on her side. She, and only she, could know she had little or none of her father in her, that she wouldn't be here today and gone tomorrow.

It was with a feeling of utter peace that she moved out into the aisle. As they emerged into the stone vestibule, in this rugged but beautifully designed church the pioneers of more than a century ago had raised, it became the happiest of occasions for the Drummonds, as the people crowded round to meet their new granddaughter, so recently found for them.

She was glad she didn't have her father's colouring, for people to remark on. Instead they kept saying how anyone would have known her for a Drummond, that she was the living image of her grandfather and of his twin sister, the long-gone Anna. But she was still more glad when someone said, 'But you have your grandmother's dimples.' She wanted Kitty to have some share in her.

The minister was outside, shaking hands. It was a proud moment when the Drummonds presented Anna. Sophy sparkled. 'What a wonderful thing it was that Mr. and Mrs. Forbes went to Fiji and met you! I so hoped and prayed that you'd come and be able to stay – Mrs. Drummond told me all about it over the phone. Sorry I've not yet been out, but I was away in Dunedin for a committee meeting at the Hall, and when I got home there was a lot of sick visiting to catch up on. But I'll be out tomorrow.'

Calum was behind them. 'I should hope so! I feel neglected. I've never been sick enough to warrant a duty visit, and when I am, what happens? You're away. I looked really fetching in my capelline bandage . . . now I'm down to a piece of sticking-plaster it's not half as romantic.'

Sophy's sapphire eyes sparkled. 'From what I heard you weren't exactly a cot case. The lambing continued just the same. I thought Philip would have had to have done double duty there, but apparently not. Besides which, chump, you know I have to be careful not to favour one lot of parishioners more than the other, and I'd not blame anyone for thinking Strathallan got more than its fair share.'

Calum chuckled, 'Well, under the circumstances it's no more than any member of your flock ought to expect.' Anna looked keenly at him. What did he mean? Yes, his glance to Sophy was pointed, affectionate. She looked quickly at Sophy. Her colour had risen a little.

All of a sudden it seemed to Anna that a cloud must have passed over the sun. She glanced up instinctively. There wasn't as much as a feather of cloud in all that blue. She became involved in more introductions, and, just before they left for home, saw Elizabeth and Rossiter Forbes coming towards them.

They both kissed her. Elizabeth said, 'Oh, welcome home ... I'd have been over before, but right in the middle of lambing I had to hive off to Dunedin to speak at a florists' conference. Their speaker couldn't come. Anna, you look as if you are already part and parcel of the community. Or so I hear ... rescuing old Barney and Calum. What an introduction! Still, it pitchforked you in. I heard from the hospital that they thought you were just spot on for a Drummond granddaughter. Oh, hullo, Philip, wasn't that a marvellous sermon? Aren't we lucky to have Sophy? I do hope we have her for a long, long time.'

Philip grinned. 'Don't be too sure of that. Women ministers are at risk, you know.'

Again Anna felt the touch of a shadow. What on earth was the matter with her? Though she was pretty sure what they all meant. Calum had said at the hospital he wasn't going to the Ball as his lady-love was away. And what on earth could it matter to her?

It was a busy day. Sheep didn't observe a five, or even a six-day week. It was a case of off with Sabbath finery and back into the worse-for-wear trews. The Cannog church didn't have an evening service. It took its turn with the other smaller churches of the parish.

They came in, finally, scrubbed up, had their tea. Sunday tea was always a relaxed one, they told Anna. They sat in a half-moon round the television set, watched Walt Disney's programme for the children, ate wedges of bacon-and-egg pie, hot sausage rolls, a variety of cakes and cookies and everyone had his or her favourite drink, from passion-fruit milk-shakes and hot chocolate, to tea or coffee.

Philip hadn't come in when he left his final tasks in the mothering shed. Calum left him at the door, and looked in at the group to say, 'Start without me, I want to ring Sophy.'

Mrs. Drummond looked surprised, 'Won't she be at her tea, Calum?'

He grinned. 'I don't reckon she'll have much tea tonight. She's a bit worked up over that innovation they're trying out at the Balloch service. I just wanted to wish her well – didn't get round to it this morning.'

He was almost out of earshot when Gilbert called, 'Calum, tell her there could be ice on the Pass Road, so to watch out for it. And tell her I dinna think she should stay to take supper with any of them out there. Best to get back here before the roads ice up too much. After all, she's nobbut a lass, even if she is ordained and all!'

Calum retraced a few steps, stuck his head round the door, said, 'Not to worry. Philip and I yarned about that. He's driving her there and back. He's more experienced in Central conditions than she is. I know she was here last winter, but it was much milder than this. Of course she's so damned independent. Doesn't like to think anything might daunt her that wouldn't daunt a brother of the cloth. Silly wench!'

He was soon back. No doubt he didn't want to hold her up too long. And Sophy must've given in about Philip driving her. He looked at Gilbert and said, 'She told me to tell you she's got gumption as well as an ordination certificate and not worry about her. That if women wanted to become ministers, they had to take the rigours of the back-country same as the men.'

Gilbert chuckled. 'Aye, she's a well-plucked 'un that. And it's no' just physical courage either. Hope she doesn't defy Philip over it, that's all.'

Calum laughed. 'Not a hope! My advice to him was pick her up and dump her in his car. She wouldn't dare struggle for fear of letting the dignity of the cloth down.'

When Calum had taken the children upstairs to supervise his nephews' baths and tell all three a story, and Kitty and Anna were washing up, Anna, compelled by something she knew not what, said, 'It's a wonder Calum didn't want to go over to Balloch with her.'

Kitty hurriedly sloshed some more plates through for Anna to dry. 'Losh, lassie, I canna keep up wi' you, and I've always prided myself on being a fast one. Yes, he'd have gone all right if it hadn't been for his head. He actually confessed it was sore tonight. Third day is always the worst. Sophy is a wonderful girl. Hope she doesn't mind Philip going with her.'

Anna knew she was wonderful. What she didn't know was why she should feel envy for the first time in her life. First, that is, apart from that wistfulness she'd known as a child when she had watched other little girls playing with fun-loving fathers, tossing balls to them, teaching them to surf, to swim. . . .

She said, 'Why did Grandfather mention her two kinds of courage? I expect he meant because she'd tackle the icy roads of Central and not turn a hair, but the other—'

'Oh, because of what she'd come through. She always had a leaning towards some kind of Christian service, so took social welfare training and became engaged to a very fine divinity student. He left the Theological Hall in the November and came straight here to be our minister, Roderick Knight. They planned to be married the next year when Sophy would have finished her course. In the June he was struck down by leukaemia. If ever a girl broke her heart, it was Sophy. They were so suited. We knew her extremely well, because when she came up for week-ends when they were engaged she always stayed at Strathallan.

'She pulled herself together, decided to carry on with his work – there are quite a few women ministers in the Presbyterian Kirk in New Zealand – and she entered for the ministry. We had an older minister for a few years till he retired, and as it coincided with Sophy's ordination, the parish called her. Even the old die-hards who didn't fancy a woman minister have changed their minds by now. She said to me recently that at least she didn't face bereaved people with the emptiness of inexperience. Her gallant acceptance of something that must have been hard for her to understand, has made other people accept sorrow more easily, not to question it so much, to kick against the pricks.'

Something in Anna's heart eased. That inexplicable envy! She felt a little shame.

Kitty went on, 'But grief can't continue for aye and we're

told it's foolish, even wrong, to sit up late to eat the bread of sorrow. Rod told her himself, just before he died, that life was for getting on with. And lately I'm pretty sure healing is setting in. She's fighting against the attraction because it's quite evident that if she married a farmer she'd not be able to carry on a full parish work. At least not once she had a family. But there are other spheres of service ... and other ministers. But life, and time, has a way of working these things out. Only men aren't noted for patience. She oughtn't to take too long to decide. Some other girl could dawn on his horizon. Mightn't be a bad idea at that. Might wake her up.'

M'm. Anna couldn't imagine Calum being a patient lover. And at his age, if a man was the marrying sort, he wanted to settle down. Perhaps this situation had added to his irascibility about the Drummonds' newly-found granddaughter coming in to disrupt their lives. She was still ashamed of the envy she had known. Not that she wanted to analyse it. It was probably just a natural wistfulness. Never in all her twenty-four years had Anna met anyone with whom she'd really want to spend the rest of her life. She'd had plenty of partners, had liked several very much, but it had stopped there. How wonderful it must be, she thought, to find someone like that. To know that ahead of you wifehood and motherhood lay. Not that it was everything, but how complete life would be if that relationship could enhance the other achievements.

If one had a true career, of course, it might be different. To be as dedicated as Sophy Kirkpatrick was, or to be in the nursing profession, or the teaching, which was what Anna had craved, could be very satisfying. But Mother would have been so lonely if she had gone to Auckland University and teachers' college. Anna had simply pretended she had no ambition for a career, for higher education. Mother would have killed herself managing the guest-house on her own. So it had been a case of: 'Do with thy might what thy hand finds to do.'

Anna hung up the tea-towel, said, 'I must write Mother and Magnus tonight. I'm thrilled about this. Not only do I feel this is my home, that my roots are here, but it gives them a world of two, and I can go up once a year to see them.'

67

Kitty put her arm round her girl. 'You can go more often than that, Anna, if it's the money for air-travel you're thinking of. The estate can easily stand two or three trips a year. Tell her that. Would you tell her too, that I'm not possessive, that you'll always be free to come and go as you like and if you do finally decide to take up some career in Auckland to be near them, I'll be glad for this precious interlude, and will then look forward to you spending holidays here. And tell her I am very grateful to her – because I'm sure now I've seen how she brought up her daughter solo – that she must be a fine person herself and I feel she must have given my son at least some years of happiness in his turbulent lifetime.'

When they went back into the sitting-room Calum was down from the story-telling and he and Gilbert were watching *County Calendar*, intent on a demonstration of a new method of irrigation. Anna said she'd go into another room to write her letter.

Kitty stopped her. 'They don't like the next couple of programmes, so write your letter then.'

Anna got fascinated with the irrigating too. Kitty went upstairs to switch the children's lights off and tuck them in, then called downstairs, 'Gilbert, they want Grandy too.'

Calum looked across at Anna from his big chair, said, 'Aren't you too tired for letters? You worked like a Trojan in the paddocks this afternoon. There's always another day.'

She shook her head. 'I like to be outside then. And this is going to be a mammoth letter. I'm writing to my mother and stepfather to tell them about finding my grandparents and that I'm staying.'

He looked startled. 'Mean to say they don't know yet? I thought Kitty wrote to Fiji. I'm sure she said when she heard from you from Auckland and then confessed to Gilbert what she'd done, that she'd written there. Why didn't you tell them then?'

Anna looked at him steadily. 'It came the morning of their wedding. I didn't want any thoughts of the unhappiness of other days to intrude upon Mother then. She'd shed ten years. She looked so young . . . all in gauzy green . . . and so lovely and carefree. You know how it is when something happens like that. It rakes up things best forgotten. The mind can't help going back. It wouldn't have been fair to Mangus if her thoughts had been of anyone but him that day. When we went to Scotland, Mother and I, and I found out the Drummonds' motto was 'gang warily' I thought it fitted Mother's attitude to life very well. Because of my father. She was sweet, never bitter, but she walked warily, didn't seem to want to trust a man again. Then Magnus came and changed all that. I used to lie awake at nights and pray she'd let that old reserve go, and fall in love with him. On her wedding-day I felt that faith looked out of her eyes again, and rang in her voice as she took her vows. I wanted nothing to upset that. So I kept mum. I determined I'd see what my grandparents were like before I committed myself, or told her.'

She stopped speaking, looked at him sharply for his reply to that. His eyes still held hers, but he withheld comment. It irked her.

She had an edge to her tone, 'It's very disconcerting when you get carried away and reveal your inner feelings to someone who's asked why, then doesn't comment. What's the matter with you?'

His eyes searched for a moment or two longer as if he needed to assure himself this was truth, then that dark face broke up and the fans of laughter-lines about his eyes deepened. He stood up and came across to where she sat at the table with the lamp on it.

He couldn't help a chuckle. 'Oh, Anna, you're so funny! You have such an angelic air, all cream and pink and soft two-tone golden hair and pansy-brown eyes ... and you aren't angelic at all. In fact you're a bonnie fighter. You can certainly hold your own. But this time please hold me blameless. You were thinking I didn't understand, that I thought you were putting on an act. Anna, get this straight: my silence meant only one thing. I was touched to think a modern girl could be so understanding, would put her mother's happiness first. And that, even though a very disturbing thing had happened to herself. So I couldn't find any words. Will you accept that as true?'

She was intensely conscious of him standing closely above her. She bit her lip. 'Sorry, Calum. I'm being too touchy where you're concerned. I thought you weren't giving me any credit for what I'd done, that you'd thought me secretive, not telling. Mother.' She grinned at him. 'But don't you think you're a bit tough on the modern girl, generalizing about her like that? I think lots of girls would have acted that way. I mean, wouldn't the Reverend Sophy have done just that?'

His face softened as if the very thought of Sophy was pleasant. 'Yes, she would, but then Sophy doesn't fit into the ordinary run of girls. She's someone very special.'

Anna dropped her eyes, picked up her ballpoint nervously, said, 'Well, I'd better get on with it. Calum, why don't you tilt that extension chair back and have a doze? A bit of rest now would stand you in good stead tomorrow. Don't crack too hardy. Most chaps would have had a day or two in bed after a crack like that.'

He hesitated a moment, then did as she said. By the time the Drummonds came back he was lying back, sound asleep, his open book on his chest, his dark face relaxed and even boyish.

Anna told Lois and Magnus the whole story, beginning with the likeness Elizabeth and Rossiter Forbes had seen, and omitting the actual nature of her arrival. She said that her mother's in-laws were kindred spirits and she and Magnus would adore them and when their year was up, or sooner if they could get leave, they must come over to meet them. 'You would both love it here and the grandparents would make you just as welcome, Magnus. You could have marvellous holidays, absolutely relaxing, after the tension and long hours of the operating theatre.

'I wish you could see it right now, with spring lying all over the meadows and the willows greening and the garden bursting forth in new colour and blossom every day. I don't know which I love most, the garden, the hills and the mountains, or the house itself. It looks as if, like Topsy, it "just growed". But I'm gradually finding out how it came to be, in the pioneer glimpses Grandy lets fall from time to time. At first it was a sod cottage, clay turfs, with tussock mixed in to bind it, just a shelter. But the first New Zealand Drummond wanted a stone house, like his forebears back in Scotland, so he didn't build in the wood that would have been quicker, he hewed his own stone out of the hillside. You can see the places he took it from, Mother. He built this large two-storey house slowly, adding to it as his family grew. His wife's name was Kirsty, but their first daughter was Anna, after the Annabella of long ago. There's always been an Anna here till Grandy's sister died. Now there is again.

'Mother, you wouldn't think I was any less yours because I've found my grandparents, would you? Because you and I have had such a marvellous relationship over the years, but it's pretty good to know your family tree. Besides which, in Grandmother and Grandfather you'll find kindred spirits. I think Dad must have subconsciously picked someone of the same calibre as his own mother. Gran is so happy about you, I can't tell her enough. She feels you must have given her son the only real happiness he could have known in his adult years.

'So I'm staying. I'll probably take a job at Roxburgh Hospital. We're too busy lambing just now. I've a feeling this will make you worry less about me. You were such a chump taking so long to say yes to Magnus because of me. I've got side-tracked. I was describing the house.

'It's on a slight rise, a ridge on the hill, so the drive sweeps up to the front door and down again. They built there because in torrential rain, which is seldom, the creek below can flood. Native and European trees mingle and shelter it from the west and east. Its back is to the south where the bad weather comes from, and it faces the sunny north, which lies open, between hills. A creek meanders through, and it looks as if for all the world a much mightier stream of long ago had carved its way through so that the sun could shine all day on the spot where Strathallan was to rise. They built it foursquare like those Georgian homes we saw in Britain, with small-paned windows, painted white, which show up against the natural stone.

'The windowsills are painted turquoise blue and the roof is made of Welsh slates and the front door is shining black with a brass knocker that I recognized immediately, from that sketch I took of the Drummond crest. A goshawk on a coronet with expanded wings. They sit on the gateposts too, carved in stone and thrill me every time we sweep between them. Each side are small modern wings, which soften the severity, and as they are single-storey, they have low-gabled roofs. They couldn't get Welsh slates of course, now, but they got some modern tiles that were black and blended

71

well, though Gran said they looked rawly new at first, but now lichens are clinging to them, they don't look so alien.

'You may wonder why they went on adding, with only two of them here, but the bigger annexe was added so that some day, when age means they can no longer manage the big house, they could install a manager's family here and go on living in the new part.

'I was so glad when Gran told me this. She said, "I could never take Gilbert away from Strathallan. I'd like him to be able to look out on Drummond pastures and Drummond flocks, till his day is done." Isn't that a poetic thought, Mother?

'There are hollyhocks climbing up against the house and I'm dying to see them bloom, and rambler roses too. The flowering currants and japonicas are all rosy and coral-pink and everywhere are forsythias like fountains of gold. I'm learning new names as fast as I can. The lilac has tight dark buds on it. I told Grandy how you'd once said you longed for the come and go of the seasons, for winter giving place to spring, and the scent of lilacs after rain, and he straightaway rang up a nursery in Roxburgh and ordered twenty lilac bushes, to plant each side of some natural stone steps that lead down to the brook, so you can walk between them when you come. They ought to bloom next year. So when Magnus's appointment with the Hong Kong clinic is finished, you have a rendezvous with the lilacs. They are to be palest mauves, deepest purples, and the all-white Persian lilacs.'

She paused and thought for a while before she added the next item. She ought to say something about how Strathallan was run. It took some thinking about because for some stupid reason, a reserve had crept into her outpourings. Then she scratched away. Get it over and done with, Anna.

'You'll wonder what the set-up is here. Well, Ian Doig, with his wife Betty, and three adorable children live in a new house on the estate. I haven't met the mother and father yet because Betty's mother in Dunedin is very ill, and she and Ian went down there before I got here. There are twin boys of five, Mac and Bill, and Maggie who's seven. They're imps of Satan, the boys, but such fun and quite biddable. It's just that we never know what they'll do next, and they have to be continually rescued from mud and water and trees.

'Ian's younger brother, Calum, is the farm manager and I expect when he gets married, he'll take over the big house. The Annexe is big enough to entertain you in, though – it has three bedrooms – so if he's wed before you come there'll be plenty of room.'

Well, that was one hurdle over. She'd taken it lightly. Hurdle? Why was she using that expression in her thoughts? She wrenched her mind away from this analysis, realized she was very tired, yawned, looked up, said, 'There, I've described Strathallan to them, my darlings, till they ought to be able to see it in their minds' eyes without need of photos, but remind me to take some coloured ones just the same. And some of you and Grandy, Gran. I've assured them you'd love to have them here for a holiday. I'll go and make our last cuppa. I know where everything is now.'

Calum didn't open his eyes till she brought the tray in. They listened to the late news, went to bed.

After Anna brushed her hair, she sat looking into the triple mirrors of the dressing-table. Three Annas looked back at her. One who had been Anna of Fiji; one, the centre one, who was now Anna of Strathallan; and that other one, in the right mirror, who was that? An apprehensive Anna, who shrank from the knowledge in her eyes. It was the Anna who'd never been in love before. Not till now. But what good could it do her?

Calum Doig had said he was 'spoken for'. She'd thought he'd meant an engagement. Seemingly it wasn't quite that, yet. Imagine anyone hesitating ... over a man like Calum Doig? Was Sophy really so dedicated to the ministry that she wanted nothing to come between it and herself, as a husband and family must to a certain degree?

If that was so, she simply didn't deserve Calum! She didn't know the meaning of love! Suddenly Anna banged her brush down, said to her mirrored eyes: 'You absolute idiot! A week ago you didn't even know he existed! Three days ago, when you first met, you positively hated the man. You've always scoffed at attractions as sudden as this. You must be mad! It won't last. It *can't* last. It's something born of the fact that he's here at Strathallan, in the home of your people, and that he loves it, even as you do. But he belongs to Sophy. Fancy falling for a man already spoken for!'

CHAPTER FIVE

SOPHY rang them quite early the next morning, asked for Calum. He came back to the breakfast-table, said, 'Sophy can't come out till lunch-time. Old Mrs. Meadows died during the night. She's over there now. And Peter Hollings is coming out of hospital at ten. Mrs. Hollings doesn't drive, so Sophy's going to take her over to get him. She said not to bother too much about lunch if you're going to be busy in the lambing paddock, Kit.'

Anna loved the way he called her grandparents by their first names. It must make them feel years younger. She pulled herself up. It was ridiculous the way her thoughts busied themselves about Calum all the time, now. She must remember she was supposed to gang warily. She mustn't let her runaway feelings blind her to the fact that the Doigs were extremely well entrenched here. Yet, in all fairness, why shouldn't they be? Till a month or so ago, nobody knew the Drummonds had a granddaughter.

As far as they were concerned, this could have been an ideal situation for them, someone they'd known all their lives to manage the estate. And if – when – Sophy married Calum, they would love their manager's wife even as they loved him. They already loved her as their minister, a gay and gallant lass.

So naturally Calum, and perhaps Ian and Betty, would have viewed with apprehension the fact that an unknown descendant was coming here, presumably to inherit. But Calum resented her less now. He was a just man.

Today was warmer than before, to Anna's delight, for as yet she wasn't used to these knife-edged winds that blew through golden rays of deceptive spring sunshine from the white tops about them. But once you began working with the ewes you became warm enough.

They had a few lambs and ewes to match up in the shed, so they came back a little early. On the way, in the Rover, Calum asked Philip about the service at Balloch. 'Did the older people really like it?'

'Like it? They just lapped it up.'

Anna said, 'I take it that it was a youth service, guitars, a bit of swing, or something? But presented so that the older—'

She got no further. They guffawed. Philip said, 'Wrong tack, entirely, Anna. Sophy's pretty astute. She felt that these days with so many innovations for the young folk, geared to their ideas, the older members were feeling a bit out of it. It's been most noticeable that while winter weather can account for some of them staying in of nights, some who didn't seem to know what bad weather was have dropped off. She didn't want the Balloch service to get this way. Cut off as it is through the Pass – did you know Balloch is a Gaelic name for a pass? – they've been a close-knit community, well mixed in age. So she decided on a short devotional service, with the older ones then taking over and digging down into their pasts, and their parents' pasts for stirring and hazardous tales of other days.

'Central Otago has a history anything but tame, you know, so it was no prunes-and-prisms stuff. Yet through it all they underlined the fact that these daring goldminers and settlers gave the church a prominent, even central, place in the community. Some of them opened their eyes a bit when old Jake Donnelly said that from what his father told him, the permissive society of today had nothing on some of the wild doings of those days. The dance-hall girls came in the train of the forty-niners from California, and it was a real Wild West Show at times. That the oldies with a bit of principle had a deal of temptation to face and to overcome. They're so keen now, the youngsters, they've decided to have a display when lambing's finished, of the relics and heirlooms harking back to those days, at a re-enactment of the old-time soirées the church put on. They want as many as possible to come in costume. Actually it was my mother's idea and she egged Sophy on.'

Calum chuckled in a teasing way. 'Heavens, Philip, that was quite a speech! Must be catching. Before you know where you are you'll be doing a bit of local preaching.'

Philip made a threatening move towards him. Kitty, in a tone of rapture, said, 'Oh, Anna can go in Gilbert's grandmother's best silk gown – Kirsty's. It has a bustle, Anna, and it's brown watered silk with sort of panniers of cream lace, and cream net sleeves from the elbows, frilled at the wrists.

75

It would be just lovely with your brown eyes.'

Calum said, 'Have you any others, Kit? There'll be a great demand for genuine pioneer stuff.'

'Yes, though some not as old as that, but all lovely. Still, as Balloch and Crannog weren't only settled by the first ones to come here, all fashions should be represented. There were some who followed who were just as hard-working, just as determined to wrest a living from this bare, rock-strewn country. So their dresses graced many a later soirée.'

'I had Sophy in mind,' said Calum. 'Not belonging to the district, she won't have anything.'

Anna said quickly, 'She could have the brown moiré. I could pick another. With her lovely coppery colouring, the brown would be ravishing on her. I mean she couldn't take rose-pink for instance, so her choice would be more limited. Redheads need the right colouring.'

Calum said very quickly, 'Oh, no, Anna. That's a kind offer, but an early Drummond gown should be worn by a Drummond. Gilbert would be disappointed otherwise. Besides, the parish will fall over themselves to provide their minister with a suitable gown.'

'They already have,' said Philip, grinning. 'My mother's offered Sophy her great-grandmother's wedding-gown.' He turned to Anna. 'My great-great-gran came out on the *John Wickliffe* with the first Scots settlers to Dunedin. The journey took months – long enough for that eighteen-year-old girl who came aboard fancy-free, to fall for one of the ship's officers. He wouldn't let her set foot on shore till she wore his ring. He came back on the next voyage, a year later. She couldn't have a white wedding-dress, of course, but someone on board had a length of the most beautiful blue material. I'm no judge of materials, but it's sort of gauzy. Sophy will look a dream in it.'

Calum said, 'Didn't Victoria want it? I remember your mother mentioning this idea, vaguely, before Victoria took off.'

'No, Mum's got it all in hand, whether Victoria wants to go or not. She's to wear Dad's great-gran's dress. Deep cream lace. Dad would die if it was anything but a Sherborne gown.'

Calum said, 'We'll have to hog-tie Victoria. She's here one moment, gone the next, Anna. A real career girl. She's an adviser to a firm of New Zealand interior decorators and is more or less a freelance. Philip's mother can always do with her help at home when she's not on the move. But we never know where we are with her. She's a top-notcher in her own line, so the firm usually lets her work to her own time-table. She's up in North Canterbury at the moment, re-designing one of the old homestead interiors.'

It sounded exciting, the soirée. Crannog wasn't the Sleepy Hollow it appeared at first sight. As they reached the shed a rider came up the drive on a superb chestnut mare, a slim figure in trews, with a yellow polo-necked sweater under a bottle-green windcheater ... a girl with coppery hair not piled smoothly and demurely on her head as yesterday in St. Christopher's pulpit, but tied back carelessly with an emerald green gauzy bow. Sophy.

She rode almost up to them, swung down, opened a gate nearby and sent the mare in with an affectionate slap on her rump, to join two other horses there. Oh, yes, Sophy Kirkpatrick was very much at home here.

She had a bunch of letters in her hand and the morning paper from Dunedin. She had collected them from the mailbox as she came in. There was one for Anna with a Hong Kong stamp on. 'I'll have that for my stamp club, if it's not spoken for, please,' said Sophy.

By the time they got to the kitchen Anna had it open and began to read eagerly. She made an exclamation, read on, then caught her grandmother by the shoulders and danced her madly round the kitchen with Kitty laughing helplessly and imploring her to tell her what was wrong. 'Or right,' she added, 'by the look of you.'

'Isn't it just marvellous? The most fantastic stroke of luck! Grandfather, come in here while I tell you. It's from Magnus and Mother. Instead of going to Auckland when he's finished his year overseas, he's been appointed to a position in the Med. School in Dunedin. It's what he's always wanted. Oh, I'm glad I didn't get my letter posted. Listen to what Mother says: "You must make your own decision, of course, and if you find yourself a job in Auckland that you love, I won't ask you to leave it, but I can't help thinking how lovely it would be if you fell in love with the South Island on your travels and took a position in Dunedin or somewhere near. I'm hoping Auntie Ed knows where to forward this on, so you can look round while you are down South."

'Oh, my dears, isn't it marvellous? We'll be in the same island and only a hundred miles apart. They'll be able to come up for week-ends. I'll be able to spend some with them. Oh, it's the best of two worlds for me. How lucky I am!'

After the excited talking died down, Anna went out to the wash-basin on the back verandah to scrub up. Calum was there, on his own. 'So you really have made up your mind to stay, Anna?'

'But could you doubt it?' she asked, her eyes holding his. She wished she could read that expression. Blue eyes were so inscrutable. Brown eyes seemed to mirror every change of feeling.

She decided on candour. 'Calum, I do undertand this was a difficult situation for you. Yours is a life-long association with the Drummonds. You've been as a son to my grandfather. Naturally, you'd expect to carry on when they go. Tell me, because I'd like it clear, hasn't that always been understood?'

He was drying his hands on a hard khaki linen towel, his eyes fixed on hers. 'Yes. So what?'

She said softly, her pansy-brown eyes holding his frankly, 'Then you have nothing to fear from me. I rather think that when my grandparents built that Annexe on it was so that when you get married, you and your wife could take over the homestead and they would live there, part of the homestead still, but leaving a new wife her home to herself. Right?'

'Right. That was the idea. Why?'

'Because that's the way it'll stay. Nothing is changed. I'll probably take a job in Roxburgh Hospital with a bit of luck, and live with Gran and Grandy in the Annexe. If I can't get that sort of job, which I'd like best, I'll see what the hotels can do; it's a tourist area, so I guess I'd find something. I've no diploma for it, but I'm a trained caterer.'

He said slowly, 'You will be Gilbert's heir. It's going to—'

She held up a hand. 'Calum, till six weeks ago the Drummonds didn't even know I existed. They'll probably want to leave me a legacy. It would be only natural. They might even want me to take and treasure some of their pioneer pieces, which I would do for their sakes, and maybe I could inherit the Annexe – more than that I will not take. You've worked for this. You've kept the estate going, you and your brother. I will not be put in the position of the cuckoo-in-the-nest.'

They heard Philip coming and immediately rushed into small talk.

Anna was aware of very mixed feelings during the meal. She so liked Sophy, but was intensely irritated that she could be so indecisive about marrying Calum. He was very gentle with her, surprisingly so when gentleness wasn't something you associated at first with that hawk-like face. Under that beaky exterior must lurk compassion. Pity for all this girl had been through must have softened him towards her.

Suddenly she thought of what Grandfather had said about enjoying verbal sparring when she and Calum had been bickering about her possible aid in the lambing field. He'd said, '*This* one won't agree with all you say.'

But would the Reverend Sophy agree with all Calum said? Weren't ministers given more to debate than sweet accord? Or did they keep that for their pulpits, for their Presbytery or Synod meetings, and was Sophy all sweetness and light when she was with Calum? It was odd. Especially when Grandfather had sounded as if he thought all this agreement was rather dull for Calum.

Oh, what was she pondering on this for? She must stop thinking about him. About them. That way lay emotional disturbance. But she was glad she'd made it plain to him that Anna Drummond would be no stumbling-block to Sophy and Calum taking up residence at Strathallan. Calum wasn't the sort to take no easily from someone he desired for his wife.

After the meal she found Kitty and Philip deep in conversation in the kitchen. They cut off quickly as she came in, looked guilty, then, she thought, relieved. Gran said, 'Oh, we thought you were Sophy. Thought we'd been copped. I'd had an idea. Philip thinks it might work too, if you're sport enough to give it a go. If—' she cut off as Sophy and Calum came in, carrying their dishes.

All Grandmother could say was as they were piling in the truck, and a whisper said in Anna's ear, 'Follow Philip's lead, will you? Play up to him.'

Anna said, 'You mean to – to help things along – with Sophy and—'

'Sh!' said Kitty, and added brightly, 'Ah, here you are, Sophy, in you go.'

Well, it was obvious Philip and Kitty had decided to throw Calum and Sophy together more. Maybe Sophy was so busy it was all work and no play, and Anna would be roped in with Philip for a little light relief. She'd find out more later. She didn't need to. Like Gran said, she followed Philip's lead.

But Sophy was always fun like this on Mondays, Calum said to Anna during the afternoon, watching Sophy playing a trick on Philip. She'd come up behind him, unseen, with another newly-born lamb just as he delivered a ewe of one and bent to assist its second one into the world. She quietly laid the odd-one-out beside the first and tip-toed away unseen. Philip took quite a time with the second twin. By now they were all watching him, grinning. He managed it at last, the ewe struggled to her feet, and Philip turned round to see how the first had fared. His eyes just bulged, an incredulous look went over his face. They could see the thought clicking into place: 'Triplets? . . . but I don't remember—' Then he looked sharply at Sophy who was wearing a too-innocent expression and he shook his fist at her and took after her. He chased her clean round a clump of willows and out of sight.

They emerged eventually, Sophy wiping tears of laughter away, but pretending to be angry with Philip and quoting:

'Oh, it is *excellent* to have a giant's strength,
But it is *tyrannous* to use it as a giant!'

Calum's eyes were alight with laughter too. 'What did you do to her, Philip?'

Philip's dark hazel eyes twinkled into slits. 'What do you think I did? Forgot my reverence for the cloth and clouted her! Sophy, you get that lamb back to its poor demented mother right now. There's enough bleating going on round here without that.'

Calum said, 'I'll get it. Come on, Sophy. I'll save you from any more manhandling. He's a wild chiel when he gets his dander up.'

Philip started after them. Impulsively, Anna caught his

hand. 'No, don't, Philip. Leave them be.'

Philip gave her a peculiar look.

She said, 'It's a nice change for Calum. He and I don't always hit it off. We're always getting off-sides with each other.'

He looked amazed. 'Why, Calum's very easy to get on with.'

She dimpled, looked mischievous. 'Well, perhaps I'm not. We rub each other up the wrong way.' She paused, said, 'Though I—'

She'd been going to say: 'Though I think we've got our wires uncrossed at last,' but Philip came in with, 'What a pity! I thought we might have made a foursome up for a musical in Alexandra either Wednesday or Thursday night, depending on Sophy's engagements. It's a repeat of a very successful performance by a local playwright and cast. Called *All Roads Lead to Arrow*. About Arrowtown in the gold-rush days.'

Anna didn't hesitate. 'Philip, I'd love it. But any chance of you saying *we* were going, and would they like to make up a foursome? It would be more pointed. That's what Kitty's after, I think. It would create an atmosphere quite different from the parish outings and so on. I think Kitty feels Sophy takes her work just a little too seriously. I mean, everyone needs a break. Nothing like an atmosphere of romance.'

He burst out laughing. 'This'll please Kitty no end — plunging in!'

At his laughter the other two, the lamb now restored, turned round. Philip and Anna were still hand in hand. Calum and Sophy stood very still for a moment, strangely. Then they looked at each other rather uncertainly. As if they were exchanging a shared idea.

Anna knew inward laughter. Love was supposed to be catching Perhaps Calum and Sophy were too prosaic, too cautious A faint tremor went through Anna. *Could* one think of Calum as prosaic? Given the right circumstances, she thought Calum and she might have struck sparks off each other.

Perhaps, though, Sophy was slowing him up. Probably she hadn't always been like that. Her grief, no doubt sometimes too heavy to be borne, had stilled some spring of joy in her. Her work, too, had more than likely made her inclined to take things too gravely, to weigh up the pros and cons at length. But at times her natural lightheartedness would bubble to the surface as it had when she'd played the joke on Philip.

Philip's pressure on her hand was insistent. He pulled her after him, making her bound with him from tuft to tuft of the springy turf of the paddock. They reached the others.

Philip said, 'I've just asked Anna to come with me to Alex on either Wednesday or Thursday night to see *All Roads Lead to Arrow*. I know you two have seen it before, but I could see it half a dozen times myself. How about you making up a foursome?'

Calum and Sophy looked a little strained. Strained or puzzled? They each demurred a little. Philip said a little roughly, 'I'm sure you haven't got both nights tied up this week, Sophy. It's time you got off the hook more. Plenty of male ministers aren't so single-minded as you. Even the married ones take time off to escort their wives and children to all sorts of performances. You aren't indispensable to the parish, you know.' (Oh, yes, Philip was on Calum's side all right.)

Calum grinned. 'He's right, Sophy. I've been preaching that at you for long enough, too. So has Kitty, and just about everyone else.'

Sophy gave in. For the rest of the time no one was as gay as she. Philip stayed for the evening meal too. Anna found out that the manse at Crannog had a glebe, relic of the days when the minister had covered the parish visiting with a gig, not a car, and had needed somewhere to pasture his horse. Sophy rented it out to a farmer for grazing, but her mount roamed at will among his wethers. 'Riding's so good for me, after sitting at my desk long hours. It will be idyllic tonight, riding home in the cool spring twilight. Riding home with me, Philip?'

He shook his head. 'Not tonight, I'm afraid. I want to be back here early tomorrow morning so I'll have to take the car, and besides, I've promised to show Anna the mysteries of the differing grades of wool in the farm offices. But I'm sure Calum's dying for the chance.'

Calum opened his mouth, closed it, said hurriedly, 'Too right. Sophy, how about us riding up Blue Spur before we take your road home? I bet you've not seen the daffodils down by the Crannog Dam this year? They're more numerous than ever and the light catches the water at sunset.'

Anna noticed Kitty concealing a smile.

Philip and Anna spent a matter-of-fact hour with the wool samples in the farm office, but there was no chance of private conversation because Gilbert couldn't stay out of it. His whole manner revealed his delight that his granddaughter was interested in this, and that it was perfectly natural because she was Anna of Strathallan. She had a pretty shrewd idea Kitty wouldn't have told him of her machinations. Once or twice she had the idea that Gilbert himself was thinking that if only Anna and Philip were attracted to each other seriously, then Strathallan would be safe in all the years to come. That those of Drummond blood, if not of name, would always farm here. But she didn't feel an atom of anything even approaching love for Philip. He was good fun, that was all.

She gazed madly at the samples, tried to take in the unfamiliar terms, make some kind of intelligent replies and all the time in spirit she was riding beside the sunset-stained waters of the dam, the perfume of daffodils and lily-of-the-valley rising to them. Kitty had planted the lilies long ago. Now tourists came from far and near to see them, Philip told her. He'd said in front of Calum and Sophy as they mounted, 'I'll take you to see them another time, Anna. Perhaps by moonlight. We'll stick to the wool samples tonight.'

When they'd finished in the office, she wrote her postscript to her mother's letter telling her how glad she was Magnus had the post in Dunedin. She was glad she had that to do. She was in bed long before Calum came home. No doubt Monday nights at the Manse were duty-free too, for Sophy. Was Calum making the most of his time? Had that aura of romance she and Philip had tried to create softened Sophy a little? But it was pretty feeble. They ought to think of something much more effective to help Sophy make up her mind. It was worth a try. If Calum loved Sophy, and she didn't think he was the man to love lightly, then he ought to have her.

Sophy had been in the parish a year and a half. Had Calum courted her, to no avail, most of that time? There was a betraying moment when Anna said to herself, 'Oh, if

83

only I'd come here two years ago! I wonder if—' and she had bitten off the wish that had come unbidden to her mind. That was stupid.

Gran and Grandy were delighted about the outing. They were so transparent, the darlings. They must think that if she had some social life, it would be a recompense for the stir and gaiety of the guest-house. They were adamant that the four should make a night of it. 'Sophy is so rarely off the chain,' said Kitty, 'and I would like to see her a little less careworn. She's over-conscientious. Calum, you're to finish early. Gilbert and I can manage anything that crops up after that and it's always best to whisk Sophy out of the district before anything happens in the parish. I don't mind the urgent things interfering, but the really trivial makes me cross. So make it a dinner-party first. Anna, you'd like the chance to wear one of your long dresses, wouldn't you?'

Sophy liked it too. She sounded just like any girl when she rang Anna about it. Calum said to Philip, 'As you're nearer Crannog, how about you going over there, and we'll pick you up, Anna and I? You can leave your car in Sophy's drive.'

Philip shook his head. 'No, we're taking my car to Alex. It was my idea, so I'll carry it through. I'll bring my things over here in the morning, and we can all go into Crannog for Sophy.'

The men certainly didn't look like horny-handed sons of the soil when Anna came downstairs into the big lounge where they were standing by the fire. They'd looked up to watch through the open door her progress down the last half-dozen steps and their widened eyes were a tribute to the picture she made. Her dress was in two shades of purple, simply made, with a deep wide square-cut neck edged with bands of white *broderie anglaise,* and above it she had a piece of Celtic jewellery she'd brought back from Scotland with an amethyst gemstone set in its scrolls and symbols.

Nevertheless, as she watched Calum's face in the rear-vision mirror, from where she sat in the front seat of the car with Philip, she thought he looked grim rather than happy. But why, when he was having a night out with his lady-love?

However, the look disappeared when they drew up on the

manse drive, and Sophy came running out on to the lighted porch, as eagerly as any girl. She wore a long deep blue skirt, and over it a tunic-style blouse with full bishop sleeves, pattered with a smudgy effect in blues and greens, peacock-bright. It had a high Chinese neckline and she needed no jewellery at all with those eyes like sapphires above the blue shadings. Her hair was piled high with a twist of tendrils in front of each exquisite ear.

Anna hadn't even had time for a trip to the hairdresser, the day had been so busy; she'd simply washed her hair herself. Her half-fringe slanted across her forehead in its dark-gold and pale-gold streaks and fell softly just to her shoulders, and was turned inward in a page-boy style. Given a black velvet suit she'd have looked exactly like one of the Princes in the Tower, Calum had thought.

Calum didn't kiss Sophy as he greeted her . . . so the sunset over the dam hadn't worked a spell. He just took both her hands, held her off from him a little and said, 'We'll be the envy of everyone in the hotel dining-room tonight.'

Anna missed the fact that Sophy had instinctively taken a step towards the front of the car, then drew back as Calum's hand cupped her elbow and edged her towards the rear door.

Despite Calum's compliment to Sophy, she could sense that the two in the back seat weren't at ease. Their talk had a hint of reserve. To cover it up, Anna and Philip chattered madly all the way with what must have sounded like fond raillery.

It was a delightful evening . . . on the face of it. Lovely to dine in this dramatically situated town, encircled by dark jagged hills, with an immense lighted clock silhouetted against the rock face of one of them. They had a superb dinner to start with, and a musical treat to follow, with the added spice of it all being based on local history. They relaxed and conversation coming home was four-pointed and more natural.

Till Sophy asked them in for coffee. Philip hesitated, said, 'Calum will have some, no doubt. You could run him home later, Sophy. Fact is I know Kitty won't sleep till her one ewe lamb is safely in the fold, and I want to show Anna the moon over Crannog Dam. I reckon it'll be perfect about now. Night-night, you two.'

The two in the back got out as bidden, went inside the manse. Philip laughed all the way down the main street. He was in very high spirits. 'It's working! See the look on Calum's face, Anna? Gosh, you're a sport. And Sophy doesn't know what to make of it.'

Anna couldn't see how this would help the reluctant Sophy fall into Calum's arms. It was more likely to put her back up. It was too pointed, marooning Calum there without transport, so Sophy would have to drive him home. Yet perhaps Philip knew them better than she did. But men were so lacking in subtlety, and Philip seemed even more lacking in finesse than most. It was one thing to try to create an aura of romance and get Sophy away from the parish but another to leave a couple alone like a matchmaking mamma!

Suddenly all Anna wanted was to be at home at Strathallan, tucked up in bed. But there was this blasted moon. What did it matter if daffodils were paled to ghost-blooms by its blanching light, or if a heady perfume stole up from the water's edge if the wrong man walked by your side?

She was thankful to say goodnight to Philip at the front door of Strathallan. He grinned at her in his disarming way. 'Thanks a million. See ... what did I tell you? Grand-mamma is waiting up for Red Riding Hood. Exit the wolf!'

Sure enough there was a light on in the lounge. She opened the door, reproof on her lips, then stopped dead. It was Calum. He smiled at her a little mirthlessly, waved his hand towards the table Kitty had set out with a flask of coffee, sandwiches, biscuits. 'Help yourself. You're a bit earlier than I thought. Didn't Philip take you to his place for supper?'

'No, of course not.' She sat down and rather nervously began to pour out. A used cup stood there too. She said, looking at it, 'Didn't you have coffee at the manse after all? Or did you feel like another?'

'Of course I didn't have coffee at the manse at that hour. Philip must be mad. It would have been quite different if we'd all stayed. Talk about the fierce white light that beats upon a throne – wasn't that what Tennyson said? – it's nothing to the light that beats upon a manse, especially when the minister is a young and beautiful woman. So you didn't go to Philip's place?'

86

She looked at him over the rim of her cup. 'I said I didn't, Calum. Why ask again? I'm not in the habit of telling lies. Is it because I'm my father's daughter that you have to ask twice? Just because he was a born liar it doesn't mean I am.'

He waved an impatient hand. 'Of course I don't think you are. It was just that you certainly took your time about coming home despite the fact Philip told you Kitty would be waiting up. I sent her off to bed. But of course, it was some moon, wasn't it?'

'I suppose it was,' said Anna without spirit. She was being made to feel guilty and she didn't like it. She added gloomily, 'But that grass was absolutely soaking. I was perished. I can't even feel my feet. My toes will probably drop off with frost-bite. I thought I'd *never* get Philip away!'

He was off his feet in a moment, a laugh escaping him. 'Oh, Anna, you're so funny. You disarm me when I'm most mad with you. Let me see your feet.'

He lifted the purple skirt, saw the inadequate shoes, the sodden stains, swore. 'Philip must be raving mad. If you catch a cold, Kitty'll sort him. I'd not be in his shoes for anything.' He laughed. 'Nor in *these* shoes, the rubbishy things. Why didn't you tell Philip it was no time to be wandering through daffodils – and you accustomed to a tropical island!' He had her shoes off as he spoke, and his hands, warm, rather rough, were rubbing her feet. It felt wonderful. She looked down on the smooth dark head and had a strong impulse to place her hand on it. It didn't last half long enough.

He went running off and came back with a huge red plastic bowl of hot soapy water, a towel over his arm, and a pair of farm socks that he dropped in front of the fire to warm. He knelt, lifted her skirt over her knees, drew her white bloodless feet into the benediction of the warm water. He dried them as deftly as any mother, drew on the socks. They were pure wool of Kitty's own spinning and knitting and they felt marvellous. She almost purred with creature comfort, sticking out her feet to the fire and looking like some absurd child.

Another laugh escaped Calum. She looked up at him inquiringly. He said, 'You look such a quaint combination of Cinderella-in-the-kitchen, and the princess-at-the-ball, with

87

those great big socks sticking out from under that purple frill.'

She pulled a face. 'I certainly lost my slipper tonight! Things didn't go a bit the way I'd hoped they would. Philip's just got no finesse.'

His eyes narrowed a little. He began to speak, checked, suddenly pulled her to her feet. 'Come on, off to bed while your feet are still warm.'

There was a very low light on the landing upstairs. Her room was first. Instinctively, for no reason at all, they both paused, as if all hadn't been said that should. She put a hand on the landing rail, looked up at him, uncertainly, wistful. Should she apologize, or – no, perhaps it was better to leave it be.

While she hesitated he made up his mind to say something himself evidently. She was surprised to see his lips twitch. He was amused then, not angry at their efforts. 'Tell me, Anna, when you were at school, did you always fight other kids' battles?'

She blinked. 'Yes, I'm afraid I did. Not always wisely. At times I used to founder in the mud, like I did tonight. It drove my mother mad. She said my heart always over-ruled my common sense.'

She'd never seen that hawk-like face so tender. It was elder-brotherly. He continued: 'So, did Kitty tell you about Sophy's state of mind? Or heart? Of her indecision?'

Embarrassment made her blush. 'Yes, Calum.'

This time he laughed out loud. 'So you decided to pep things up a bit? Who thought of it, you or Philip?'

'Well, it was Kitty and Philip really. I just fell in with it. And I *do* love Sophy, Calum.'

He smiled. 'Yes, it's easy to do. And she does take herself too seriously. Well, you had the best of intentions, only—'

'Only it flopped badly, didn't it?' she said miserably.

'It wasn't your fault it flopped, it was Philip's. He was so transparent. I think you had Sophy guessing for a bit. She was intrigued. But when you drove off she burst out laughing.'

'Oh, dear, will she be horribly cross with him?'

'No. Mind you, she asked me if I was in the plot too but my conscience was clear on that.'

'Did – do you think it furthered things at all?'

'I don't know. I was a bit mean. You can tell from her sermons how much quotations mean to Sophy. I fired one at her. Asked her had she read much of Addison. If so what about his saying: "The woman who deliberates is lost." She was quite impressed.'

'You mean because she was amazed you should have read Addison?'

'Yes. I didn't dare tell her I'd come across it in a cryptic crossword I was doing one night I couldn't sleep.'

Anna thought privately that sounded like a bit of intellectual snobbery on Sophy's part. Did Calum, intellectually not measure up to Roderick Knight? But Calum had a degree from Lincoln College. Perhaps in Sophy's estimation that didn't count for as much as an Arts degree.

Anna said in a small voice, 'I don't think I'll go to church next Sunday. I'd feel such a fool.'

Calum caught her by the shoulders. 'You'll go all right. Sophy's got a great sense of humour. She said it looked as if we needed saving more from our friends than our enemies.'

'She'll need a sense of humour. Nobody really loves matchmakers. And people should be left to make up their minds in their own good time. I'm sorry I got caught up in it.' She tilted her face towards his. 'And what about your sense of humour, Calum? Does it only amuse you, or do you really feel angry with me . . . inside?'

'Good lord, I'm not angry at all. Why should I be? You acted from the very best of motives. I think it was sweet of you, even if it back-fired. Good night, Anna. Don't lose any sleep over this lot.'

Taking her quite by surprise he bent down, brought one hand up, brushed her fringe right aside, kissed her lightly on the forehead, just as she had so often seen him do to Maggie when she was going to bed.

Suddenly he said, as if impatient, 'Oh, go on off to bed, Anna Drummond.'

She was surprised to find herself shaking a little. Not because he'd kissed her. Oh, no, that kiss had been as passionless as a mother kissing her sleeping baby, just a lullaby kiss. No, her knees were shaking at the effort it had been not to move nearer, to kiss him back. Oh, how stupid! Go to bed, Anna of Strathallan, take off your purple gown and his big thick clumsy farm socks, get into that lovely bed, warmed by the electric blanket your dear grandmother would have switched on long ago, and count your blessings ... you have a family, a home with its roots deep in the soil, something lasting and permanent ... don't cry for the moon.

Anna sprang into bed, pulled the clothes over her head and *stopped* counting her blessings. The smaller delights and compensations were nothing when the one thing you desired above all others was out of reach. If she gave way now to this utter misery that was swamping her, she might be better able to face another day tomorrow.

CHAPTER SIX

TRULY enough the ordinariness of the day overlaid the poignancy of the night before. Mother had always said her salvation had lain in having more to do each day than she could possibly accomplish, and that the first unbearable smart always wore off.

By Thursday fewer lambs were coming and the weather was so good, with none of the capricious showers usual in the New Zealand September, they had fewer problems. The ewes in the mothering shed condescended, mostly, to feed their rejected offspring, or in cases where they'd lost their own, gradually accepted foster-lambs.

In the afternoon Kitty took Anna off to the Forbes' property, Pukerangi. Kitty said, driving along, 'It means The Hill of Heaven, and that's just what it is to Elizabeth. I think I told you it was a case of second marriages for both Ross and Elizabeth. I feel it was foreordained they should marry as compensation to both of them.

'As you'll know from her books, Elizabeth lived at Lavender Hill. She created a paradise out of a wilderness there. Lazy Larry, we called her first husband. His land was every bit as good as other orchard land round here, but he even let some of it go back to gorse. He didn't replant when he should and would have neglected his trees completely had Elizabeth let him. She slaved day and night for her family, writing books about floral arrangements and making a garden and building up a small florists' business here. I used to see her doing his work as well as her own, and could have choked him. We'd see her spraying, picking, pruning by day, yet if we passed coming home from Roxburgh late at night, her study window would be lit, trying to get a book finished. Such lighthearted books too, we don't know how she did it. It may sound callous, but when Larry died, after months of devoted nursing on her part, we were glad for her sake, even though she'd been too loyal to utter a word against him.

'Rossiter's case matched hers. A whining hypochondriac of a wife, always moaning that she should never have married a farmer. That I agreed with . . . for the farmer's sake.

Ross was so patient with her. Funny, the only time I ever liked that woman was when she had her last illness. The others were imaginary, mostly. This she bore rather patiently.' Kitty chuckled. 'I think she found compensation in the fact that now she had a genuine call on people's sympathy. Ross went off on a world trip to put a gap of time between losing his wife and asking Elizabeth to marry him. Silly chump didn't say one word to her. Elizabeth fretted. Finally Fergus MacGregor, a young friend of hers, took a hand. He wrote hinting that Elizabeth was thinking of an overseas trip, and he hoped she might meet someone on board ship to revive her interest in life, that she'd not been looking well ... my goodness, how that worked! Rossiter Forbes was back here before you could say Whangamomona, and swept her off with him to Spain to finish his world tour.'

Anna thought: 'So all meddlers don't make a mess of things.'

It was wonderful to be visiting the round-faced merry Elizabeth. Who could have imagined the twenty-five years of her first marriage had been so tough? Pukerangi was so truly named. Its lower slopes were girdled by lines of poplars that wound in and out of its contours, delightfully punctuated by copsy clumps of trees in every hollow, where silver birches and rowans whispered woodland secrets and primroses and violets patched the ground with gold and purple.

Its symmetrical hilltop, ringed by a formation of rocks exactly like a coronet, gave it a regal appearance and a cloud leaned down to touch its crest lovingly today, as if to identify it with the sky itself. But the garden, about the old farmhouse, was its chief glory, built on terraces afoam with all the flowers of spring. It seemed as if every crevice sprang a bloom, Nature illustrating her abhorrence of a vacuum.

A stream, diverted by Rossiter, under his wife's guidance, meandered through, dropping from terrace to terrace in a series of pools, where waterlilies spread green saucers, and purple iris fringed the edges. It added a cadence of its own to the birdsong that sounded ceaselessly from spinney and grove.

Anna said, 'Oh, what creation must have gone into this, what years of work, to make a hillside that must once have been as bare as those others, blossom like this.'

Kitty said, 'Do say that to Elizabeth. She waxes a little impatient with the well-meaning folk who say: "Ah . . . obviously you have green fingers." As if a garden grows by magic, not toil.'

They swept uphill to where the entrance porch, pillared over the drive to provide shelter, was at the side of the house and held another car. As Kitty drew up behind it, her voice was warm with pleasure. 'You're going to meet the man who played Cupid so successfully – Fergus MacGregor. I hope Jeannie is with him.'

She was; four people came out eagerly. Jeannie looked no more than ten years older than Anna, and looked as if she had a fine zest for living. Fergus would be about forty. You knew instinctively that this would be a happy marriage.

They owned an orchard nearer Roxburgh and had a pigeon pair, David who was eleven and Louise who was nine. 'Though we always think of ourselves as having four really,' Fergus said to Anna, 'because Jeannie's young brother and sister have always been with us. Peter's an engineer at the Hydro, and Teresa's teaching in Alexandra. When we heard Kitty was bringing her granddaughter to Pukerangi today, we decided on an afternoon off. We've been spraying and grafting till we're sick of the sight of an orchard tree. I'd rather look at Elizabeth's prunus blossom.'

Rossiter carried Anna off to look at his sheep. 'Calum tells me you're a sheep-farmer to your fingertips in spite of having been brought up on a tropic isle. Good for you! Fergus, coming?' He grinned at his wife. 'We won't keep her too long, but I'm sure Kitty's dying to have you and Jeannie to herself so she can sing Anna's praises without bringing the blush of modesty to her cheeks.'

Anna's cheeks were already warm with pleasure because Calum had commended her. Considering the start they'd had, and the animosity it had bred when she had heard him deploring her imminent arrival, when they were at the hospital, they'd progressed well along the road of amicable friendship. Friendship? Well, that was all it would ever be on Calum's side. On hers it was a strong attraction that was going to be grubbed out, root and crop, however harrowing the process was going to be.

Anna couldn't help laughing inwardly ... even her

thoughts ran in farming terms these days.

How marvellous to be accepted like this, striding over the paddocks with knowledgeable farmers, one of their fraternity; she knew she belonged here, with generations of sheepmen behind her from the hills and glens of Scotland.

They came back with appetites sharpened with the keen air, to hot scones and redcurrant jelly, shortbread stamped with Scots thistle moulds, apple shortcake and tea. As they paused on the verandah to scrub up, she heard Jeannie say, 'I wish she had more go in her. I'm sure that's why they've never set a wedding date. It's as if she's never forgotten her first love.'

It seemed as if a cold finger touched Anna's heart. If that were so, would Calum ever know perfect happiness?

Elizabeth's voice was troubled too. 'There are women like that, who love deeply only once. Pity. Still, when they do get married, we may be proved wrong. Only Calum deserves better. I could shake her!'

All the way home something bothered Anna. Suddenly she pinned it down. Sophy was full of spirit. Why did they think she had no go in her? Or were the three women who were discussing it wiser because they had known marriage themselves? Perhaps they recognized Sophy's animation in the things of her career, but felt she was lukewarm as far as Calum was concerned?

Philip hadn't taken Calum's scolding much to heart, it seemed. He said to Anna laughingly, 'The boss didn't approve of our little plot. He told me not to be such a damn fool and definitely not to involve you. He said I was about as subtle as a steam-roller, which is very likely spot on. But oh, boy, I'm not going to church on Sunday, believe me. Calum wasn't exactly complimentary, but Sophy was really withering. I'll give her time to get over it. I'm having a week-end away.'

Anna said, 'Why, when I told Calum I didn't think I'd go to church, he said not to be stupid, that Sophy had a sense of humour.'

For a moment Philip looked grim. 'She has, as far as your part in it is concerned. Not for mine.'

'Why? You haven't seen her, have you?'

'Not seen, heard. She rang. She was incensed, but more on your behalf – at first. Said it wasn't fair to a girl to use her like that and she didn't want to see you hurt.'

Anna blinked. '*Me?* Oh, she thought I might take you seriously. Oh, Philip, I do hope you told her it was my idea too. I don't want you blamed for the lot.'

He sighed. He must like to stand high in Sophy's regard. 'I'm afraid it's nothing that can be sorted out quickly, Anna, but thanks for trying. Sophy thinks it was sweet of you, so you needn't feel embarrassed about meeting her.'

Anna wrinkled her brows. 'Then why are *you* shy of meeting her?'

He shrugged. 'Oh, well, it's a matter of timing. It's business too. Had a ring from a chap who has a high-country run in South Canterbury. He's going to be in Dunedin at the week-end and would like to see me. He wants another man and his team of dogs up there. I'd fancied it two or three years ago, and he knew that but didn't want anyone then. But not a word to anyone here. I have to find out a bit more about it, then think my way through it for a day or two. And Sophy just could feel embarrassed in her pulpit on Sunday so soon after ticking me off.'

Anna was appalled. 'But, Philip, they can't do without you here. Calum said the other day how glad he'd be when Ian got back, that they didn't always like working at this pace, and he thought Kitty and Gilbert were looking tired.'

'Yes, I know, but you can always get men for here, so easy of access to Central towns. It's different back in the Alps, and I think it might do me good to get away. I've been considering it for some time. I'm suddenly fed-up with things. But not a word.'

She promised.

It made her feel restless herself. It was such a fair and lovely place, Strathallan, but there were undercurrents. She herself worried because Calum must feel ousted because of her; he was not only in love with someone who seemed to put career before marriage, but because of Anna he might feel his future here was uncertain. If she herself married a farmer, *he* might want to take over Strathallan. Not that Calum need entertain that thought: the farmer she wanted loved someone else . . . but the idea was bound to occur to him.

Philip was restless and wanted the challenge of the high-country station life. Only Grandmother and Grandfather seemed perfectly happy. Or was perfect the word? More like happier than of yore. True, they now had their grand-daughter here, but there was always the remembered bit-terness that their prodigal son had gone away, but, unlike the Biblical character, hadn't come back.

Calum went out after dinner, saying he was going to Crannog. Was he bound for St. Kit's Manse? It would be a relief to know that Sophy *had* decided to marry him, then she wouldn't be tormented by the faint hope she felt was so unworthy, that Sophy might stick to her career and in time Calum might turn to herself.

If he did, she would take him, even knowing she was second-best. Sometimes second-bests turned out happiest in the end. She'd heard of cases like that. Oh, stop dreaming, Anna. You're no less than a fool!

When Calum came home, much earlier than she'd ex-pected, he found Kitty, Gilbert and Anna deep in discussion of the past.

Till now Kitty had forborne to ask Anna much about what she remembered of her father, what she knew of the situation as it had been between him and her mother. She must want to know how her boy had spent those years, but Anna thought it was because they were rarely alone for long without Gilbert, and for her husband's sake Kitty wouldn't bring up yesterday's sorrows.

But tonight it was Gilbert who did. Perhaps with the telepathy that exists between two partners of a long and happy marriage, he sensed there were things Kitty hungered to know.

Out of a companionable silence he said, 'Anna, would you like to tell us about your father . . . how he met your mother, where they lived, what Alex did? But tell us the truth, don't spare us. We know he was unreliable, spendthrift, had no sense of responsibility. Though the knowledge of his physi-cal bravery at the end compensated us a great deal.'

Anna said, 'I'll tell you what I know, though of late years Mother didn't speak so much of him. I do know she loved him dearly when they were first married. That they were almost deliriously happy. It was later, when money got tight and Mother couldn't work because she had me, that things began to go wrong.'

'Aye, that adds,' said Gilbert. 'But why did they have more at first? Did your mother have a very good job?'

'Not particularly. Just a run-of-the-mill wage, but her adoptive parents left her a house and a small legacy. She lost her parents when young, and their childless neighbours adopted her. She had only this bachelor uncle in Fiji besides. They were not young when they took her, so they died before she was married.

'Mother and Dad lived on in the house for a while, then Dad fancied a citrus farm. It took all the money from the sale of the house and meant a big mortgage. Dad, I'm afraid, was lazy. That's why I felt a fellow-feeling for Elizabeth Forbes today. Certainly they had bad luck, but, in spite of the fact that growers' hazards did set them back, they could have survived except that Dad—' she hesitated.

Gilbert raised his dark brows that were so like Anna's and filled in for her, 'But Alex couldn't stay away from the race-meetings?'

'Yes. Was he like that here?'

'He was, I got him out of debt time and again. More fool I. I didn't want to see the Drummond name besmirched. I should have been firmer, I can see that now. I forgave him too readily, too often. Forgiveness is fine till a weak character trades on it so much that it makes them weaker still. It's kinder by far to put a bit of backbone and independence into them. Go on.'

'When Mother's uncle left her the guest-house she saw it as a godsend. It was something she could manage, even with a small child. It would get him away from his racing friends, give him a new start. It was also an exciting, glamorous setting, and Dad was so keen at first, she had high hopes. But of course it was hard work. They couldn't afford a big staff to start with and Dad thought some of the tasks were too menial for him. So he started spending more and more time away. The life there can be a lotus-eating sort of existence. There were other forms of gambling.'

She decided to say nothing about the wine and the women. 'Mother thought she was going to lose the guest-house too, and that was all she had to bring me up on, to support herself and her husband. She put a notice in the *Suva Times* that she would no longer be responsible for debts contracted in her name. She must have been desperate to do it. In a week Dad was gone, taking with him all that could be turned into cash. It upset Mother terribly. Wondered had she been wise, that he might go from bad to worse. But she got over that, because without the drag of his constant debts, she made the guest-house pay, extended it, modernized it, educated me as far as I wanted to go. That was all, till news of his death reached her.' She hesitated. She didn't want them to know he'd discarded his parents to the extent of even denying their existence. 'If Mother had known about you, had any idea where you were, she would have been in touch with you, have let you know you had a grandchild. She'd probably have tried, in the early years, to bring you together again.'

Gilbert said, 'Aye, lassie, I'm sure she would. We've searched our hearts many's the time, to find out where we'd gone wrong. You canna help doing it. You ask yourself were you too strict at a time when gentleness would've perhaps answered better. Were you too soft when discipline and putting your foot down might have been the right method? And you canna know.'

Kitty nodded, dry-eyed. She'd lived with this so long she'd learned to bear it. 'I used to find myself going back over the years trying to pinpoint just where we lost his confidence, when he first began lying to me, deceiving us. Aye di me, but he was such a dear little lad, bubbling over with the sheer joy of living, rushing in from school, eager to tell us all that had happened.

'I know he got in with a bad crowd. We tried to turn him from them without antagonizing him too much, but we never learned how. We felt hampered by inexperience – I expect most parents do. But even now there are times when I long to know how he spent his last years. And it always comes back to me, "Where did I fail"?'

Before Anna could search for words that might give some measure of comfort, they came from Calum. He'd come in, unheard.

'Oh, Kit,' he said, 'don't you realize you suffer more than you need from the fact that Alex was your only one, your all? So you feel your failure is a total failure. Can't you see what I mean? There's a perfect example of it in our family. Mother and Dad have three of us, Ian, Blair, me. Far be it from me to hold Ian and myself up as exemplary characters, but you know what Blair was like. Mother always says what a comfort you've been to her, because you understood as no one else did. He was weak, irresponsible – flawed in the making somewhere. If he'd been their only child they'd have felt as you do. I wish I'd realized this before. But because the two of us turned out reasonably decent, Mum and Dad, even though they fret over Blair, put it down to some throw-back and they feel they've only had thirty-three-and-a-third per cent failure with their family. They're not always tor-menting themselves with such questions. So from now on, you cut it out, do you hear?'

Anna would never forget the look that crossed the two faces she so loved. A new truth, a saving truth, had dawned on them. Calum crossed to the fire, took off his shoes, put on the slippers Kitty had by the hearth for him, said, 'Now, that's all the soul-searching we're going to do tonight. How about a game of five hundred?'

No one would have guessed at any inner conflicts disturbing the Reverend Sophy's breast on Sunday morning. Anna wondered how long she'd spent on that sermon. It was mas-terly. It made a hitherto inexplicable Old Testament inci-dent come alive for Anna. Sophy built up the atmosphere moment by breathless moment, once she'd given them a sketch of the historical events that had led up to it, making them see the times in their own century, understanding the old prohibitions, the shibboleths, the customs that seemed harsh now, but were accepted then, things ingrained into a godly people. But a state of judgment, rather than mercy.

She made it seem inevitable then, that the God of Love and Mercy had to be born into the world to reveal Himself as He was. She had still incorporated the flashes of humour, the quotations from poets, but it was an inescapable presen-tation of a case for Christian living. For the first time Anna wondered if this section of the community didn't need Sophy more as their pastor, than as a farmer's wife.

Outside Sophy's eyes twinkled as they met Anna's. 'You looked extremely thoughtful in kirk ... I noticed you. I sincerely hope you weren't hatching up any more Machi-avellian plots.'

Anna laughed too, but ruefully. 'That was the trouble. Ours wasn't in that class. Kid stuff. And, Sophy, I wasn't thinking of anything but the points of your sermon. It made me wonder how I'd ever had the nerve to try to influence you in any way. Oh, if only there was some way for you to be a wife *and* a minister! Oh dear, I'd better stop, pretty nearly everyone's out, but this is no place for a conversation like this.'

For a moment Sophy's face changed, it was just a quiver, but in that instant Anna saw again not the severity of the upswept hair-do and the black of the Geneva gown, but the laughing girl in the sapphire blue dress of the Alexandra musical.

Sophy said in a low voice, 'Anna, come over and see me some time when I'm on my own. Ring first to make sure. I'm not as sure of myself as I was. Sometimes I'm terribly lonely. And I— Oh, here's Mrs. Middlemarch coming. Come and see me this week. I've got to the stage where I think I'm just being selfish. Oh, good morning, Mrs. Middlemarch. Your flowers were perfect, with that use of the native flax as a background.'

Anna thought she ought to be glad. It looked as if Sophy was coming to a decision. She must make herself glad that Calum looked like getting his heart's desire.

She had no opportunity to talk with Philip on the Monday. Gilbert was trucking some heifers to Cromwell and took her with him. 'The orchards are a picture right now, the peach and apricot blossom is out. We go through Alex, and it's a garden town that you've only seen in the dark, and then through Clyde, with an air of still dreaming over its days of gold, and through the Cromwell Gorge. I want you to see Cromwell as it is now, before the dams alter it beyond recognition of us old-timers. I want you to see the confluence of the Kawarau and the Clutha, such turbulent rivers that they don't mingle till well downstream. I know we need the power and that changes have to be, and that no doubt in time we'll find new stretches of beauty, but—'

It was a day of sheer happiness for Anna. She pushed all other concerns to the back of her mind. Grandfather was delighting in having her all to himself for the drive, and later, in introducing her to all and sundry, men who had known him and his father before him in some cases.

On Tuesday morning Philip was across at the sale, leaving early straight from his own home. His father worked a few acres and wanted him to buy some stock in. Philip rang Anna late the night before, but very briefly. He said guardedly, 'Anna, don't give anything away in your answers, but I thought I'd like to tell you I have been offered a job on Draviemore in the Mackenzie country, but I've got till tonight to think it over. This chap is going to ring me at home then, after ten.'

Anna wished she could have talked it out with him, tried to persuade him not to leave Strathallan. She liked Philip. They might not get as good a man again. But it was Philip's business, and possibly Calum's as manager, and she dared not say a word.

Anna went round the sheep with the two men, Calum and Gilbert. Kitty came too. There wasn't the same need, lambing was tailing off now, but they liked being outside. She and Kitty came back earlier than the men, with a ewe and her lamb they hoped would do better with each other in a pen. Kitty said, 'Would you like to go over to the kitchen and start the lunch? Switch on the infra-red griller and put the sausages under it, and pull the soup on to the fire. I'll see if I can persuade this one she has a purpose in life.'

Anna was slicing bread when she heard a light step behind her. She turned. Here was a girl about her own age, or a little older, tall, with an elegance of dress and carriage, and she was extremely like someone Anna knew. She tried to catch at the resemblance ... dark chestnut hair, hazel eyes, patrician features ... before she could pin it down, the girl spoke, smilingly. 'You're Anna, aren't you? Mother told me all about you. I'm Victoria.'

Anna said, 'Oh, of course. I couldn't think who you were like ... Victoria, Philip's sister.'

Then the girl said easily, 'Yes, and Calum's fiancée, of course.'

Anna felt rooted to the floor. It was just as if the words this girl had spoken had dropped a stone on to an ice-surfaced pond and splinters of crystal sound had shattered the silence. She didn't know how long she stood there, just looking at Victoria Sherborne, trying to make sense of it, till she became aware that Victoria was looking at her quite strangely; aware too, that she mustn't, on any account, let her tongue spill out the words that were rising in her throat.

She mustn't gasp: *Why, I thought he wanted Sophy!*

Afterwards she felt weak with relief that she'd managed to dam them back.

Victoria said, 'What's the matter? You look as if you've come all over funny! Did I startle you? Sorry, I thought you'd have heard me coming.'

Anna managed a little laugh. 'Do forgive me staring, but you're so incredibly like Philip, it was like seeing him dressed up as a girl.' She swallowed, said, 'Does my grandmother know you're here?'

'Yes, I saw the door of the shed open and went in. I'll put my bag in the guest-room and come and help you, Anna.'

It gave Anna a chance to recover. This girl must never guess. She might think Calum had been making up to Sophy. But what – why – had everyone been talking about *Sophy*? It didn't make sense. She hadn't time to work it out now. The men must soon arrive. Anna found herself saying: *Help me, God, to appear natural. Keep it from showing.*

Victoria came back, took a look at the table where as yet Anna had no more than table-mats out, went to the cupboards, began getting out the necessary china, cutlery, jam and butter dishes, deftly, with the speed born of familiarity. 'I just got home this morning after Philip had gone. I stayed in Lawrence last night. I decided not to ring Calum and just walk in on him for a surprise.'

Anna's mouth felt dry. She wished Kitty would hurry and take over. This girl could ask her some question yet that would betray her into revealing she hadn't known she and Calum were engaged. That would sound peculiar, even suspicious, to any girl. Given time, alone, Anna would be able, by going back in her mind, to recall each piece of conversation, or gossip if you like, to work out how in the world she'd managed to hassle things up like this!

But it wasn't Kitty's step they heard next. It was Calum's, and Anna wished herself a hundred miles away. Oh, why hadn't Victoria come yesterday when she and Grandy were safely at the saleyards? Now she'd have to witness their meeting after a fairly long absence from each other.

He spoke before he reached the door. 'Are you there, Anna?'

She couldn't reply. She would have choked. She and Victoria were both staring towards the doorway but with very different expressions. Victoria was smiling, anticipating his surprise.

And surprise it was. He just stared. 'Why, Victoria, I thought you weren't coming till next week.' There was the faintest of pauses, perhaps because he knew they were not alone, then without as much as a flicker of his glance in Anna's direction, he swiftly crossed the room and kissed Victoria.

Certainly it was only the sort of kiss one would give in front of other eyes, but Anna had difficulty in controlling her breathing, making it appear as if nothing to her, as if she had known all along he was engaged to Victoria. He'd been so open too, had told her all along he was spoken for.

It wasn't fair, it just wasn't fair, to have to adjust oneself with lightning rapidity to a completely different circumstance. Victoria went on explaining that she'd wanted to surprise them, adding all the trivia one inevitably does, passing on the regards of their mutual friends in Lawrence, asking him this and that.

Then she turned to Anna, saying, 'Calum wrote and told me that all his fears about you fitting in here had fled, that you've made the Drummonds very happy and that you're going to stay. How perfectly lovely for them! It makes up to them in such a big way for Alex clearing out. It's so terrible to be left behind, to find life empty.'

Calum was standing beside Victoria, one arm along her shoulders, and Anna saw a nerve jump in his cheek. The next moment she thought she'd imagined it. Because why should he flinch from that remark? This was a glad moment for him. His fiancée had come home to him after weeks of absence. Fortunately Kitty and Gilbert came in then and under the general talk Anna got her feelings under control.

It was only when she was outside again with the older folk, leaving Victoria and Calum together, that Anna knew why she now felt more desolate than before. It was because when she had thought Sophy was hesitating, there had been a faint ray of hope for herself.

Suddenly she almost recoiled as another angle hit her. Till now, selfishly, she'd been totally concerned with the situation as it affected herself. But now . . . who then had they meant Sophy was swithering over? ... Of course ... Philip! That was why Sophy had rung Philip in a fury and told him not to use Anna. Anna had wondered that Calum and Sophy had so soon caught on to the idea that she and Philip were bent on creating an atmosphere of romance for them. That they'd hoped romance might be catching. The other was so blatant it would've hit them in the eye immediately. Philip's idea had been: 'If *you* won't go to watch moons with me, Sophia Kirkpatrick, I'll get myself a girl who will!' Oh, heavens to Betsy, what could she do?

At that moment Anna remembered the rest of the conversation Sophy had had over the phone with Philip. Anna recalled it now with the utmost clarity. After Philip had told her about the high-country offer, she'd detained him long enough to ask curiously, 'Tell me, Philip, how did you and Sophy part on the phone?'

He'd looked grim one moment, devil-may-care the next. Really reckless. 'I finished up telling her it was no business of hers. That she had a pretty good imagination if she thought we'd been putting on an act, and why should *you* do such a thing anyway? Don't look like that, Anna, I know it wasn't the truth, but I was past caring. I told her she had a nerve even thinking of it, that on my part it was a very genuine attraction and I'd thank her to keep out of it.'

No wonder he hadn't wanted to go to church, and had gone to Dunedin. What horrible timing – why on earth had that man from Draviemore turned up with his offer just when they'd all got at cross-purposes? If Philip closed with it, Sophy and he might never come together. Sophy would fill her days with parish work just as she had done with study, to ease her grief at the loss of Roderick. Philip would take on possibly dangerous mustering jobs and live a rough, if satisfying, life in the back country. And he'd probably marry the first girl to cross his path, on the rebound.

Anna's mind felt like an ant-heap with thoughts scurrying to and fro. Oh, if only she could do something! But what? When Victoria and Calum came back to the paddock, she went across to Kitty. 'I'm going back to the house for a bit. I want to ring Sophy if I can get her. There was something Philip wanted me to tell her.'

Kitty surveyed her granddaughter's flushed face. 'Just as well not to forget any message from Philip for Sophy. But you may not get her just now, love.'

Anna said, 'Say nothing in front of the others. It's private.'

She thought she'd try to get hold of Philip first. He might be back from the sale, though she doubted it. The Sherbornes had a lovely home, Kowhai Bend, nearer Crannog. Philip's father was the County Engineer, but liked enough land to run a few sheep on. Anna liked his mother very much. She was sweet.

She must go warily, though. Philip mightn't have told his mother he was thinking of making a change and a mother oughtn't to hear it from a stranger. Oh, dear, there were so many people to consider. But she must stop Philip closing with that offer. She was fairly sure that would be the right thing to do. She'd tell him this might be the very moment to press his cause, not give up. That Sophy had confessed she was lonely, that she wanted to chat with Anna. She might have been angry with Philip on the phone, but could now be having second thoughts.

Philip's mother was young-hearted and gay, and she sounded so happy because Victoria was home. Anna simply said she had something to ask Philip, when would he be home if he wasn't there yet?

'He'll be lateish, Anna. He's having dinner in Clyde on the way home, with friends. But he did say he'd have to be in by ten as he's expecting a ring from Tekapo then. Anna, you might know. Has there been any friction between Calum and Philip? I wondered if Philip might be thinking of going up the high-country. I mean, this Tekapo ring. They've been wonderful friends, but I wondered if Philip may think it's not wise to have a brother-in-law as boss.'

'Oh, no, Mrs. Sherborne, they've been just as usual, the best of friends.'

'Then it's this business of Sophy. I expect you've noticed. If Sophy wants to be single-minded and wedded to her career, I expect we must make the best of it, but if ever there's a girl I'd like as my daughter-in-law, it's Sophy. Not that that means a thing. I've tried to tell myself that Philip will get over it if she finally turns him down flat, that he'd eventually meet someone else, but I'm whistling in the dark, I'm afraid. Oh, how much better it was when they were little and one could pick them up and comfort them. Goodness, I sound like a doting mother, and I'm not, really.

'Only when you have a family, you feel so helpless some-times. It's easier to bear your own troubles than your offspring's. I did try to tell Phil a few weeks ago that if Sophy wouldn't change her mind, there could be someone else for him in the years to come, but nobody believes that till it happens, ever. Besides, it mightn't with Philip. My two take after their father, once they love it's for keeps. Oh, Anna, I shouldn't be unloading this on you, but even though I've only met you twice and you're so young, there's some-thing about you that makes it easy to talk to you. Kitty and Calum and Elizabeth Forbes have all said so.'

'Calum said so? I can't imagine it. He and I clash a bit!'

'Well, he did. He came over here to see if I'd had a letter from Victoria, because he was worried that he hadn't had one. But of course she was on her way back. He said then that Kitty and Gilbert were opening out as they hadn't for years. That they were different persons now. Of course, not knowing them before, you'd be unaware of it. You don't know how happy it's made our whole community.'

Anna felt warmed, comforted. 'Mrs. Sherborne, I wonder if you'd ask Philip to be sure to ring me as soon as he gets in. I don't like to sound mysterious, but I'd like it to be before he gets that ring from Tekapo. I can't say why because it would mean breaking a confidence. And don't worry too much right now. I've got a feeling things might come out all right. I mustn't say any more. I can hear the rest coming in. Bye-bye.'

That was a polite evasion. She didn't want to say too much. She got no answer from the manse. She tried the hospital, only to find Sophy had done her afternoon visiting and had departed on her parish rounds. Well, she'd try again tonight. She didn't know who to tackle first. Perhaps, from sheer necessity, it would have to be whichever one she got hold of soonest. She really needed something a little en-couraging from Sophy before she stopped Philip taking the Draviemore position.

Victoria, naturally, stayed for the evening meal. Anna kept going to the most private extension, the farm office one, but the manse phone remained unanswered. Perhaps Sophy had stayed to tea with someone.

With this problem on her mind, Anna felt a little remote from the pain of seeing Calum with the girl who was going to be his wife, the wife who would live in this lovely old house, in this very kitchen where the first Drummond wife had hung up her smoked hams, her bunches of herbs, made her oat-cakes, her girdle-scones, baked her crusty loaves . . . where William Drummond had brought his first weak lambs to revive in front of an older stove than this. No doubt later it would impinge on her numbness, but for the time being she must set straight her unknowing part in this recent estrangement between Sophy and Philip.

Calum said as they finished their apple-pie, 'Now Victoria and I will wash up. You all go and watch TV and we'll bring the coffee in when we're done.'

Naturally he'd want Victoria to himself for a bit. Anna was thankful. She sped to the phone and got Sophy, who, by her muffled voice, was having her tea.

Anna came to the point without preamble. 'Sophy, I've just got to see you. I've tried to get you all the afternoon. May I come over now? Is it too much to hope you're free?'

Sophy swallowed and her voice sounded clearer. 'You can come any time you like. Anna, are the Drummonds okay? Is anything—'

'No, nothing's wrong. It's nothing to do with Strathallan folk.'

She heard Sophy take a deep breath. 'Anna, I'm sure it's to do with Philip. Is he all right? Has he had an accident?'

Anna made her voice sound surprised. 'He should be all right. He went to the Cromwell sale. He's having dinner with friends at Clyde. But – oh, I'll explain when I see you. Quite soon.'

She slipped a brown windcheater over the frock she'd changed into for dinner, picked up her car keys, came in jingling them. She said lightly, 'I'm off to the manse, Grandmother. Remember that message I had for Sophy? I've just got her now. She was just having her meal. I want to see her before she gets called out again.'

She was glad Victoria and Calum were still in the kitchen. But as she swept past the entrance she saw Calum come out on to the front porch, put up a hand as if to stop her. But she wanted no questions asked. She'd *never* confess to Victoria that she'd thought Calum loved Sophy. That could arouse doubts.

Sophy had the porch light on for her. She tapped, found the door unlocked and went in. Sophy called from the study. 'I'm in here, Anna.'

Sophy had a slightly defensive look about her. Anna thought she had decided to receive her in this room to give the interview a more formal background. As if Sophy wanted to stress the fact that she was a minister, that she had a career. She was in a blue tweed suit she wore often for visiting. It had a white blouse under it, shirt style, with a black tie at the throat knotted like a cravat, rather a severe garb.

She stood on the hearthrug, a fire glowing redly behind her, her hands behind her back. Anna hesitated and all her carefully prepared opening dissolved from her mind like the mists of morning. Sophy looked so remote, so sure of herself, Anna's knees began to shake. She thought she ought not to have come.

CHAPTER SEVEN

SOPHY managed a stiff smile, said, 'It's all right, Anna. I tell you it's all right. I know exactly what you've come to say, and I admire you for having the courage. It's quite all right with me. I made my decision some time ago. Philip is entirely free. I know you'd never poach on anyone else's preserves – you're too honest. I recognized your integrity from the start. You've got the green light to go ahead!'

Anna boggled at her, then burst into laughter, really mirthful laughter that wouldn't be gainsaid. Then she managed, 'Oh, Sophy, Sophy darling, everybody, I repeat *everybody* gets their lines crossed. I thought—' she broke off and giggled again – 'I thought you were trying to make up your mind about *Calum,* not Philip!'

It was Sophy's turn to boggle. 'Calum? Calum and me? Why, he's engaged to Victoria, to Philip's sister. How on earth could you—'

Anna waved agitated hands. 'Sophy, let me explain, or we'll never get it sorted out. My grandmother, telling me how much they think of you, told me about your loss – about Roderick – and added that she thought you were fighting a certain attraction. I thought it was for Calum.'

Sophy's blue eyes were intense, but puzzled. 'But why? I mean Calum and I have never—'

'Well, you see when I thought Calum was drunk, Maggie said – oh dear, I'm not telling it well – the night I met him, and he'd swerved off the road. I thought he was drunk—' she saw the eyes watching her widen in incredulity. 'Oh, don't interrupt me, Sophy, or I'll never get it straight. And someone will be bound to ring you, or call, and I'm terrified you and Philip keep on crossing your lines – I know he wasn't drunk, but Barney's beer had smashed all over him and when Maggie heard us telling the family, *she* thought he must have been and said: "Whatever will Miss Kirkpatrick say?" Calum later told me he was spoken for, so I thought this Miss Kirkpatrick must be the one he meant.

'Grandmother said you were very fond of Calum – he seemed very concerned about you the night he thought the

Balloch road would be icy, then when you came out to Stra-thallan – oh dear, I'm getting out of sequence. That day just after lunch, I copped Kitty and Philip talking about the situation. They thought it was you and were most relieved to see it was me. Of course I thought it was you and Calum they were talking about. Evidently Grandmother thought a spot of jealousy would help you make up your mind. I can see that now, I didn't then, because you and Calum began bringing the dishes out. They whispered to me just to follow Philip's lead.

'When he asked if I'd make up a foursome for the musi-cal, I thought he wanted to create a less – a less – um – ecclesiastical atmosphere, more a courting atmosphere, to encourage you to fall into Calum's arms. That incident after Philip had chased you round the paddock and I caught his hand gave colour to it. You and Calum had such a peculiar look on your faces. No wonder! I can see now that Philip thought you were jealous. I hope you were, Sophy. Oh, dear, I ought to be called addle-pated Anna – but it's not my fault nobody mentioned Victoria other than as Philip's sister.

'I thought if Philip was trying a spot of matchmaking, he was being stupidly obvious about it, trying to leave you together for coffee and so on. Then that night when I got in, Calum was waiting up for me and ticked me off for inter-fering. But nobody crossed their t's or dotted their i's.' She stopped, because she was out of breath.

Sophy looked as if she was afraid to believe that a tangled web was being disentangled, her eyes had lost their watch-fulness, her stance its air of defence. She moistened her lips. 'Go on, Anna, don't stop there.'

Anna spread out her hands in a despairing gesture. 'You've got to do something, Sophy, and do it quickly. Philip told me of your conversation over the phone – that you'd twigged he was trying to rouse you, but then he got so flaming mad it hadn't worked, he insisted he *was* serious about me. I feel awful, it's bad enough feeling the cuckoo-in-the-nest as far as Calum and the estate is concerned, without feeling the spanner in the works with you and Philip. I promised him I wouldn't tell anyone but I'm breaking that promise here and now. He went to Dunedin this weekend to see the owner of Draviemore, a high-country sheep station near Tekapo. That man's ringing him tonight about ten to see if he'll take the job he's offered him, or not. Sophy . . . are you going to let him go?'

'I should just think I'm not! I'll ring his mother and say he's on no account to take that call from Draviemore before he sees me. I'll ask her to send him over here as soon as he gets in.'

Anna's eyes were ashine. 'Oh, Sophy, does this really mean I've not done so much harm after all? Does it mean you're willing to give up your career? That after all, you think marriage—'

Sophy had held up an imperative hand. Her copper-coloured hair gleamed in the lamplight like a newly-minted penny, her eyes held a dreamy look, as if she'd glimpsed a happiness just waiting over the horizon for her. She said softly, 'Oh, Anna, that was never more than a smoke-screen. It wasn't my career. I know I could still be a part-timer, an assistant minister. It was something else.' She paused, and Anna felt her mind was turned inward. 'Roderick told me life was for getting on with. I think he saw what was ahead of me more plainly than I did. I thought that I was doing just that . . . in service in the same field he'd had to relinquish.

'I've been fairly wise for other people who have been bereaved, but not, I think, for myself. The plain simple truth is, Anna, that I didn't think it would be fair to Philip to marry him while my thoughts still turned constantly to Rod. I hadn't quite stopped grieving for him. Oh, I've been wilful about it. Even when I knew I was weakening, I'd go and get Roderick's photo out of the drawer, look at it, re-live the past.

'That night we went to the musical I'd have given anything to have been sitting in the front seat with Philip and you in the back with Calum. When Philip paid you a compliment at dinner, about your purple dress, I nearly burned up with jealousy. Don't look so unbelieving, Anna, I did. I'm only human. I can't wear purple. My hair looks almost orange if I do.—and clashes hideously. Lilac, yes, not purple. And – when he said he wanted to show you the moon over Crannog Dam it was the last straw. I couldn't bear to think about it.

'On the way home with Calum I asked if he thought Philip was doing it on purpose and he said he thought that was obvious, but that he'd wring his neck if he hurt you over it, but that you might just have been asked to do it, and I'd better put a stop to the silly nonsense pronto. When I rang Philip, and – well, scoffed at him for doing it, he got really mad and pretended it was for real. And just today, when I realized he hadn't come near me, or rung, I got myself into a fine state imagining it was true. I don't know why he didn't fall for you, Anna. You're much less complicated. But suddenly I knew that without Philip life would be dust and ashes, like fish without salt. That Roderick belonged to yesterday, Philip to my present and future. Philip's face even got between me and my prep for next Sunday's sermon. And I had to admit to myself that I'd probably be a better minister if I was a wife – Philip's wife.'

Anna felt that Sophy's radiance reached out and touched her too. They stood regarding each other for a moment or two.

'So what now?' said Anna at last. 'You've got to move pretty fast. I said he was to ring me the moment he got home. I think I'd better get back to Strathallan, though it won't be for some time yet. He'd told his mother lateish, but he'd be in by ten for this ring. Sophy, you'll be here, won't you? You won't get tied up with anything?'

Sophy said simply and convincingly, 'Anna, if anyone needs me, domestic trouble, or a death or severe illness, I'd just have to go. But if that happens, and you can't get me, tell Philip for me that I love him, that I've come to my senses.'

'Yes. Oh dear, isn't it complicated? Let's pray it doesn't happen that way. When Philip rings Strathallan, I'll say I've seen you, that I have made it plain to you it *was* a put-up job to make you jealous and that I found you breaking your heart because you'd come to the conclusion it was for real. That'll bring him hot-foot to the manse, though if I were you I'd get straight in his car and go and find a moon. There aren't any telephone connections to the moon yet, thank goodness.'

She had turned to go and stopped dead as a bell rang. 'Or doorbells either. Sophy, I'll get it. If it's urgent I'll let 'em in. If it's somebody to say she'd rather take the cake-stall than the sweet-stall at the Spring Fair, I'll say you're out. Don't look like that, it'll be on my conscience, not yours.'

She started again for the door, but it flew open.

Calum! She would so much rather it had been Philip.

He said, striding in, and standing before the two of them, 'What's going on?' They were struck dumb, thinking of the explanations.

He caught Anna's arm. 'Come on, out with it. You're fighting other people's battles again and you'll get hurt. I'm here to see Sophy and Philip don't use you as a battle-dore.'

Anna burst out laughing. 'I think you mean a shuttlecock, Calum.'

He waved an impatient hand, began to speak again, but Sophy came to life, seized his hand, held it. 'Calum,' she said, and there was that in her voice and eyes that made him narrow his gaze. 'She won't get hurt. When you burst in, I was just on the point of asking her to be bridesmaid to Philip and myself.'

It was Calum's turn to boggle. Then he swung round on Anna, 'Is this true? Did you manage to sort it out, to per-suade Sophy that—'

Anna suddenly felt miraculously carefree. Calum would fix it with Philip so there were no more crossed wires. 'She didn't need any persuading. She'd realized she loved Philip long before I got here. Her only problem was to know how to communicate it to Philip who'd obscured the issue by insist-ing to her that he was really attracted to me!'

Sophy was still clinging to Calum's hand. She gave it a little shake. 'It wasn't so much making a decision as coming to myself. To knowing myself. I'm going to be frank. I think Philip's parents and the Drummonds and you should know it. Otherwise they might think Philip was marrying someone who loved him so little she put a career before him, before love and marriage. I wouldn't like Philip's mother to think I didn't love him as he deserves to be loved. It was just that I wasn't quite sure I'd got Roderick's loss out of my system or not. But when Philip took Anna to watch the moon over the daffodils, I knew, oh, I knew!'

Calum's dark face crumpled into laughter. He said, 'If only you'd known . . . she came home as cross as two sticks because there was a heavy dew and she got her feet wet. She announced to me that she would probably lose all her toes from frostbite. And then I bawled her out for what she and Philip were doing to you.'

For a moment his dark-blue eyes looked into Anna's pansy-brown eyes, remembering. He smiled at his thoughts. Anna had the same thoughts. He hadn't bawled her out, he'd chided her gently, he'd washed her feet, dried them, put warm socks on her – his own. He'd kissed her, as he would have kissed Maggie.

Calum thought of something. 'Didn't you see me rush out on the porch tonight to try to stop you, Anna?'

'Yes. But I thought if you knew what I was doing you'd think I was meddling.'

'No, I didn't even know where you were going. I heard the car start up just after I answered the phone for you. It was Philip. He wanted you urgently, said he'd had a message from you to ring him and he'd got in early because the friends he was going to have dinner with had gone down with 'flu. I went to ask Kit where you were off to in such a hurry. She had a funny look on her face, said you'd been trying to get a message to Sophy all afternoon and had now gone to the manse, but she had a certain feeling you wouldn't want Philip to ring there. I thought I'd better come and sort it out, but it looks as if Anna has pulled the right rabbit out of the hat. I take it you've been in touch with Philip yourselves by now, if the wedding's fixed?'

Both girls gave way to mirth. Sophy said, 'Poor Philip, he doesn't even know there's going to be a wedding yet.'

Calum regarded them suspiciously. 'You're having me on.'

Sophy calmed down. 'We were trying to work out how I could see him without half the parish round. What did you tell Philip?'

'That Anna had gone to Crannog to get some fruit and would be home soon. Anyway, Philip said he was going out seeing he had a few hours to spare. He said to tell you when you came back he'd ring before ten all right. I thought I'd better come and try to find out what was happening, to sort it out if necessary. It so often happens that the one who tries to put things right gets the rough end of the stick, and I didn't want it to be Anna. She's not had a very good time between the lot of us. I didn't give her much of a welcome when she first came.'

Anna felt happiness well up in her. Calum might be promised to Victoria, but he had a caring concern for other people too. It would be all she'd ever have, but it was better than nothing.

Calum said, 'But for heaven's sake ring Philip now. You may just get him before he goes out. Put him out of his misery. Sophy, better just tell him if he likes to come over, he may hear something to his advantage. Say we're all here to get things straightened out.'

Anna said uncertainly, 'He might get as mixed up as Sophy was. *She* thought I was coming over here to confess I'd fallen for Philip – she was being all noble about it. Told me Philip was free. If he sees us all together, he might say something in the heat of the moment he'd regret later. I think *I'd* better ring and tell him everything's okay. Sophy, I don't want to do you out of a proposal, but—'

Sophy said calmly, 'I had my proposal long ago and I fluffed my lines. I'll take things Philip's way this time. Go ahead. I've been too sure of myself till now. It comes with people asking your advice all the time, bring you their problems. It makes you big-headed. And when it comes to your own affairs, you have no more sense than a baby! Go ahead. I don't care where we meet, or who interrupts, just as long as he comes.'

Calum stood with folded arms, a smile playing round his lips, while Anna, from the back of the study desk, so that she was facing them, dialled the number. Suddenly she bashed the receiver back on its cradle, looked aghast. 'What if I say the wrong thing? What if this time *I'm* trying to play God?'

Calum said, 'Anna, get on with it. I'll back you any time.'

Their eyes caught, held, disengaged. She dialled again.

Philip answered, she said simply, 'Philip, it's Anna. I'm going to ask you to hear me out. But get this into your head first, because what follows is complicated: *Everything is all right.* I'm ringing from the manse. When you've heard me out I want you to come over here. I don't care where you are going, this has priority. Calum's here too. And Philip, drive with care. We want no accidents on the happiest night of your life . . . to date. No, Philip, don't interrupt.

'You see, I was all mixed up or I'd never have consented

115

to our little deception. Nobody explained it properly or I'd never have gone to watch that wretched moon with you. I thought it was Calum Sophy was trying to make up her mind about.' As she heard Calum bark out '*What?*' she realized that they'd not told Calum that yet. She said imploringly, 'Oh, Philip, don't shout like that in my ear – Calum's the other side doing the same. It's the first he's heard of it too. Yes, he's here too. Calum, be quiet. Let me tell Philip. So, as I thought I'd thrown a hefty spanner in the works and you'd been daft enough to tell Sophy you really were attracted to me . . . well, yes, daft and all, it worked! She got beautifully jealous. Only Philip, it wasn't her career that was standing in the way. She wanted to be fair to you. She had to be quite sure she'd got over Roderick. When you paid me that compliment about my purple dress she went all green-eyed. Thought she'd lost you, then hoped you were just doing it to make her jealous. That was why she fired up on the phone. But when you were absent this week-end, she developed doubts. Oh, she's been just a poor, mixed-up girl, not a minister of the cloth! Now is that enough, Philip? Are you on your way? Calum and I will stay here to keep all parishioners, dead-beats and what-have-you away from the manse door – just long enough for you and Sophy to settle your differences once for all, then you can take her out under the moon – if there's one – and this time you won't be with a girl who'll tell you off because there's dew on the daffodils. *She* just won't care. Ouch!'

She put a hand to her ear. . . . 'He's certainly on his way! He didn't say as much as goodbye.'

Anna looked at Calum, whose face expressed bewilderment, and told him exactly why she'd thought what she did. 'There's just one thing, though. Now, stop laughing! I don't want Victoria ever to know I thought that. I don't want to rouse doubts in anyone else!'

Calum said, 'Victoria? Well, perhaps it's a good thing she's at Strathallan and not at home. Philip might have let it out to her. Anna, when *did* you find out I was engaged to Victoria?'

'Today. When she walked in and said: "You're Anna, aren't you? I'm Victoria." So I said, "Oh, Philip's sister," and she just about knocked the legs from under me by saying: "And Calum's fiancée." Anna then achieved a really amused laugh of which she was extremely proud. It wasn't till later that she remembered Sophy had laughed, but not Calum.

But he said, 'How on earth did you manage not to spill the beans?'

'By a superhuman effort. I didn't want to appear an utter fool.'

'No,' he said quietly, 'we all hate to look foolish, don't we? Sometimes I think we'd rather be thought wicked than foolish. Odd, isn't it? Oh, that sounds like Philip now.'

Calum strode to the front door. But it wasn't Philip's voice the two girls heard, oh no. It was Mrs. de Paget's. It had to be, of course. Hearing it, they froze. Sophy said, 'Oh, no, Anna, not tonight. I love my parishioners ninety-nine per cent of the time, but not tonight. She's a darling, but—'

Mrs. de Paget was a dear, bumbling old soul, very garrulous, and without a scrap of malice in her, but she never knew when to go home. Everyone who saw her coming knew it would be an all-night sitting, but she was so kind, nobody would hurt her.

They heard Calum's voice pointedly raised. Oh, they were to take a cue from him. 'Oh, hullo, Mrs. de Paget. Come on in. Anna and I dropped in to see Miss Kirkpatrick about something but we've struck a bad night. She's got an urgent appointment coming up in a few moments. A long and important discussion. But she's asked us to make ourselves a cup of coffee and make an appointment for another night. But come along into the living-room and have a warm-up. It's a cool wind, isn't it? This way.' As he passed the slightly ajar study door he called, 'Come on, Anna, your time's just about up. We'll have a cup of coffee and be off. I'll say goodnight from here, Miss Kirkpatrick, to save interrupting the business later.'

Sophy put a hand to her mouth to stifle laughter. She said in a whisper to Anna after she called out goodnight, 'Calum always knows what to do, doesn't he? I'd trust him to take over any situation. See you later.'

Calum had whisked Mrs. de Paget down two halls and into the living-room at a breathless pace, with his hand under her elbow. He didn't want her recognize the voice of the next caller.

Sophy's table was still set with one table-mat, a plate with a chop-bone on it, and a bowl containing her dessert which she'd not had time to start, evidently.

As Anna came in she heard Calum say, 'Oh, poor Miss Kirkpatrick, she's not even finished her dinner. Oh, well, it's like being in a doctor's household, I expect. I remember when the Wellesleys were here, Mrs. Wellesley said James often missed a meal. We'll wash her dishes up for her when we've had our coffee. Anna, switch that kettle on again, and we'll just use instant coffee.'

Mrs. de Paget reminded Anna of some of the talkative guests they used to get in Fiji; Anna had always preferred them to the very reserved ones, even if at times you could ill spare the time to listen. But they were less strain and enjoyed themselves so.

But she had just paused in her first fine flow when Anna and Calum, whose ears had been pricked above the sound of her voice heard a car door bang, footsteps that positively leaped, the front and study doors closing with slams, and then silence. They hoped that silence meant only one thing ... that the minister was being well and truly kissed.

Mrs. de Paget cocked her head on one side, listened, said, 'Oh dear, that sounded like someone in desperate trouble. I do hope there hasn't been a tragedy in our midst, or anything difficult for a young woman to handle.'

Calum said hurriedly, 'Oh, Miss Kirkpatrick has such a calming effect on everybody, she'll be all right. I think from what she said, it was something that had to be dealt with hurriedly. It could be that who ever it is has to discuss things with her before a committee arrives or something. She leads a busy life. When we've had our coffee, we'll run you home, Mrs. de Paget. We'll just have to see the minister another night. Nothing urgent about our business. What about yours, can you make it another time?'

'Oh yes, surely. It's not business with me. It's just that I get a bit bothered about that lonely bit of a lassie at times. It's a great big manse this and a bit solitary-like with the glebe paddocks at the side nearest me and the Church Hall on the other. I drop in occasionally. She enjoys it. And by the way, I'd rather have tea than coffee. I brought along some of my oatcakes with me, so you can have one each if you like. And I've a pasty in my basket for her dinner tomorrow. Would you put it in the pantry, Calum?'

To Anna's surprise, Calum bent down and kissed Mrs. de Paget's cheek. 'You're a pet, Pagie. I'm sure she'll just love the pasty. And we'll all have tea. I've a thirst on me that no coffee will satisfy.'

They didn't bustle her away, even though they were dying to know how things were going in the study. They listened to two or three stories of the old days that Calum, at least, had heard many times before. Bridie de Paget's husband had been the son of a French goldminer who'd struggled against bitter odds in the eighteen-sixties, to win gold from the pitiless gorges, with his stake near Chamonix. Anna was fascinated. To hear stories handed down by word of mouth, to just a third generation of listeners, of what was then unexplored country almost, harsh and cruel, and realize that one now lived in an atomic age, held magic indeed.

Finally Calum caught her eye, they rose and washed the dishes, put Bridie's offering of love in the fridge and left a note to say where it was, and they escorted her out of the back door.

Bridie said comfortably, 'Well, at least she canna be lonely if she's in the thick of discussions on the business of the kirk. And I've enjoyed this bit crack with you two. Anna is a new audience for me. Will you come and visit me sometime on your own, Anna?'

Calum had switched off the outside light so Bridie wouldn't recognize Philip's car. It was hardly likely that she, of all people, would have missed seeing in what quarter the wind lay. More than one in the parish had observed Philip's attraction with a shrewd and pleased eye.

Anna had to admire Calum. He must have been dying to get back to find out how things were between the two starcrossed lovers, and to keep other callers at bay, but he saw the old lady into her little stone cottage, switched on her lights, asked if she had plenty of wood and coal in, and stirred her sleeping fire to a good blaze.

Bridie looked at them affectionately. 'There's lots of folks criticize today's young 'uns, but I find them much as they always were. Even the very young. You've given me a very pleasant hour or two, Calum, you and your lass. Thank you.'

Anna had a pretty shrewd idea Mrs. de Paget wasn't often

set back or even conscious of the clangers she must at some time drop. Anyone who chattered as much as she did would have a fair average. But as she realized what she'd said, her weatherbeaten cheeks deepened several shades, then she said, 'You'll have to excuse an old woman who gets a bit muddled now and again these days. I'd forgotten it was Victoria. It's just that—' she left her words hanging.

Calum's voice was smooth, reassuring. 'Not to worry, Bridie. After all, Anna's family now, a very natural mistake. She's Anna of Strathallan.' He added: 'Clan connections, you know, if not blood relations to us. We even wear the same tartan. Doigs are sib to Drummonds.'

In the brief ride back to the manse Anna realized she'd misjudged Calum and his brother's family from the start. They had the right to wear the Drummond tartan.

Calum parked his car by Philip's, sounded quite a tattoo on his horn, leapt out, opened Anna's door. 'Best to give them fair warning,' he exulted.

Sophy and Philip had the study door open, and were hand-in-hand. They didn't need to ask were things finalized.

They went through to the living-room and everyone tried to talk at once. Finally Calum held up his hand. 'Let's get down to brass tacks. When's the wedding going to be, and what are you doing about this?' His comprehensive gesture embraced the manse, St. Kit's, the parish.

Philip answered. 'Sophy will carry on fully, for say, a year.' He grinned wickedly. 'We'll be married in January and live here. I'll keep on working at Strathallan. That'll give the parish time to look round. If, when our family start to come along, they want Sophy as an associate minister, we can leave the manse to the full-timer, and by then I think we should have been able to restore the old stone house on our property. I've always had a yen to. It would please Dad. He has always loved it, and as it's historical— he's got a conscience over it, but he's been too busy to do anything about it. Even if St. Kit's doesn't want an associate, there are plenty of vacant parishes not too far away who'd be glad of Sophy helping out as supply. It would satisfy her, but not take all her time.'

Anna was radiant, the pansy-brown eyes shining, the dark

and light hair glowing above the emerald green of the soft mohair dress she was wearing, girdled with gilt. They all looked at her and Calum laughed. 'I believe she's fought other people's battles all her life. She gets a bit mixed-up at times. Don't you, addled-Anna, but somehow it comes out all right. Just imagine how apprehensive we were when we heard she was coming to Strathallan. Instead, she's achieved the happy ending none of the rest of us could manage.'

So she had ... for Sophy and Philip, but not for herself. ...

Philip said, 'Let's all go over home. You gave us a good hour or more alone. My lady mother is going to be very cock-a-hoop. She predicted long ago that I'd finally get Sophy if I persisted. Even Dad said if I had any sense I'd bludgeon her into accepting me just as he did with Mother after Al – after another chap let her down and she wasn't going to trust anybody any more.'

Philip and Calum looked fleetingly embarrassed. They both rushed madly into other speech. Anna thought she'd examine that switch later. But she didn't want anything to mar Sophy and Philip's betrothal night.

She said, 'Victoria ought to be in on this. Where is she? Still at Strathallan? But she must just think it was sheer coincidence I was here when Philip came over and did the bludgeoning. Let's ring her. I hope she doesn't feel left out of all the excitement.'

'She won't,' said Calum. 'Victoria doesn't get at all het-up over such things. I sung out as I left that I'd better try to catch you – I'll say I realized from something Philip said that things were coming to a head and he was going to the manse, and I wanted to whisk you out of it. We can make a good story out of it, say we didn't get away quickly enough, and had to entertain Bridie. Do you want Kit and Gilbert in on the celebration too, Philip? Victoria could drive them over. You've got you car here to drive them back, Philip. Oh, we've cars galore. There's Anna's too.'

Sophy said, 'Victoria must be our other bridesmaid, of course I've already asked Anna. Yes, Philip, I'd got that far before you arrived. Calum will be best man. How about Ian for the groomsman?'

Philip said, 'Have a heart! Give Anna a bachelor, not a married man. One good turn deserves another.'

Anna said, 'You dare! Ian will do very nicely. I've had best men thrust at me before. At a wedding in Fiji. It was so obvious what my best friend was after. It made me go off this chap before I met him. I just loathe matchmakers!'

They all doubled up. Philip said, in gasps, 'Oh, Anna, you're *so* funny. *You* saying that, the arch-matchmaker of all time! Well, it all sounds fine to me, though I'm in such a state of happiness, if you proposed old Barney for the groomsman I'd probably say yes. Mother will be most relieved to find we've got it down to the last detail. Of course it could be that by then Victoria will have to be a matron of honour. How about it, Calum? Any date fixed yet? Or should we make it a double wedding?'

Calum said quietly, 'That's over to Victoria. I told her some time ago I'd leave the date entirely to her. She knows what commitments she's got in her job. But before we go over to your place, Philip, Sophy's got to have some coffee and some oat-cakes. She didn't even finish her dinner and she's had a lot of excitement. Make it quickly, Anna, while I ring Victoria and tell her to take the others over to Kowhai Bend.'

Sophy said, 'And ring your parents too, Calum, they must be in on this. Oh, your poor mother, Philip ... an engagement party at a moment's notice, and her cake-tins are probably at a low ebb. It always happens that way.'

Calum said, 'Oh, Mother'll take stuff over. So will Kit.'

Sophy and Philip drove off. Calum said, 'Leave your car here, Anna. We can drive over tomorrow and pick it up. Come with me.'

She shook her head. 'No, I'd rather take it. I'll follow you because although I know the way to Kowhai Bend from Strathallan, I don't from Crannog.' She looked up at him and in the light from the street lamp outside, thought he looked a little strained.

'Tell me, Calum, I'd rather know. One could drop a brick otherwise. When Philip caught back a name tonight – about his mother – was it my father who let her down?'

He hesitated, but not for long. He reached out and took hold of her cold hands. 'It would be silly to lie. Yes. But then Henry Sherborne was waiting. It doesn't have to matter to you. Nobody, least of all Grace Sherborne, is going to think any the less of you because you're Alex's daughter.'

Anna said, 'No, I could never have told from her manner to me. She's really sweet. But—' she caught her lip between her teeth for a moment, to still its trembling, then went on again, steadily, 'But it does hurt to know one's father caused so much unhappiness. That's something you can't possibly understand, Calum. Because you've had a secure family life.'

He said patiently, 'Oh, Anna, have you forgotten Blair?'

She had. 'Oh, Calum, your brother. But surely he couldn't have done such havoc as my father did?'

He said, 'He was the middle brother. Older than me. Havoc? He was engaged to Victoria. He just cleared out. Can you imagine what that does to a girl? She'd got as far as planning a home. You know she's an interior decorator, don't you? Even though she hadn't the experience she has now, she was still mighty good. She dreamed day and night of the home they would make together. She planned to have them take over some old place and do it up. Then Blair just cleared out. Left a note saying he wanted to see the world, not be tied down to domesticity.

'He roamed the world, spent longest in Canada, then went to Britain. He finally married there. My mother still yearns after him. But she was very happy when Victoria and I became engaged. And don't you think it will mean a lot to Grace Sherborne that Alex's girl brought her son and the girl of his heart together, when the rest of us failed dismally. Even though she'll only know you spurred Sophy on by making her jealous. Not that you thought I loved Sophy. You're right in saying Victoria shouldn't know. She's suffered enough doubts in her life.'

Anna returned the pressure of his hands. He caught the gleam of tears in her eyes. 'Oh, Calum, you've a genius for making things look right for me. Just like you warmed my frozen feet that night. I felt chilled to the bone just now when I realized my father had treated Philip's mother badly. But now I feel all warm again. And you did it by telling me your own private family anguish. Did you —' Oh, no, she mustn't ask had he always loved Victoria. She began again. 'You said it made your mother very happy when you and Victoria became engaged. You mean she wanted Victoria as a daughter-in-law?'

He said slowly, 'She never said just that, but she always thought that if Blair had married her, he might have settled down. He would have, too, because Victoria's got what it takes. She's a real home-maker.' His voice held pride, admiration.

'Then I'm glad it had a happy ending. And, if Blair is married now, too, I expect your mother feels better about him?'

'Yes, in a way. He seems to have realized at last that he'd have to stick to one job, one line. He was fast becoming a jack-of-all-trades, master of none. He's gone back to farming. Not his own farm, but he works on a model dairy and health food farm in Surrey. It used to be a stately home. They keep it going and make it pay by going in for this specialized production. Blair got interested. He never cared for sheep. He lives in the village surrounding it. Most of the workers do. Houses are provided. He's got two children. Mother's dying to see them. We'd like her to go over, but she won't leave Dad. He'll retire from the Hydro in a year or two and they'll go then.

'Blair's been writing home more regularly lately, and more warmly. He was such a casual beggar. I think being a family man must suit him. He writes reams about the kids now. But he never mentions his wife. It makes Mother uneasy. Shortly after Blair married Yvette a friend of Mum's went to Britain and visited them. Mum really pressed her to tell her how they were managing. This friend finally confessed Yvette was a flibberty-gibbet. Mother said drily, "Well, perhaps that's the type he deserves. If he'd got someone as unselfish as Victoria, he'd have leaned on her all his life." Now we're inclined to think this is what has happened. He writes a lot about his work now. He really likes it. He wasn't on even speaking terms with hard work before. Well, let's off and make merry. I'll make sure you're tailing me all right, Anna.'

Her thoughts weren't of Sophy and Philip. They were with what Calum had left unsaid. Had Calum been glad when Blair had left the field to him? Or had it been later, when Victoria had got over the first bitter sense of loss, that Calum had found he loved her?

She had the vague idea that her grandparents didn't

wholeheartedly approve this match. What had Grandy meant when he'd said Calum needed someone to spar with verbally? Strange comment that. Surely it was better if sweet harmony flowed between a man and a woman? Or was it? Mightn't it be a little like a dewless morning? Like an egg without salt? On which romantic thought she saw Calum turn in at the gate-posts of Kowhai Bend, looked beyond to see lights coming in that direction. That would be the three from Strathallan. Calum's folk would take a little longer. They had to come from the Roxburgh Hydro Village.

Well, Anna, this is it. It's been quite a day. Just imagine, even twelve hours ago you had no idea Calum Doig was engaged to Victoria Sherborne! You're always a bridesmaid, never a bride. Oh, who cared ... there was more to life than love and marriage.

CHAPTER EIGHT

EVERYONE laughed because Philip's mother kissed Anna first, then the engaged couple. 'Well,' said Grace Sherborne, 'Philip said on the phone that the whole thing was due to Anna. She seems to have the knack of making people happy.'

Anna laughed, flung out her hands, said deprecatingly, 'Oh, please don't. It makes me feel like a Belladonna. And I never did like that child.'

They all looked puzzled. Then Calum said indulgently, 'You're at it again, Anna-the-addled-one, you mean Polly-anna. Belladonna is a drug. Or a lily. Beats me how you achieve the results you do, you mixed-up creature.'

She flashed round on him, grinning. 'You get addled too . . . you called me a battledore and you meant a shuttle-cock!'

His eyes were alight with laughter, remembering. 'So I did, it's one up to you!'

Suddenly Anna caught a strange look on Victoria's face. She was looking at Calum as if seeing him in a new light. Then slowly she began to turn, to look at Anna. At least Anna was sure that was what she was going to do. Anna turned swiftly away and said to Kitty, 'I'm getting the credit for it, but at first I had my wires crossed too.' She said it in a low tone, under cover of the congratulatory chatter going on. 'I may sound as if I've played Cupid, but believe me, I nearly goosed the whole thing by being so blind, so addle-pated. I'll tell you later. Not a word to anyone else.'

It was a very happy gathering, informal and heart-warming. Anna felt part and parcel of this community now. Dermid and Judith Doig came in, added their quota to the general rejoicing. Anna had thought of them as a fun-loving couple, hospitable, out-going types. Now, with a more intimate knowledge of the way they'd worried over Blair, she saw lines of patience and a little sadness beside their mouths. Mouths were so revealing. But it was only in repose that you could notice it. She sat down on the arm of

Dermid's chair. He slipped an arm about her. 'Don't fall off, lassie. From what my son tells me, you've been prime mover in this.'

She twinkled. 'At one stage I was scared Sophy would regard me as the snake in the grass. Philip merely pretended he was taking an interest in me, and Sophy fell into his arms.'

Dermid chuckled. Anna added, 'I only hope it doesn't go to my head. I might start playing Providence and get all Crannog by the ears.'

'Not you. You've just no idea of what you've accomplished by just coming here. Kit and Gilbert are different persons. Kit's got back the spring in her step, and Gilbert can do nothing but talk about you. Before that he thought he was going to fade out of life, with no descendants to carry on at Strathallan. After all, Calum and Ian are not blood relations.'

How sweet they all were! How extraordinary that she'd met with no resentment from anyone.

Dermid continued, 'Just look at Calum. You'd think he'd been responsible. He used to be like this long ago. He and Blair were such pals. He missed him horribly. Oh, well.'

Anna smiled. 'Calum can take a good deal of the credit. He kept parishioners at bay in the most noble fashion, till Philip and Sophy got things signed and sealed.'

It was very late when they got back to Strathallan. The neighbour's daughter they'd got in to babysit with the children was in the little spare room fast asleep. Kitty and Gilbert had laughed all the way home about the mistake Anna had made. Kitty said, 'It was my fault and Philip's really. We assumed she knew the situation. Well, it worked. No, we won't say a word to anyone. As you say, it could make Victoria wonder a little. And it's very hard at any time to know what she's thinking. She's a dear lass, and her first experience didn't give her much faith in men.'

Anna didn't sleep till she heard Calum come in and tiptoe past her room to his. It was more than an hour later. Oh, well, Calum would have had lingering goodnights to say to Victoria ... not only was this the night her brother celebrated his engagement but the first night of her return after weeks of absence.

Life would settle down again. There wouldn't be any more foursomes, that was for sure. At least there would be, but they would consist of Sophy and Philip, Victoria and Calum. The dawn was greying the sky before she slept.

They let her sleep it out. Only Kitty was in the house when she woke. She couldn't believe she'd slept through the accustomed uproar as the twins and Maggie were breakfasted and got off to school; that neither cockcrow nor the bawling of a calf newly parted from its mother had wakened her.

Kitty laughed. 'I crept in and you looked so exhausted I felt it would be downright cruel to rouse you. Matchmaking can be an exhausting business, and often after such excitement, one can feel a little flat.'

Yes, of course. That was all it was, this weight on her spirit.

Kitty went on, 'We've had a ring from Ian. Betty's mother is out of hospital and her other sister has arrived down from Napier to nurse her when convalescent. So they'll be home tonight. I wondered if you'd come across to their house with me, air it and put some flowers in. There'll be baking to do, too, to fill up their tins. I'd been keeping ours full in case they got home soon, but I took it all over to Kowhai Bend last night. But between the two of us, we can whip a few things up quickly. The men are going to be busy, but I wondered if you'd mow their lawns while I cut the edges.'

It was good to be so busy. One couldn't feel quite so – so what? Quite so lost? How stupid, Anna. What have you lost? Nothing that you ever possessed. No, but when she'd thought it was Sophy Calum loved, there had been that faint chance that – Oh, Anna! It had been a forlorn hope at best and not a very admirable one.

Strathallan became a place of wider activities and interests with Betty and Ian back. The children still managed to be underfoot at the homestead a lot and they regarded Anna as their own special property.

Betty said, 'Anna, enough's as good as a feast. You're far too good-natured by far. You hardly ever say no to them whatever they want you to join in. Don't let them impose upon you.'

Maggie came round the corner just then and was most indignant. 'Mum! We don't impose on her. We don't pester either. If Anna's busy, she tells us and we go away. But we always know she wants to come. And she just loves tadpole-ing . . . just imagine, she'd never gone tadpole-ing in her life. And she likes finding out things and says if it wasn't for us she'd not know half enough about New Zealand. We found some silver-eye nests for her yesterday, hanging under the pine branches, down in the triangle copse. But she was the one who spotted that one was hung with spiderwebs, all the rest were horse-hair. Gee, we'd like to see them doing it with web. How come they don't get all sticky and messed up? We're going to build a hide in the copse next year so we can watch. Anna says we can't now or we'll disturb them.

'And she's such a sport. She didn't mind a bit when she fell in the creek when she was hanging over trying to see into the kingfisher's tunnel. We wouldn't keep asking her to come if we thought she was only doing it to please us. And you know Bill and Mac don't take too much notice of other people as a rule, but they really *mind* what *she* says. Because she isn't frightened to spank their bottoms when they do dangerous things.'

Betty burst out laughing. 'Well, that's the best recom-mendation of all. Maggie, I cry peace. I know I sounded mean but all mothers are scared their offspring make nuis-ances of themselves, but I think you're right. Anna seems to really enjoy your company.'

Anna looked almost apologetic. 'You see, they know I'm on my own. I mean you've got Ian and Calum's got Victoria, and nobody else has first claim on my time. And I love it. I could ramble for hours. You see, I never had anyone in the family to play with. I used to bring children home after school, but they always went home again, and it's marvellous to know that all the hills we explore belong to us.'

'Okay, but tell those devils that when you've had enough, they're not to persuade you to keep going. They just regard you as their very own personal property.'

Anna laughed and departed with them. She just loved Betty. It was probably true what Grandmother had said, Betty wouldn't suit the homestead. She loved everything up-to-the-minute, brand-new furnishings, strong colourings, a clinical-looking kitchen. When she picked up a pair of butter-pats she didn't see, with her mind's eye, Kirsty Drummond dexterously turning out grooved curls of home-made butter still with ice-cold drops of water on them; she merely said, 'Thank goodness we get ours straight from the dairy company these days.'

When she saw Anna flinging the rose-and-thistle rag mat outside for shaking, she didn't see it as a replica of Kirsty's, and generations of Strathallan Drummonds as small children squirming their cold toes in its warmth and softness as they dressed before the old range, glowing red, on mornings of snow or hoar-frost. She just said, 'Real dust-traps, aren't they? Give me something you can vacuum.'

Nevertheless, Betty was fun. She mightn't be one for reading poetry or dreaming over the gold-miners' robust past, but she looked well to the ways of her household, and had a sort of wholesome prettiness and commonsense that was restful. All your friends couldn't be kindred spirits, and Anna had soon realized that as far as Strathallan was concerned, Betty didn't resent her appearance at all. There wasn't an atom of jealousy in her. Anna's last suspicions about the way the Doigs had dug themselves in here, dissolved. She needed to gang warily no longer!

It was only as far as her feelings for Calum were concerned that that still applied. Often she'd find her eyes lingering on him as he stretched out in one of the big wing chairs after dinner, reading or watching TV. She liked his comments on the documentaries, on the world scene, the country calendar series, the political issues of the day at home and abroad, and, closer at hand, his tolerant yet at times strong views on local affairs.

She liked it best when, rarely, perhaps after a harder day than usual on horseback, or the tractor, he'd drop asleep. Then she could watch him unobserved. It was strange how that rather granite-like face would soften then, look a little defenceless.

One night when Kitty was upstairs and Gilbert was busy in the farm office, she indulged herself in this study of his face. Perhaps he'd been working too hard of late. Those grooves in his bronzed cheeks were deeper, surely, than when she'd first come to Strathallan? Certainly he was leaner. The curved lines each side of his lips were emphasized when he laughed, but tonight they suggested weariness and patience to her.

She thought he'd driven himself too hard during October, and though she had chided herself for being fanciful, she'd thought at times he only just held leashed some impatience, as if he disciplined himself, checked something in him that wanted to be uncurbed. Oh, well, some said a long engagement was a strain. There was something immensely appealing about Victoria. She was five years older than Anna, she'd found out, but Anna often felt protective towards her. Odd that, but the make-up of a person could affect one's maturity. Calum had said he was leaving it to Victoria to name the wedding-day. Anna had a strange feeling that Victoria was perfectly happy to be just engaged, not to advance another step.

Anna wondered what it meant. There were women, of course, who because they suspected they were sexually frigid, preferred a long engagement, not wanting to totally commit themselves to anyone, instead of looking on marriage as entry into a new and delightful world, where romance and passion and deep need of each other could be blended into one. Anna checked her thoughts. How did *she* know all this? Then she conceded the answer. Because she so loved Calum. Because that was how she would have looked on marriage with him.

No one living at Strathallan could possibly be cynical about marriage. Kitty still turned eagerly at Gilbert's step as he came in from the fields, lifted her face for his kiss as if, like a man working in the city, she'd not seen him all day. Once, when her grandparents hadn't known she was inside, she had seen Gilbert catch his Kit to him with an abandon Anna thought she'd witnessed hitherto only on television. She had realized, with a lift of the heart, and a little envy, that the passion of true love could last right into old age.

She could have found that with Calum, she knew, but long before she had come here, Calum had asked Victoria to be his wife, and these moments of tenderness when she could watch him unaware, were all she'd ever have of him.

At that moment Calum opened his eyes, fully. It wasn't the look of a man just struggling up from the haziness of slumber, it was the alert look of someone who'd been awake some time but hadn't raised his lids.

There was a long shared moment of eyes looking into eyes

across the distance between Calum's chair and the couch on which Anna sat.

Calum said swiftly, 'Anna, what is it? You look wistful and lost. Like that old tag, Anna-where-art-thou? Where were you, Anna? Back in Fiji? What's biting into you?'

The spell broke with his words. She blinked, pretended to be surprised, said, 'I think I must have been far, far away. Just dreaming.'

He sounded abrupt. 'That's what I mean. Dreaming of what? I've never seen you look like that before. You've been so happy-hearted, we take it for granted you're glad to be here. Content with this life. Are you homesick tonight? You looked lost, wistful. It's all right for us, we've been born and bred in this district. But for you it amounts to a foreign land. Tell me, Anna, don't bottle it up . . . are you homesick?'

(Oh, no, she wasn't homesick, because home was where the heart was, it was said, but she must go along with that. Because he must never guess. She couldn't stay on if he knew.)

So she said, 'I am, just a little, sometimes. But my grandparents must never know.'

He came to sit by her, took her hand. 'Oh, Anna, no one would have guessed. Tell me what you're most homesick for? Is it the heat, the colour, the palm fronds against the night sky? Soft Fijian voices, coral reefs . . . oh, yes, I've been there. How odd I didn't know about you then. If only, like Elizabeth and Ross, I'd picked your guest-house, we'd have met sooner. I'd have recognized you for Gilbert's granddaughter for sure, especially as you bore the name of Drummond.'

She didn't know why she had to ask that first, but she said, 'Was Victoria with you? Were you on a cruise?'

'No. It was long before we were engaged. I was on my own. I flew. I'd had my appendix out and they didn't want me hanging round the farm trying to do things I wasn't fit for. I loved Fiji. You haven't said what you miss most, Anna.'

That was easy, 'Oh, the sound and sight of the sea, Calum. The feel of a boat under me.'

He nodded. 'I can understand that. Living away inland like this must make you feel cut off from an element that's second nature to you. We must get you up to the lakes sometime. They're immense, their beds gouged out by glaciers in the ice-age, sheets of water as blue as the seas because snow-fed. I've heard people who live by the sea say it's the only place they could ever live, if they had to go inland.

'It's been all work and no play for you, lambing's like that. But even the tailing's behind us now. We'll have a day off soon – that's a promise. We'll go down to the sea.'

He heard Kitty coming downstairs singing softly, as she so often did these days. She had a lilt in her voice again now, because her son's daughter filled that emptiness in her heart.

He returned to his seat, picked up his book. Anna said, 'I must go up to my room and sort out some stuff for Maggie. They're doing a project on Polynesian arts and crafts. She came home all starry-eyed about it, knowing I'd be bound to have something. They're having a display, and are each doing a strip, cut from magazines, for a wall decoration.' She slipped away.

By now the trunks she'd stored at Auntie Ed's had been sent down here. Since Mother and Magnus would be in the South Island next year, they were better in safe keeping at Strathallan.

She sorted through tapa-cloth, wood-carvings, coconut shell curios, strings of shell beads. The brochures were at the bottom of this trunk, she thought. Maggie would cut them up and paste them on cardboard tomorrow night under Betty's supervision.

Oddly enough, though she'd used homesickness only as a cover-up for her real feelings, these things did give her nostalgic pangs tonight. Oh, she knew that had Calum been free, and if he had loved her, she'd have known no nostalgia at all – but they lived closely here, in the same house, so that she had grown highly tensed about it, always on guard.

Suddenly an almost unbearable longing for her mother swept her. They'd been such pals, so close, and they'd had such fun. Mother had been her whole world when she was a child. And, here were the brochures. How gloriously coloured they were! Small Maggie would be delighted. How she loved Maggie, with her Highland colouring so like Calum's. The small daughter she might have had herself one day if – oh, stop it, Anna. Then at the bottom she saw her mother's scrapbook. She took it out and went across to the chintz-petticoated chair that an early Anna Drummond had fashioned out of a cheese crate and goose-feather filling long, long ago. She'd curved the back and buttoned it and Anna loved to use it.

She could faintly hear Calum's voice downstairs. He must be phoning. She began leafing through the pages. It was full of clippings of poems, things about Fiji, the occasional bit of publicity about the guest-house from the *Suva Times*, a few cartoons that had taken Lois's fancy. At times, infrequently, she had used it as a journal to enter up some milestone in her daughter's life, or something interesting about some guest, famous for something.

Anna wondered if she ought to be dipping into it. Lois might have used it as a wailing wall. But if it had been very private, Lois would have taken it with her, surely. Tonight, swept with longing for her mother, this brought her near. The first entries were full of her joy in her small daughter. Anna wondered, as she read on, absorbed, how Lois had managed to keep from writing out her anguish, her disillusionment. Was it in case Alex had come across it, and his image of himself be damaged? No, she found the answer to that when she turned a page and found a note that recorded the inscription of an old sundial. 'I record only the sunny hours.' Beside that Lois had written, 'And so do I, in this dear book, record all I find of compensation and inspiration'

Then Anna found a poem that had a whole page to itself and carried a comment that revealed a lot. It was called *Message* and had been cut from a *Good Housekeeping* magazine. It read:

'From this ploughed field the young sweet corn shall spring,
　　These frozen clods yield to the tender seed,
And pulsing Earth, with all her myriad gifts,
　　From Winter's paralysing grip be freed.

This rotting mould shall bring forth loveliness,
　　These leafless branches bloom in bridal white,
And where the moon now gleams on frost and snow,
　　The briar rose shall scent the summer night.

Then down these sombre walks where you have kept
　　Your foolish trysts with bitterness and pain,

New joys shall spring; and all old sorrows yield
  Before the healing tide of time again.'

Under it were two comments, one in faded ink, one in
recent ball-point. The first said, 'I wonder?' The second
said, 'New joys *did* spring. Thank you, God.' And the date
under it was the eve of her marriage to Magnus Randal.
That poem had meant as much to Lois as that.

Anna felt strengthened, happed about with her mother's
love and understanding She wished her mother could have
known that she too had received comfort from that poem,
and by the knowledge that her mother had indeed found that
healing tide, the young green corn springing. Perhaps for
her too, new happinesses would lie ahead in the years to
come. She must put all thoughts of Calum away from her.
He was betrothed to Victoria whose first love, long ago, his
own brother, had jilted her.

Victoria, then, had felt as Anna did now. But worse, because she had known Blair's love. Could one miss what one
had never had? Anna turned swiftly from the thought. She
would fight this attraction and never, never betray herself or
Victoria.

Victoria was so right for the mistress of Strathallan.
Unlike Betty she loved the old, the historical, had exquisite
taste in antiques. Naturally, when she was the Otago rep-
resentative of that top-class firm of interior decorators. She
was so knowledgeable about every kind of Colonial an-
tique.

Nothing in Strathallan of sentimental value would be
thrown out. She would gather choice pieces of her own about
her, and the homestead would be loved and cherished as it
had always been. Anna felt there was great comfort in that.
And she would be part of it, still, living in the annexe with
Kitty and Gilbert.

Anna went downstairs walking tall, secure again in her
own resolve not to betray herself. When they were having
supper Calum said, 'I was talking to Victoria on the phone,
down at Te Anau. She's found an old homestead full of
treasures down there. It overlooks the lake, some distance
out. She was scouting for items, but got overcome with the
enormity of ever removing a thing from this place. So she's
talked them into restoring it and running it as a showplace

for tourists. She'd landed the job, so her firm will forgive her for not securing the stuff. They're three sisters, who felt it was getting too much for them to keep up on a reduced income — as they'd sold a lot of the land. It wouldn't take much to restore, and they'd make a packet out of tours. That's just Victoria. She'd never bulldoze people into part-ing with things she feels ought to be retained in their own surroundings. I said to her it's just as well she's so valuable to her firm that she can get away with these things. She laughed, said she'd been in touch with them and they'd said it would be the best possible advert for them. What a girl! She'd never do a mean or wrong thing.'

Anna thought her grandparents looked a little excited. But that was absurd. Why would they? No, they had more the look of people about to spring a birthday surprise on a dear child. Equally absurd, because nothing eventuated and they retired fairly early.

She woke to a tap on her door, not an urgent one, a dis-creet one. Someone evidently didn't want to disturb the rest of the family. She said 'Coming,' and went quietly to the door. Enough light to show her a fully-dressed Calum, but not in farming gear, more like sporting garb.

Her eyes, above purple pyjamas, were enormous. 'What is it?'

'Surprise, surprise! I cooked it up with Kit and Gilbert last night. I'm taking you down to the sea today, to "the flung spray and the blown spume, and the seagulls crying". Throw a dressing-gown on and come downstairs. I've got breakfast all ready. But not being the world's best cook, I started the bacon too early and don't want it frizzled. Don't even stop to wash your face or brush your hair. You can shower after.'

She blinked sleepily at him, hooked the white towelling robe that was on the back of the door down, tied it round her, and crept downstairs in his wake. She looked like a child in the short jacket, rubbing her eyes with the heels of her hands. He laughed at her indulgently.

'Good girl! You didn't stop to reason why, you just obeyed. Can't stand girls who'd rather die than appear with-out their faces on and their hair slicked up. But you're one of the lucky ones I'd say. Your hair is hardly ruffled.'

She laughed. 'It's so thick the layers just lie on top of each other.' She looked at the table and all sleepiness left her. 'How odd, I'm starving, yet it must be still about the middle of the night.' She swung round to look at the old schoolroom-type clock on the wall. 'Just four o'clock, why, Calum, do we have to be so early? And what sea do you mean?'

'The Pacific, of course. Your sea. The one that washes the beaches of your beloved Suva, but a good many degrees colder. Not that it will matter today, we won't be swimming. We're going out in a launch belonging to a good friend of mine. It's a hundred miles to Dunedin and about another twenty-five to Karitane. That's why we had to rise so early. This chap's only there at weekends. I've spent many with him, so I know how to handle the boat Can't promise you a coral reef, but there's a quite tricky bar.'

All of a sudden the bright, warm kitchen wavered before Anna's eyes. She blinked rapidly, realized Calum had seen the tears, said, 'Oh, this is stupid of me. Only it's – it's so kind. I—'

He said, deftly sliding rashers of bacon on to the warmed plates, 'Why not kind? Don't I regard you as the sister I've never had? You live in the same house, like the same things.'

It steadied her, cooled her emotions down. Of course. It was a *brotherly* thing to do. That was all it was to him.

He pulled out a chair for her. 'I didn't say you were homesick, just that you suddenly had a yen for the sea. Kit and Gilbert immediately suggested I take you to Bull Creek, out on the coast from Milton, a glorious spot, but I thought if we went to Karitane, you could actually go out on the sea in Doug's boat. I rang round while you were upstairs last night. Didn't want to say anything till I was sure we could have the launch.'

Ring round. Oh, yes, he'd been talking to Victoria too. She reached out for the marmalade. She must be quite candid. 'Calum, you did mention it to Victoria when you were talking to her?'

'Yes, of course. That was why I rang her.'

Anna was busy cutting her toast into strips so didn't look up.

'You asked her if it would be all right, I hope?'

He said softly, 'I get it. You feel you disturbed Sophy over Philip – you don't want Victoria to get wrong ideas too!'

She looked up then. 'Yes, of course. I appreciate the brotherly concern, Calum, as long as Victoria recognizes it for that. You see, if I was engaged to you – I mean if I was engaged to a man – and he took a girl out for a whole day, I have an idea that I'd get jealous. But if she really does understand, then—'

'She does. Not to worry. Nothing upsets Victoria. She sent you her love.'

'Nothing upsets her?'

'Well, nothing now. Things used to. But she was educated in the University of Hard Knocks, so she's got a fair idea of the fitness and relevance of things and doesn't read ulterior motives into everything I do '

Anna felt slightly put in her place.

His voice crisped, 'Now, if you don't want another cup of tea, off for that shower. Kit said she'd slit my throat if I allowed you to as much as wash a cup, and you're to leave your bed too. We want as many hours of daylight as possible and by the time you're ready the sun will be up. Nice if we'd been able to see it rise, but we won't make it.'

'Like to bet on it? I had a bath last night, I'll skip the shower. I'd rather have the dawn.' She was off like a lintie.

He had the Avenger at the door by the time she came down in white trews and sweater with a high roll collar and a turquoise-and-white spotted kerchief knotted triangular-wise round it, turquoise and white sneakers, and an Alice band in black to confine her hair a little.

How glorious to be off the chain after the close devotion to farm chores of the past weeks. Anna thought that to watch the dawn come up with the man you loved – even if he didn't love you in return – was surely something.

It came up with sudden splendour, as if aware it had an audience, just before they reached Roxburgh. Calum drew the car into the side of the hill-road to watch it. Just two of them in all that glory of light and colour . . . as if the world was being made new for them alone.

A silver streak split the sky ahead of them to the east horizontally, then, before sixty seconds had passed, great ochre rays seemed to shoot up out of the slit, and the darkness above it rolled back as the rays widened. It paled from the centre rapidly through shades of inkiness to a pearly grey that was more an absence of light than any hue at all, all depth of shade emptying and ebbing before the onslaught of the mighty sun.

Then nature rushed in to fill that vacuum with banners and billows of pulsing, changing opalescent colours, the night retreating hastily in the bowl of the sky, to its furthermost edges, and disappearing over the horizon from north to south.

It was just as if some stage lighting expert had turned on rainbow beams to bloom and fade to delight the two people who had time to watch. Clouds were outlined in fiery light, blues infused the grey of the dawn sky, and those mysterious lights switched and rayed from copper-rose to amethyst, to baby-pink and deepest fuchsia ... another switch and the clouds were purple and then turned to coral above a stretch of sea-green sky.

'The world put that on specially for us,' exulted Calum, as he let in the clutch and drove off. 'I ordered something extra good in the way of sunrises, but that exceeded all I hoped for.'

They turned a corner and there below them lay immense sheets of colour, the pink and apricot drifts of acres of fruit orchards, and heavy on the air was perfume from an old gnarled pear-tree close to the road, surely the very essence of spring itself.

The orchards patched the whole hillsides. They looked to the left below them and there was the aquamarine of the dammed-up Clutha River at the Roxburgh Hydro, with its colour turned to silver as it cascaded down the spillway. 'I'll take you across to the works soon,' said Calum. 'Dad mentioned it the other night. He'd like to show you through. He's so proud of it you'd think he'd conceived and carried the whole thing through himself. We'll all have to visit him more frequently soon, anyway, because he'll be on his own for a couple of months. Mother's off to Britain to visit Blair.'

Anna was delighted. 'How lovely for her. She's not seen him for many years, has she? Has Yvette written and asked her to come to see the grandchildren? Won't Blair be excited?'

Calum said quietly, 'Blair doesn't even know she's coming. She wants to give him a surprise. I'm a bit uneasy about it. I'd hate her to get rebuffed. She's off as soon as she's finished with her immunizations. Evidently she'd been thinking of it for some time. She's got her passport and visas and what-have-you. She and Dad will still take an overseas trip when he retires, but she feels she must go now. That something impels her. I can't imagine what's stirred her up so suddenly. She's just going to arrive in London, give herself a couple of days to recover from the trip, and then give Blair a ring.

'I can't make it out. He's been writing more frequently than he's ever done Just nice chatty letters, especially for Blair. Ian and I, now, when away from home, write screeds. Blair never did. I said this to Mother the other night. She just looked at me strangely and said, "Yes, he's writing very newsy letters. It's what he doesn't say that bothers me." I expect she means because he never mentions Yvette.

'I said to her that it could be in case she passed them over to us to read, as she does, and he doesn't quite know how Victoria would react to much mention of his wife. Mother looked quite angry and said, "Oh, surely not .. now she's been engaged to you so long. That ought to be water under the mill." Which I suppose is fair enough. But she's got the bit between her teeth.'

'How does your father feel about it?'

'Oh, Dad's a great scout and has always understood Mother. He'd only have to say, "Oh, Judith, I can't bear you to go without me, do wait," and she'd stay, but not Dad. I said to him couldn't he stop her, that I was afraid she might find a situation she didn't like, that Yvette might make her feel unwelcome. Dad said: "Son, I feel it's been laid upon your mother to go. She'd bide here till I retire, I know, but something bids her go and go she must. I'd rather feel lost without her than have her fretting." ' Calum was silent momentarily, then said, 'I rather envied him his complete confidence in her doing the right thing.'

Could he mean he wasn't so sure about Victoria? She said slowly, 'I find that most endearing, Calum. But perhaps that sort of confidence only comes after half a lifetime of marriage. He may not have been so sure of her judgment in, say, their engagement days.'

'Why do you say that, Anna? As if reassuring me?'

She turned away as if something had just caught her eye.

'Oh, did you see that profusion of clematis? . . . Look, absolutely smothering that old stone hut. It's just a galaxy of pink stars.'

He didn't repeat his question He must have thought better of it.

Roxburgh was hardly stirring yet, except for the milkmen. Anna's eyes swept the rounded shoulders of Mount Benger, with, on its lower slopes, winding ribbons of rows and rows of lombardy poplars in full green leaf. By midday it would be lying in a blaze of sunshine with its bright-roofed houses, vari-coloured, set in gardens so vivid they almost hurt the eye. Private orchards decked the houses with pink and white, grapevines trailed on supports.

'Calum, this is such a dear little town. It blends the new and the old so beautifully. The old gold-mining haunts aren't so derelict here as in others. They're restored and treasured and it seems to have such a happy, neighbourly atmosphere. It has a personality all its own. I call it the marigold town, because it's all golden now, in spring, and from that painting of Grandy's over our mantelpiece, it's burnished gold and burnt orange in the autumn. It's more gentle and dreaming than some of the other more rugged parts of Central.'

They drove into the sun as the miles rolled by. Anna wound down her window so they could hear the birdsong resounding in the glad chorus of early morning. They went over the Beaumont bridge with its really vivid green-blue waters swirling around the pattern of rocks islanded in it. As Calum went on recounting the history of every landmark, Anna marvelled that ever there should have been pioneers to cross these waters on horseback, or on frail punts. . . . Lawrence was stirring to life, beautifully circled by its hills, with old inns, restored, that could have told many a lawless tale, many a tragedy . . . a place that could remember the first discovery of gold, a road that could remember Anthony Trollope's plunging coach-horses on a night of smothering snowdrifts, a place of silver birch avenues, of poplar avenues where beneath the trees, shortly, there would be drifts of lupins as colourful as if rainbows had fallen from the sky.

'Remind me to take you to Gorge Creek on the way to Alexandra to see the wild lupins there next month. There's one patch entirely composed of shadings from palest lilac to deepest purple. Then in other places are the whites, the golds, the blues, the rose-pinks, all mixed like the ones here.'

The hills became lower, and there were deep-red ornamental apple-trees in the gardens, early rhododendrons from pearly pink to purple and a deep flourescent red; wistaria hanging royal plumes round verandah posts, old-fashioned cottages with white-painted Victorian iron lace-work between the posts, prosperous-looking farms with flocks as dazzlingly white as if they'd been bleached, sleek cattle herds, geese waddling down to the little steams.

They wound through the Manuka Gorge, a small one by New Zealand standards, with just a tiny willow-choked rivulet threading through it, but this was an ice-trap in winter, Calum said.

Every quivering leaf added its music to the day. Oh, yes, it would be a day to remember all her life, a glad, rainbow-hued day. Something she would remember when she was eighty. At the thought she laughed aloud.

'Yes?' asked Calum.

She chuckled again 'I found myself thinking I'd remember the beauty of this day when I'm eighty and tried to imagine myself at that. It's almost impossible. Even Grandmother's nowhere near that yet, so I've nothing to pattern myself on.'

Calum agreed. 'Very hard to do. I've heard quite old people say they can't imagine they *are* old. Till they meet their contemporaries! That they feel much the same inside and don't know where the years have gone to.' He paused. 'Now me, I'll have a most severe look. I'll be more beaky than ever. Do you know what Maggie told me the other day? That my side-face was just like those schist rocks near Alexandra! You remember those eroded ones, all scarred by the weather into sharp angles? She's dead right. I could see it myself. But you, Anna—' he paused, 'you'll still look like your grandfather. Your hair may be white too, but it'll always be streaky, I warrant, with that bit of dark-gold showing underneath. And your eyes will still be this purply-brown of pansies.'

Her laugh was derisive. 'Oh, Calum, how absurd can you get? Who ever heard of purple eyes?'

'I said purply-brown. Like those pansies of Kitty's by the

back steps. They're supposed to be brown, with golden edges, but in reality they have a purple tinge. When the sunlight's right on your eyes they aren't brown and they aren't black, they're pansy-coloured.'

Anna was giggling helplessly. 'It doesn't sound old-ladyish enough.'

'Well, I'll concede that perhaps you'll be a little stiff in the joints, because you've spent so many springs in wet paddocks at lambing-time, and your knuckles might be a little knotted too, and you'll have the brown spots of age on the backs of your hands, but you'll always grow young again when spring comes back to Strathallan. Like Kitty you'll always be out eagerly looking for the first primroses, the first violets, for the return of the dotterels to the river-beds; looking to see if the starlings have built again under the water-tank, and of course they will have. Generations of starlings will never disappoint you, Anna.

'And your grandchildren will gather round your chair in front of the kitchen range for you to hear their spelling and to help them look up information in the encyclopaedias, and stick their stamps in their albums. That's how you'll be when you're eighty, Anna; and you'll still dip into long-loved books of poety before you go to bed, so that your dreams will always be pleasant.'

Her grandchildren? But for that there'd have to be a grandfather. Who would he be?

The main road was ahead of them now, so they turned left to join the stream of traffic from the south, and passed over the Tokomairio River to come into the township of Milton, where the streets had the name of poets loved long ago. . . .

'This was the town Anthony Trollope and his wife were very glad to reach that snowy winter August night in 1872. It was here they were given great kindness, dry stockings provided for Mrs. Trollope in front of a huge fire, and they were given a good hot dinner, and brandy-and-water.'

They stopped beside the waters of Lake Waihola where sometimes world championships for rowing were held, to drink scalding coffee and sample Kitty's shortbread beside the wide spreading waters that drained the hillsides. Not a blue, snow-fed lake like the ones that drained the mountains further inland, but cool, pewter-silver waters fringed with bullrushes and weeping willows.

143

Just over half an hour and they were driving through Dunedin, a graciously architectured city, now inevitably becoming sky-lined with square concrete blocks of buildings that indicated progress, and over the Water of Leith to climb a hill and take a main highway that dipped and swung round some quite massive hills, some of them heavily forested.

The vast expanse of Blueskin Bay and the Pacific beyond came suddenly into view, a shimmering diamond-bright sea that reached out limitlessly. Anna caught her breath at its sheer, glimmering beauty in the early morning sun, its restlessness and freedom freeing her spirit. Calum let her gaze her fill in silence. They dipped down into the Waitati Valley and suddenly, among the *totaras* and *kowhais* by the boulder-strewn stream, there was a flash of white and a soaring.

'Heavens,' said Calum, 'I'd have thought it was too late for one of those, but it is. Anna, this must be put on specially for you. It's a white heron, the *kotuku*, so rare that its name means the pure white heron of a single flight. But now they are heavily protected their numbers are increasing. But we see them here mainly in winter – this side of the Alps. By November they'll all be over in Westland at the Okarito Lagoon, where they return every year – even from the North Island – to nest in the same *kowhai* trees there.'

He laughed. 'There's an old legend, though I can't vouch for its truth, that the year you see your first *kotuku* means you get your heart's desire before it ends. How about that, Anna?'

The pang that tore through her was almost physical. Heart's desire ... this could be the year she had to witness the wedding of the man she loved, to another woman. This year, or next year?

'We turn east here, beyond Waitati, to the shore road on the north of this big curving bay. Some day we'll stop short of here and I'll take you to Doctors' Point, so called because so many of the medical bods in Dunedin have weekenders there. It's the most glorious beach.'

The road they took twisted and curved back over the main south railway line, following the contours of the hills, and had farms whose emerald paddocks ran right to the edge of the cliffs and *kowhais* golden with pendulous blooms drooped graceful branches earthwards. Gnarled old *ngaio* trees leaned away from the east winds that swept up from the sea, and sprinkled the sward with fragile daphne-like flowers from among their five-fingered leaves.

They came up over the top where the famous Truby King's original Karitane Hospital stood, for the care of the not-so-strong babies, and again Calum ran the Avenger into the side of the road so she could drink her fill of contoured beauty.

The Pacific here curved into the land in twin indentations, one bounded by a crumbling long razor-edge of cliffs that reached out an arm to shelter the Karitane River sweeping out to sea, and on the far side of the second curve was the pinkish bluff of the Waikouaiti Headland.

'As far as I'm concerned,' said Calum, starting up, 'this has everything, the surf on this side of the razor-ridge, rocks to scramble over, shells for the children to gather, hills to climb, a great stretch of shore for riding on if you can get hold of a horse, and the boat-harbour at the other side with the fishing-boats coming in over the bar, through the channel, and a very safe lagoon type of beach there for the children. Ian and Betty bring the children here whenever they stay with her mother in Dunedin. In fact if ever I can afford it, I'll buy a holiday house here myself.' He would bring his and Victoria's children here.

They swept down towards the beach, turned up a narrow lane and ran through a stand of magnificent blue-gums to the back entrance The front one, Calum explained, was just a hillside path of boulders that served as steps down to the boat-house.

Anna loved it from the moment Calum took an enormous key and unlocked the door. It was a darling house. It was wide-set because it had to follow the line of the hill and it was steep. It was a curious and fascinating blend of the old and the new. Whoever had modernized it had done it with great taste. They'd exposed the beamed ceiling and restored the wood to its natural state after some Philistine had painted it. Two rooms had been thrown into one, so the sitting-room end was slightly above the dining end, and they had put wide landscape windows each side of the French windows so that almost the whole wall was glass. These opened out on to a long planked verandah, with a rail to it that looked like teak, Anna said.

'It is teak,' said Calum. 'Old Captain Bluenose who built this house got it from a ship that was being broken up.'

'Captain Bluenose? Oh, surely that wasn't his name?'

'No, his name, believe it or not, was Gamaliel Macallister. Don't you think that's a most euphonious name? He was a seafarer from Nova Scotia. Bluenose is a name for Nova Scotians. You know, like they call people from our West Coast the Coasters, or the Tynesiders Geordies. He had a sister in Port Chalmers who was widowed, long before the days of adequate pensions. So he came here and built this to satisfy his love of the sea but was a chandler at Port Chalmers, so he could support her and the children. The beginning of the century, it was. My friend Doug Fenton bought it, and he and Marjorie restored and modernized it. She's almost as good as Victoria. I must keep an eye on the tide. Anna, it's incredibly early for lunch, but in terms of how long since breakfast, we're well past our time How about it?'

Her eyes sparkled as they looked over the sea. 'Yes, of course. Anyway, it's gloriously mad once in a while to turn the timetables upside down. You said you packed some food last night. What?'

He brought out cold sliced mutton, farm-grown, therefore as tender as chicken, early tomatoes, curls of lettuce, mayonnaise, cheese, some of Kitty's home-baked rolls, butter, jam, tea-bags.

They stacked the dishes to do on their return. Calum said, 'I come here often. It may be cool on the water. Doug's wife said for you to help yourself to anything of hers you may need. In Fiji the winds blow from the Equator – here, from the South Pole. What about this over your top?' He handed her a sea-green sweater in a bulky knit. She pulled it over her head, shook her hair free.

He picked up a yachting cap, set it on his crisp black hair. It was the first time she'd seen him in anything but the old woollen cap he wore for lambing. It really did things for his profile, that peaked brim. She turned away, lest her eyes reveal too much.

The sun was so hot, beating on them from the north as it worked towards its zenith, it didn't seem possible it would be cool on the water. Calum took her hand to help her down

146

the sandy boulders, covered with slippery pine-needles from the giant trees overhead. There were just a couple of flowerbeds against the house, blazing with geraniums and marigolds in a glorious clash of colour, and the rest, to make it easy to look after, was matted with ice-plants, carpeting it with yellow and crimson and cyclamen.

The white wicket gate led to a public beach path. They - jumped down a natural formation of rock steps to the boathouse. The launch was well kept, with beautiful lines. A couple of fishermen came along, recognized Calum, gave him a hand, and in a few moments they were heading out along the well-marked channel

Anna recognized immediately that Calum knew how to handle a boat, that this was something he must have grown up with. The hours spent on the water were unalloyed delight. They skirted round the coast for Calum to point out various features and he promised her she could explore them closer at hand, from the land, when, during the summer, they always spent some time here as a family.

She shivered as he pointed out the scene of a long-ago massacre, Goat Island, which wasn't quite an island, but was joined to the mainland by a narrow neck, only wide enough for one warrior to traverse at a time ... there was a deep blow-hole on one side, and a curving scimitar of a beach on the other, and it jutted out into the open sea. They had guarded that narrow bridge ... not knowing that in the mist of a swirling snowstorm, the raiding tribe had come upon them from the sea and scaled the cliffs

She said, 'It seems incredible on a day like this, all blue and gold, and almost cloudless. A scene of peace.'

She looked up as a soaring gull's wings caught the light in its flight. 'Perhaps that's why they keen so sadly. Never a sadder sound than that. Keening over limitless stretches of water.'

He nodded. 'Didn't some poet long ago write of that ... the bird singing of "Old, unhappy, far-off things"?'

This was true companionship. Something Anna had missed all her life. Most other girls had had fathers who had shared that sort of thing with them.

He took the wheel from her, his hairy forearm brushing hers, warm from the sun. He pointed out a rock. 'I've never found out if it has a name or not to the local inhabitants. It must be the last, hardest peak, of what was once a headland, reaching out into the bay. Back on the shore, it looks like a bust of Queen Victoria. So I always call it the Empress Rock. I wonder how many thousands of years it is since that headland was here, with turf on the top, and native bush thick with singing birds? I wonder if a *moa* ever roamed there. See those great jagged spires rising out of the sea under the razor-back? I suppose some day their softer rock will be eroded away, and they'll be just the size of the Empress. I wonder who'll look at them then and wonder about them as we've done today? A time when we and this boat and all our dreams and hopes will be dust and ashes.' He gave a short laugh. 'What a ghoul I am! Why think of mortality on a day like this?'

She smiled, standing beside him, braced to the swing. 'I don't call that ghoulish. When you realize this sea has pounded those cliffs for millions of years, one is more conscious of continuity. It makes me feel at one with all who've ever lived here, the *moa*-hunters, the small Morioris, the spirit of all those Maoris who leapt into the cruel sea on that day of snow and violence, their happier years, the eeling parties, the years of peace when tribe ceased to war against tribe, when generations of children, European and Maori, played together on these beaches. Later these same beaches must have seen crowded troopships, with *pakeha* and Maori soldiers on board, sail past here from Port Chalmers to fight in European tribal wars . . . waging them in France and Italy and the Middle East and the Islands of the Pacific.

'But the best memory of all, for me, will be of old Captain Bluenose, who built a sturdy house on a steep hill and left me, someone he never knew, the legacy of a happy, happy day, with salt spray on my lips and the feel of a wheel under my fingers. Oh, goodness, I never talked like this to anyone in my life before! Calum, why don't you stop me?'

His hand touched hers briefly. 'Don't get all reserved on me, now, Anna. We didn't get off to a good start, though it's only hilarious to recall now, but we've become so – such friends. I'm glad you voiced your thoughts about continuity. I've never believed that some day earth will be no more, that God will destroy it all eventually. It makes Him out to be an arch-vandal. How could a Creator destroy? I think He's more likely to bring Heaven down upon Earth. Ever think about that? With all Earth's war-scars healed.'

Anna was enchanted with the idea. 'Oh, Calum, why don't you express that to Sophy, she'd find a text for it and preach on it, I'm sure.'

'I came across a text once that bolstered up that belief of mine, but I've been too shy to mention it to anyone – till now. It's in the Book of Revelation. The first verse of a chapter. Twenty-one, I think. "And I saw a new heaven *and a new earth.*" ' He laughed, said, 'I dare not finish that. I've just realized how it goes on.'

She said, 'You've got to, Calum. I'll only look it up when I get home if don't.'

He laughed. 'You'll hate it. "For the first heaven and the first earth were passed away, and *there was no more sea.*" '

She laughed too. 'I see. Well, it wouldn't be heaven for me without sea, but I do understand how John the Evangelist felt. He was a prisoner on Patmos, suffering ghastly tribulations, and that glassy sea he described below him was the symbol of his prison walls. And yet he had that mighty vision.'

It could have been tricky getting back over the bar, but they were able to follow the little fishing smacks beating back to harbourage. They called at the sheds and bought some fresh blue cod, for themselves, and for the folk back home.

'We'll cook ours immediately. I guess that's how you like your fish, fresh from the sea? I'll gut them and fry them while you do us a big pan of chips. I saw a chip basket under the sink. And don't for Pete's sake call them French Fried, they don't taste half as good.'

He'd known he'd give her fish for tea, had come prepared with lemons. They finished up with Kiwi fruit, or Chinese gooseberries as Calum called them, peeled and cut into thin crisp slices, their tiny black markings symmetrically centred, sprinkled with sugar, and topped with whipped cream. The percolated coffee Calum made was fragrant, ambrosial. Then, regretfully, they washed up, packed their things away.

'But we're going to watch the sunset,' Calum decreed. 'This was planned for a sunrise-to-sunset day. Did you notice that the Captain's quarter-deck, as the Fenton children call it, turns the corner to the west?'

They took deck-chairs out there, sat in absolute silence as the sun painted the sky even more vividly than at dawn, as it dropped down behind the hills so it could light another hemisphere. Suddenly the flame and tangerine and amber were gone, and the hills looked as if they drew purple cloaks about their shoulders and settled down for sleep.

Anna stood up. 'I thought nothing could have been more lovely than that sunrise, but perhaps sunset is even more spectacular. How could anyone not believe in eternity when they can see sunsets like that? As if unguessed-at pleasures lay beyond the sunset. Oh, dear, I'm at it again! Come on, Calum.'

They made faster time on the way home, because the darkness hid the landmarks that might have needed to be explained. Too fast, Anna thought, and rebuked herself. Hadn't Calum given her a whole day, full of joy and the abandon of the ocean?

The darkness was soft and velvety. Oh, yes, summer was a-comin' soon. There was something so friendly about the dark, it made you brave enough to say things, knowing your expression couldn't be read.

'Calum, there are a few things I'd like to discuss with you. I find it hard at home to get uninterrupted conversation in. It's about money. I always find it difficult as a subject, but I feel I could approach you tonight, after a day like this. You – won't take anything I say amiss, will you? I mean at first we found it only too easy to get offsides with each other.'

'We did. But it's a long time ago. I promise I won't take you up wrongly.' She thought there was a smile in his voice.

'Oh, thank you, Calum. You see, I know I get things addled. I don't want to snarl things up, this time.'

He laughed outright then. 'Fire ahead. You've spiked my guns already.'

'It's about Ian and Betty.'

'Ian and Betty?'

'Yes, you see they were away when I arrived. I surmised, because you were the manager, that Ian was younger than you. I thought he'd probably married young. But I found you were the youngest in the family. How come you were made manager?'

'Oh, I always worked at Strathallan, right from my time at Lincoln College on. Ian and Betty had high-country experience first. Looking after a place till the son of the owner was old enough to take over. By then Ian wanted a place of his own, so—'

'Then why did he come to Strathallan? Was it to help you out?'

He hesitated. She continued, 'Well, you've both done more for Strathallan than any hired help does normally. I feel it's only natural, with my father dead, and no one knowing about me, that you should inherit. Both you and Ian deserve to. I expected Ian and Betty to resent me. But Betty is sweet to me. It's almost unnatural. She's just like a sister, lets me share in the children, has never shown in any way that it has altered their standing. I think the situation must be talked out soon, Calum.'

His left hand left the wheel to pat hers. 'Relax! It's time we put you in the picture. There is no dividing fence between Ian and Betty's home and Strathallan homestead, it's true, but they are separate properties now, and Ian owns the half his house is on, but we work it as one, which is often done, with family estates. We share the woolshed, the machinery, everything. There never will be a dividing fence while your grandparents live. I felt, so did Ian, it would somehow take away Gilbert's pride in the property. He'd feel it was whittled down. But it was all that could be done when he had no one of his own.

'When I say it belongs to Ian, I'd better say he has a mighty big mortgage on it, but Gilbert did let him have it at a lesser price than if it had been on the open market. So Ian and Betty couldn't have resented you. You were pretty astute about that. They're probably glad you didn't come on the scene earlier, though. Gilbert might never have split it up then.'

'But what about you, Calum? You're manager, and ought to have the chance of Strathallan – the other half – in time.'

'I'll put you wise about that, too. I'm buying the other half of Strathallan already. Gilbert rents me the farm, I run sheep for him as well as for me and he no longer pays me wages. I put half my wool cheque every year into paying off the land. We have a special agreement, all drawn up and watertight. It doesn't apply to the homestead itself. I saw to that. It must be theirs till they go. I think you know that it occupies the very edge of the property. It's subdivided, but once again we've put up no fences. I've a feeling that Kitty and Gilbert are by no means ready to move into the Annexe. Now you're here the house has come to life for them. I want them to have all the happiness they can out of that.'

'But . . . when you and Victoria marry?'

'When that happens what's to prevent *us* moving into the Annexe? It's not exactly midget size, you know.'

Anna didn't answer, she couldn't. Then she said, brokenly, 'Oh, Calum, how I misjudged you! At first, that is. But for some time I've known you're not acquisitive. But one thing I'm determined on, you *must* get a substantial legacy. Ian too. I'll talk it out with my grandfather. You kept the place going when they thought they had no descendants.'

Calum said, 'I absolutely forbid you to do anything of the kind. I got the land cheaply too. The arrangement suits us all very nicely. Anna, there may be times when time itself must be taken by the forelock, others when one shouldn't act hastily. You've got all het-up because you distrusted me at first. That doesn't matter. I felt the same – was scared you might have come for what you could get out of the place. Even thought you might have been an impostor – but once I saw you!

'Well, oddly enough I've an odd streak in my nature. Independence, I suppose. I don't want anything dropped in my lap too cheaply. I want to work for it. And it would lessen what's legally yours. All Ian and I pay back must be left to you. Oh, I'm not stiff-necked with pride. My father gave me, and gave Ian, advances on what would have come to us at his death, to buy in our stock. That's different, it's family, and Dad's always said he'd like to see us enjoy what will be ours, while he can see it. But what I do for Kitty and Gilbert, who are the salt of the earth, and had a very rough deal, mustn't have a price-tag on it.'

Anna could see his profile in the faint light, the aquiline nose, the bony brows, the high cheekbones, the square chin and the tender mouth, and experienced recognition of the Highland pride that lived on in this man. She wouldn't want him to be less than that, even if she would have liked him to benefit from the estate.

Her voice shook a little, but she said, 'I can see you mean what you say. I admire you for it, Calum. And, though you didn't know it at the time, I'm going to apologize to you here and now for the fact that when I first came here, I felt with regard to the Doig family, I must remember the clan motto: Gang warily.'

He laughed at that. 'This day has been worthwhile, Anna of Strathallan. It's good to have been so honest with each other.'

Before they reached the Crannog turning he said, 'We *must* leave things as they are, Anna. Before long you may fall in love with some young farmer who could live with you here at Strathallan. If that happens, Gilbert can buy my half back and I'll go and farm somewhere else. Think what it would mean to your grandparents if they knew that their Anna lived here, to raise their great-grandchildren in the Drummond tradition, on the land of their fathers.'

He ran the car into the barn. She said, 'Remind me of that Calum, any time you think my fancy is turning towards anyone who doesn't qualify . . . say a white-collar civil servant in Roxburgh, or one of the engineers at the Hydro. There's no blueprint for love, and if ever I have to follow a man in his calling, I'll be very happy to think of you and Victoria at Strathallan.'

He didn't answer at first. Then when they walked towards the house he said, 'Don't forget the motto of the Drummonds is also the motto of the Doigs. Perhaps I too gang warily.'

She thought he paused, as if wanting her to comment on that. But she didn't. She felt it wouldn't be wise. But why it wouldn't was a thought she dare not analyse. Because the answer might, just might, upset too many lives.

CHAPTER NINE

GRANDMOTHER'S peony roses burgeoned in all the corners of the garden in deepest red and snowiest white. Snow-in-summer that Kitty scorned to call cerastium foamed over the rocks on the terraces and vied with the aubretia for pride of place. Azaleas in vivid coral and flame and mandarin orange blazed under the trees, as if they were burning bushes, like Moses's, and were not consumed. Guelder-roses dotted their snowballs all over their green branches and the drive that led to the road was a vision of beauty such as Anna had never seen before, lined its full length with an avenue of deep rose hawthorns.

Calum saw her standing there one morning, close under a tree, gazing up at the light filtering through it, as if she couldn't get enough of such loveliness. It was only when she began to come away that she became aware of his presence.

He said, 'You love the hawthorns, Anna?'

She turned eyes that were still a-dream up to him. 'Calum, you can't imagine what it's like never to have seen a hawthorn in bloom before. If you grow up with these things you take them for granted, but to see a tree like this put on myriads of blossoms out of tight little buds almost overnight, is like witnessing a miracle. Just look! Every branch is crusted with tiny rose-like flowers. Yet I feel as if this was always waiting for me.' She turned and made a gesture that comprehended it all, the square house sitting against its hill-side facing the willow-shaded brook, the rose-arches over the wandering paths, the fringe of lilac catmint where the cats loved to roll, the big barns, the woolshed, the new house on the flank of Tushielaw Hill where they could see Betty cleaning her windows, sparkling in the sun.

'I can't imagine now it wasn't always part of my life.'

Calum said, 'I feel as if you've always been here too.'

There was a silence between them, then he said hurriedly, 'Anna, why don't you tell Elizabeth what you just told me – about seeing a hawthorn in bloom for the first time? She's writing another garden book. As you know, those are the things she's so keen to incorporate. The human interest. You could make everyone who reads it see a hawthorn in full bloom as if they too saw it for the first time in their lives.'

Her eyes lit up 'Oh, Calum, do you think she'd like it? I'd love to think some thought of mine could be used in a book. Books are such immortal things. Long after they've stopped selling, they stay on people's shelves for generations, to delight children who were unborn when they were first penned.'

Calum, leaning on his slasher, looked down on her keenly.

'Thinking of anything in particular?'

He was surprised to see colour run up into her face. 'Yes. I – I've been browsing in Dad's room. I've never wanted to find out what he was like before, because I thought I hated him for what he did to Mother. But *she* never hated him. But gradually, the knowledge that he redeemed himself in his last hours, by such bravery, has sort of leavened it for me. He had a habit of marking the passages he liked in his books, and because he was so footloose they are still here.

'Gran caught me one day. She was so glad. She said, when I showed her some lines of poetry he must've liked, "You are seeing your father as he was meant to be." We've talked about him a lot since. It's so stupid, but I find myself hoping that in his later years the philosophy of those writers he admired – some of them lived three or four hundred years ago, and more – may have helped him find the courage he must have had to go into that mine and bring so many out . . .' Her voice trailed off.

Looking up, she saw that Calum was moved. He straightened up, shifted the slasher he was going to attack the gorse hedge with, from one hand to the other, seemed to be seeking for words. Then they heard the rattle of a car coming over the cattle-stops. They looked through the hawthorns.

'It's Victoria,' said Calum.

By now Anna had achieved a measure of success in disciplining herself to accept witnessing their kisses of greeting, their frequent departures on outings where, presumably, three would have been a crowd. It was something she had to live with, and by now she loved Victoria too much to ever let her suspect by any unguarded look or warmth in her tone, when she spoke to Calum, that she had a *tendresse* for him.

Victoria had suffered deeply long ago. She deserved the happiness she would have with Calum.

As the car neared, Anna said, 'I'll leave you to it,' and turned to go. Immediately an arresting succession of hoots on the horn began. Anna swung round. Victoria put her head out of the window, called, 'It's you I want, Anna.'

She drew to a halt, proffered a cheek to Calum, said, 'I know you've never been to Te Anau, Anna. One of the larger lakes down in Fiordland. My three ladies are well on with their plan, and the firm think I should be there just now. I'd like company. The old pets wanted me to stay with them, but I'm agin that. I like to relax away from work at night. I've got a motel booked at Te Anau and there are beds and to spare. How about you coming?'

Calum said promptly, 'You must, Anna. Betty'll give Kit a hand.'

Victoria's hazel eyes were sparkling. 'Good for you, Calum! I'd dearly love company.' She looked at Calum, 'I do miss your mother. Tell me, has she reached London yet? And Surrey? How did she find Blair and Yvette? I've been waiting and waiting to hear from you. I feel there's a conspiracy of silence about it and I find it stupid. All I want to know is how they are, if they're well, happy, settled. They must be settled, though. Blair's been in that one job for ages. Shows what happiness and the right partner can do for one. Quite different from the daft fancies one takes in one's salad days. But everyone skirts round the subject as if it was only yesterday that Blair jilted me, the stupid beggars.'

She turned to look, grinning, at Anna, but Anna had been looking at Calum. At Victoria's first words it had been as if a shutter had come down on his face. Victoria oughtn't to have said this in front of her. It should have been discussed in private It was out of character. Victoria was usually cool, reserved.

Victoria must have read her thoughts. 'Don't be embarrassed, Anna, nobody acts naturally with me any more, and every time I try to discuss it, or even just mention Blair casually, Calum shuts up like a clam. It's not good for him, not good for anyone. It's daft. People are jilted and engagements are broken all the time. It wasn't all Blair's fault, though at the time I liked to think so. I knew he was the roving type, and I was the stay-at-home. My dreams of marriage were all of a house I could decorate, not enough of the man.

'If I'd gone off with him, had the fun of living on a shoe-string in out-of-the-way places, working at anything and everything till we had enough money for the next ship-fare, air-fare, whatever you like, it would have got the wanderlust out of Blair. Everyone gets sick of travel in time, wants to strike roots. Like Blair has now. I thought only of what *I* wanted, so he upped and offed. Since I've travelled round on this job I've understood what he felt. So for goodness' sake let's be natural and if you hear from your mother about him, tell me, good or bad. After all, he'll be my brother-in-law before long, won't he. I don't want your family split because of me, or taking sides.'

Now was the moment Calum would tell Victoria he'd had a letter from his mother yesterday. From Haslemere, Surrey. Anna had collected the mail and had handed it over. Calum had gone straight to Ian's with it. She'd thought it strange at the time that he hadn't passed on any news to Kitty and Gilbert.

Calum said, 'Mum hasn't reached Surrey yet She's still looking round London. I expect it gets you that way, the hub of the universe. I'll let you know when she sees Blair. Anna, you'll love Fiordland. One word of warning though, because you aren't used to the New Zealand bush – it's easy to get lost in, so don't get off the tracks. And Victoria, if you make time for a run through to Milford Sound, make inquiries before you do, to make sure all danger from avalanches is over. And when you're waiting your turn at the Homer Tunnel, keep away from under that sheer face. I mean that.'

'Yes, darling,' said Victoria meekly. 'After all, I'm only twenty-nine. No horse-sense yet '

Calum stood his slasher against the hawthorn, said, 'I'll come up and make you girls coffee while Anna's packing. Better get cracking now. It's a lovely morning.'

Anna had a feeling he'd be glad to see Victoria on her way. What had been in that letter? Did he want to postpone telling her? Or not tell her at all?

They went via Queenstown and round the foot of Lake Wakatipu to Fiordland. Te Anau was a dream; it had a more mystical, remote air than Wakatipu, because its arms stretched away into mysterious country, densely bushed with rain forests, where less than thirty years ago, a hitherto-thought-to-be-extinct bird, the *takahe*, had been discovered in a region still largely unexplored.

Victoria's three customers were like something out of the Victorian age, despite their modern dress, Eugenie, Hortense, Letitia. They invited Anna out to their home, too, one that was set amid scenes of peerless beauty. They were so grateful to Victoria for, as Eugenie said, 'handing us happiness on a platter. We sold most of the land, but nobody wanted to be bothered with a house as big as this and we couldn't quite afford to keep it going. We hung on as long as possible, trying not to sell it for demolition. But now we can install someone to look after it, and we'll be able to share our joy in these treasured possessions with so many people. Nobody not interested in antiques is going to come and see them.

'Victoria has been so wonderful, like an answer to prayer. We'd never have known how to contact the National Publicity Studios, the Tourist Corporation ... she's got it all ready for preliminary tours for Christmas when the summer holiday season starts. She's worked so hard. I do hope her young man hasn't had to forgo too much of her time.'

But he had, to a great extent. Apart from the trips to the lakes a group from Crannog had made, and the occasional visit to Alexandra, Calum had been home at Strathallan night after night, working on wool samples, the accounts of the estate, even sticking stamps in his albums. He'd been very understanding about Victoria not being free. 'Oh, well, that's her work, and it's the breath of life to her. Besides, she's got such a soft heart, and she thinks if the old dears can have a full tourist season, it will help them tremendously financially, and pay for the initial outlay.'

Anna was revising her first opinion of Victoria. She probably wasn't sexually frigid at all. Very likely she was just reserved with Calum in front of other people. She might be much more demonstrative when they were on their own.

The old ladies had the time of their lives. Though on the doorstep of the Fiords, they'd not been through to Milford Sound for so long. 'We only use the car for going to Te Anau, or Mossburn or Gore. The other roads are too rough for us now. But we so love Milford. We did the Track, of course, in our young days, with our father and mother, several times.'

Almost impossible to think of these frail ladies tackling what was often called the most beautiful walk in the world . . . and the toughest. Three days it took, through terrain where it rained three days out of five, and streams had to be forded, heights climbed, and only rough accommodation provided. But it was the only way to really visit the fairyland of the rain forest.

Victoria said, 'You ought to get Calum to take you on one of the tramps. You have to book well ahead to join the groups. You wouldn't get in this year, but perhaps next.'

Anna said, 'You mean you'd come too? It would be such fun.'

'Depending on my work. I can't always get away when Calum can.'

Anna said, 'Oh, you must try. It would be no fun without you.' She found she meant that. She enjoyed Victoria's company immensely. She'd so missed her Fijian friends. How ironic!

They had a peerless day at the Sound, going through after heavy overnight rain that had given place to sparkling sunshine, so that every granite face streamed with the silver of cascading waterfalls that hadn't existed the day before. And Anna had never in her life seen such vertical scenery. When they came out of the tunnel and swung round and down to the right, Anna gasped as the full beauty of the Fiord – it was wrongly named a Sound – burst on her sight. The sapphire blue of its almost fathomless waters shimmered and danced below the plunging mountains that surrounded it on all sides, and one could imagine they dipped as far below the rim of the waters as reared above. Retreated glaciers flashed blindingly from the pockets high on the peaks and great hanging valleys spilled foaming waters from their laps. Mitre Peak, so symmetrical it was a photographer's dream-come-true, rose almost centred from the depths. The chorus of bell-birds and tuis soared and ascended, twanged and chimed.

Hortense said, appreciatively, 'There isn't anything quite like bringing someone here for the very first time . . . someone as awake to beauty as Anna is.'

The three ladies had the day of their lives, recalling long-ago times, revelling in the artistic and palate-stimulating food put on by a superb chef at the hotel, gazing out at this feast of beauty so unspoiled and uncluttered.

They came back to Fuchsia Downs in the twilight, with birds twittering sleepily now, and sat without other illumination till the last light faded from the sky.

It was then that Hortense mentioned the heirlooms in Sydney. They were what their father had given his youngest daughter when she married an Australian. She had died three months ago. Her only son was an engineer in Indonesia. He had just written them saying he had stored them, meanwhile, because the climate where he was living was quite unsuitable for treasures such as these – they'd be at the mercy of mildew and insects and goodness knows what. Now the aunts were to stay at the old home, he wondered if they could take them back. The only thing was that he had found it hard to distinguish between what had come from Fuchsia Downs and what antiques his mother had bought since. It would be very expensive to ship the lot over, of course, so he wondered if it would be possible for them to go over.

Here Hortense coughed delicately, hesitated, looked at Letitia, who took her cue. 'We don't feel we could face such a trip now, and the work involved, unless someone younger could accompany us. Would you feel able to do this, Victoria dear? We would pay all your expenses, of course. Hal doesn't even want Eleanor's antiques – he moves round the world, lives in primitive conditions mostly, we thought the firm you work for might like first choice of them – Hal said the money would be of more use to him. Would you think it over, dear? We won't bustle you.'

Anna wouldn't have associated Victoria with snap decisions, but lately she'd seemed so much more alive. She said, smiling at them, 'I'll do it. The firm would leap at it. And I've nothing urgent on '

Despite the unsurpassed beauty they'd left behind, Anna knew overwhelming happiness when they swept back over the cattle-stops into the avenue of hawthorns. Oh, they were still fully out. She hadn't really wanted to miss any of their blooming.

She was surprised Calum didn't go over to Sherbornes' with Victoria, though he'd had a little whispered conclave with her. He seemed very quiet. He waved her off with, 'I'll see you tomorrow afternoon, dear.'

Victoria said, 'Make it tomorrow night. If I'm off to Australia I'll have a bit of paperwork to get through.'

By the time the family at Strathallan had settled down after dinner, with their coffee, Anna was aware that not only was Calum quiet, but her grandparents too. Some heaviness of the spirit sat upon Grandy. Grandmother had shadows under her eyes.

The network news finished, they looked at the weather forecast, then, before *South Tonight* came on, Calum switched off the set. Before he could speak, Anna did. 'Are you going to tell me what's wrong? There's something, isn't there?'

The Drummonds looked appealingly at Calum. He said, 'Anna, the day you left we had a letter from South America. It had disturbing news in it.'

Anna felt the blood draining from her face. An appalling thought flashed into her mind. Was her father still alive? What would that mean to her mother? Would it disturb her new-found happiness? She clamped her mind down on that question. If he was, it could bring joy to his parents. But – she managed, 'What do you mean? Disturbing?'

Calum said, 'It's hard to explain. But tell me something first, when your mother married again, had she waited till she was widowed, or had she got a divorce?'

Anna swallowed. Then, 'Oh, Dad was killed before she married, but she'd had a divorce some time before that. She thought it was only fair to him. That if he wanted to be free to marry again, he must be. Though they took ages to find him to serve the papers to him.'

If anything they looked even more worried than before. Why?

Then Gilbert said heavily, 'Then it could be true.'

Calum said, 'Anna, the letter from South America was from a woman who calls herself Rosita Drummond. She says your father married her and she has a son, in his teens, Alexo. Some kind of an agent's letter accompanied hers, saying she had papers to prove it. A solicitor, I suppose. It wasn't too bad a letter – her English isn't perfect, so that made it a little hard for us to get the feel of it. The agent is claiming on the estate for them. Oh, not exactly claiming, but approaching us.

'If you could tell us exactly when your mother's divorce came through, it would help. Your grandfather's solicitors, of course, won't part with anything, merely on this letter. It would have to be thoroughly investigated, but at this distance, even that could be very costly. She said that only recently had she discovered Alex's parents' whereabouts. Fishy, that. But then she said he deserted her for another woman and it had taken time.'

Anna didn't mind this for herself, but she minded very deeply for her grandparents to receive more evidence of the perfidy of their only son. Another wound, another shame. She wondered how many lives her father had ruined. Oh, the pity of it, just when they'd found such compensation in the knowledge of the unquestioned bravery of their son's last hours. It was possible they'd have no legal claim on the estate. but Grandfather was so honourable, a moral claim would be just as binding to him. Two more people to keep would be a big drain on the estate.

She said, 'If it proves to be true, and they were deserted, and you want to help, don't forget that now the busy time is over, I'm taking a job in Roxburgh.' She summoned up a smile for them. 'You never know, Grandy, this Alexo might be a grandson to be proud of. He might even come here. You might find you could love him. You sent for me and I was an unknown quantity—'

Her grandfather said, 'That woman sent a coloured photo of the two of them. I can't imagine her here. Look – she looks like a woman of the cabarets to me. I'd rather keep her over there – if I have to.'

Of course, Alex hadn't been a fair Drummond. He'd not even been like his mother – he was more like one of her brothers, who'd been dark. Therefore this boy's warm southern colouring and dark handsomeness needn't necessarily come from a part Spanish heritage. He could be like his father as well as his mother.

He definitely was a handsome lad, but it looked to Anna like late teens, not mid-teens. Did they mature more quickly there? His mother was short, voluptuous, garishly dressed. But then bright colours suited Latin America. You couldn't, mustn't form a snap decision. She might be warm-hearted, justified in fighting for her son's rights. But—

Anna said, 'I don't think he could possibly be my half-brother. He's too old. He'd be born long before my mother got those papers served on Dad. This woman could be trying something on. It will have to be investigated. Look, the family papers are upstairs. I'll go and look.'

As she knelt by the tin trunk she heard Calum come in behind her. He knelt beside her. He put his hands on the edge of the trunk. They exchanged a long look.

He said heavily, 'I'd give a lot for this not to have happened. It's too much for them at their age. It may be only a try-on. I wonder in what standing that agent is held over there. I'll do as much as possible for them, with their solicitors, to spare them.'

Anna, hardly knowing what she did, put her hand over his and patted it. 'Oh, Calum, they may have lost a son, but they gained one in you. I'll be so grateful if you see them through this.'

The dark brows lifted so she could see his eyes. They were blazingly blue with emotion. 'Anna, it's not just for them. It's for you too. I will *not* have your inheritance whittled down by people who may not deserve it.' He paused, then the words seemed wrung from him, 'Oh, Anna, Anna, why didn't you come here *last* year instead of *this* year? Why? Why?'

He caught her against him, bent his head, kissing her fiercely, demandingly. There was pain as well as a lawless joy. She yielded, knew she even responded. Then to both of them remembrance and realization came flooding in. They both drew back. Anna put the back of her hand against her mouth, stared at him with wild, shamed eyes. 'Oh, Calum, what are we doing? What's come over us? What of Victoria?'

Strangely he didn't look ashamed, only rueful. 'Sorry, Anna. I've no right to involve you in my feelings. How could I? I've tried to guard against it. What fools we are! I've always wanted to meet someone I could love as Dad loves Mother, as Gilbert loves Kitty. I told myself, eventually, that I was looking for an ideal that didn't exist, that Victoria and I would deal very well together, as indeed we do. But it's hardly a grand passion. That was over for Victoria a long time ago. But I could never deal her another blow.'

Anna shuffled back. She dared not stay near. She said breathlessly, 'Of course you couldn't, Calum. I suppose these mad moments can happen to anyone. We live too closely here. I'd go away if I could leave Grandy and Gran, but I couldn't, any more than you could hurt Victoria. It will be easier when you marry and I go to live in the Annexe with them. I'll get that job in Roxburgh and we won't be together all the time.'

She had grown very cold. Calum said, his eyes fixed on hers, 'Then it wasn't just me, Anna. You too?'

She caught her lower lip between her teeth. She mustn't let it tremble. She got control, said steadily, 'Me too, Calum. But that's all that's ever to be said about it. Oh, here's the box.'

She leaned over, lifted out a cashbox, leafed through its contents, brought out some papers, scanned them. Then she looked at Calum, the old fighting spirit back in her eyes, 'They said sixteen, didn't they? Though he looks nineteen. But even at sixteen they can't have been married when he was born – look at the date.'

'Right, let's go down and tell them. We mustn't stay up here.'

No, they mustn't.

As they reached the open door Calum suddenly kicked it shut. Anna looked at him with alarm. He smiled down on her, but wryly. 'Not to worry, Anna. I just want to look at you fully, once. I may never have another opportunity. Not so close.'

She held her breath. He took her chin in his fingers, tilting it a little. The dark-blue eyes looked hungrily into hers. Then they searched her whole face. The dark-gold streaky hair slanting down in its childish bang over her brows, the short thick fan of quite dark lashes, the faintly golden skin, the small straight nose, the curved, passionate mouth, the square cleft chin so like Gilbert's that gave her face its strength. Then he said, a little smile creasing the corners of his mouth, 'Right, I've looked my fill – let's go, my darling.'

That night, when sleep finally overtook her, lulled by the sound of the rain pelting down on the iron roof of the new garage close by, Anna thought she too had something to remember. She had known a giving and a sharing in that wild kissing not experienced before and ... she would never forget the tone of his voice as he called her his darling.

Life seemed to be sweeping them along. Victoria was away at Te Anau more than at home. She seemed to be in a greater hurry than they'd ever known her. No doubt she wanted to make sure all was ready for the tourist season.

Calum spared no efforts in working out with the Drummonds' solicitors the right approaches to be made to the claimants in South America. The question of the date of birth was being raised. Anna got her job nurse-aiding in Roxburgh. She loved it and it kept her busy. Away from Calum. He and Philip and Ian were hard at it.

Sophy and Philip's happiness was lovely to watch. Their plans were going ahead so smoothly. Philip would continue to work most of his time at Strathallan, but had managed to rent eighty acres adjoining his father's place. He'd run his own sheep on this, and during Sophy's year or so with the parish, they would get on with restoring the old stone place on the property, assisted by Victoria.

Victoria departed for Australia with her three old dears, going down for them, packing for them, bringing them up to stay the night at her mother's place, giving them the time of their lives. Anna took Kitty and Gilbert over to see them. Calum's idea, he thought it would take their minds off the South American problem. Calum himself took the four women to Momona Airport at Dunedin for the first lap of their flights to Sydney.

They all watched anxiously for the mail these days. Certainly their own solicitors were handling most of it, but Rosita had written them directly in the first place, so might again.

In between her bouts of fierce resentment for the anxiety this had brought to Gilbert's brow, Kitty had attacks of conscience. If Alexo was indeed their grandson, they must provide for him. She believed that the poverty of some of these countries was pathetic. Anna didn't know what to think. As she said to Calum, in one of the rare moments they were alone, 'Even if Alexo is illegitimate, but my father's son, then it seems an injustice if he doesn't share with me.'

Calum said, 'I know, but leave it till we know. It could be

hard to prove he *is* Alex's son if Alex wasn't married to his mother. She might be just trying it on. It's so long since Alex was killed, it makes me think this has just occurred to her – or to that agent.'

He brought in a letter with an Argentine stamp one Saturday morning but didn't produce it till all four of them had finished their mid-morning coffee. They gazed at it with concern.

'All right, lad,' said Gilbert. 'You've been in our confidence all along. Open it and read it out.'

It was from Rosita. She was reproachful. How could they have doubted her so, she who had made their son so happy when his wife would not leave her guest-house in Fiji to come to live with him here, share his poverty? A wife's place was with her husband. She, Rosita, had shared that poverty, had worked long hours. It was not like New Zealand, you understand, where wages are high and hours short. Oh, but there were many temptations lying in front of a man when he had to live alone, a young, virile man, with many lonely years ahead of him. Be grateful, then, that she had kept him from those grosser temptations. That she had provided a home for him, such as it was, with three good meals a day, yes.

Of course Alexo had been born out of wedlock, she admitted that, but later, when Alex's divorce had come through, they had married, thus legalizing the child. It would take time to get copies of the papers. They would understand she dared not trust the originals to the mail – a woman had to protect her son. But her agent had it all in hand, and would send them the copies, and when they saw them, then perhaps Alex's wealthy parents would be a little sorry that they had not helped them earlier. For Alexo, was he not flesh of their flesh and bone of their bone? She had suffered much, for, after looking after Alex so well, after a few years he had left her for a younger, more beautiful woman. That was why he was up-country when he was killed. Possibly in that village they had not even known he had a wife and child. Perhaps now they knew all this, out of their abundance they would send them enough to just subsist on, till it was proved.

Kitty was in tears. Gilbert's face was drawn. For once in his life he sounded harsh. He brought his fist down on the kitchen table. 'Turn that letter over to our solicitor, Calum.

Take it in this afternoon. Not a penny leaves this house for them till it's proved beyond shadow of doubting. I *will* support my grandson when I am satisfied he is a Drummond. Not till then. Now, Kitty, dry your tears. I will not have it any other way. Calum?'

Calum said, 'You're absolutely right. Nothing must be done till facts are established, and it must go through legal channels. Otherwise it's almost extortion. In any case, you're not responsible – but I know if Alex left a son you'd take it on.' He went to tuck the letter back in the envelope. 'Oh, there's something else here.' He pulled out a postscript on a half-sheet. Rosita said on this, 'I am thinking that if I do not hear from you quickly, I will sell my furniture and bring myself and Alexo across to see you. When you look at him, so like your son, you will have no doubts at all, and I will have my marriage certificate safely with me.'

Anna felt sick. It might have been just a naïve letter from a woman who knew little of the processes of the law, but somehow it sounded like a threat. Pay up, or I come!

Calum must have felt the same. She saw the rare colour of rage fly up from his throat. He stood up. 'Well, I'm away in with this. I'll kill that idea – coming here – stone dead. Or rather Stornway will. He can cable her that until it's proved, if she does set out there can be no question of any reimbursement or compensatory payments if her statements prove unfounded. I've a feeling she's trying something on, hoping for a hefty advance payment – and if she got it, we'd hear no more. If she lives in a town big enough to rate a solicitor, then it would surely have a photocopying machine. Copies of the marriage certificate could have come with this.'

That night, when they were watching TV in an endeavour to lose their troubles in entertainment, he said, 'I've something to tell you.' Gilbert switched the set off.

Calum said slowly, 'Mother didn't want this broadcast all at once. Ian and Betty have kept it to themselves. Our friends will be told soon. She wants it just to leak out, as if Blair hadn't kept it all to himself. Doesn't want too much made of it. She rang Blair from London. He nearly had a pink fit, but *was* he glad to see her? He's coped with a most difficult situation for the last eighteen months. Mother said it has been the making of him. He works like a Trojan. Yvette left him nearly two years ago.

'I can understand marriages breaking up – I can't understand a mother deserting her children. But she did – went off to Spain with someone, completely infatuated. Only six weeks later she began having dizzy turns. They discovered she had a brain tumour. The chap couldn't take it, and lit out. She rang Blair. He flew over to bring her home and nursed her to the end. She died eighteen months ago.

'He wouldn't write and tell us because he knew Mother would go straight over to look after the children, and that Father couldn't do without her all that time, and for once he was going to prove he could stand on his own feet. Said once he became a father he wanted for them the sort of childhood we'd had – so he determined to look after them himself. He's been able to get a daily housekeeper, hardly goes out at all at nights. Mother says he's no less than magnificent. The children are very affectionate and loving. His boss – the owner of this stately home that does all the super farm produce – thinks the world of him. Dad's told her to stay as long as she thinks fit. Mother offered them a home here. Blair could take on a job as farm manager round about – but he won't have it. He's found his right niche and has great hopes of becoming farm production manager.'

The Drummonds were so pleased for Judith Doig that she had found her son so well adjusted, even though his marriage had turned out so badly. Anna wondered if they might have had a pang or two, envying the Doigs, but they didn't show any signs of that. And Blair hadn't been a waster like Alex, only footloose, irresponsible.

She was in bed before she remembered something . . . Calum lying to Victoria when she'd asked him had he heard from his mother, and how Blair was. Perhaps lying was too harsh a word. His mother had asked him to keep it to himself. He'd tell her, for sure, when she returned from Australia. Anna had had a letter from Victoria. So had Calum. He hadn't passed on a single item of news from it. He was a bit edgy these days, seemed off-colour. And he'd yelped the other day when Anna bumped his arm. She'd said sharply, 'Calum, have you strained a muscle or something? Or got an infected scratch?'

He'd said grumpily, 'Of course not. What an imagination you've got! Don't fuss, Anna. You're far too handy with that first-aid box.'

In Anna's letter Victoria had explained her longer absence. She was doing a lot of buying for the firm, over there. The three old sisters were having the time of their lives, and the treasures their nephew had stored were terrific. 'I'm just going their way, Anna. I'll stay here as long as they want to.'

Perhaps Calum didn't take such a good view of it. He surprised them one morning by announcing that he was off to Sydney. 'I may be away a week or two. I'll cable you when I'm coming back. Victoria's letters have given me itchy feet and it's a long time since I've been to Sydney. It's not a bad time to take a break now.'

He drove to Momona where he would leave his car, to fly to Christchurch for the Sydney plane. Anna did a lot of wondering. That incident in the room upstairs might never have been. Perhaps he felt a little embarrassed over it now. And he must be missing Victoria.

Despite the fact that she told herself it was easier to carry on with him away, she felt very lost and lonely.

CHAPTER TEN

SURPRISINGLY Victoria's old ladies came back alone. They rang her mother to say she was staying on for a bit, and they'd found flying such a wonderful way to travel, they hadn't minded a bit not being escorted home. She'd seen them off.

Grace Sherborne rang to tell Kitty, but got Anna instead as Kitty was out in the garden. 'At which point,' said Victoria's mother, 'I asked where was Calum in all this. They hadn't seen him. He hadn't arrived when they left. Of course he said he was going to give Victoria a surprise. You know, Anna, I think he'd been trying to write to tell her that Blair's wife had died. He came over and told us, but said not to say anything to Victoria yet. It's not easy by letter. So I think he upped and off to do it by word of mouth – much better. I'm sorry it had to happen now – for lately Victoria has come out of her shell. When Blair left her she lost all her spirit and never quite regained it. She used to be a spitfire as a child. It wasn't just that she learned to control her temper – as we all do as we get older – it was as if something had stilled within her. But you've helped her tremendously.'

Anna said, 'What? How could I?'

'I don't know, but she's somehow loosened up since you've been here, hasn't just acquiesced in everything. I can't analyse it, Anna, but just as you brought Sophy and Philip together in some mysterious way, you seem to have done something for Victoria. I do want to thank you.'

Anna felt touched almost to tears because here was a woman who might even have disliked her for being Alex's daughter. She thanked her, even while deprecating it, added, 'I think Calum must have just missed the old ladies. Victoria would probably go back to the motel to find him there. Funny if they ran slap-bang into each other in the airport. Stranger things have happened.'

Stranger things did happen, but not till nearly a week later, a week during which they thought Calum might have sent them at least a postcard.

Then one morning at the hospital, the doctor who'd attended Calum and Barney that first night gave Anna a shock. He said, accepting a cup of tea from her, 'Did Calum's smallpox injection settle down all right? I was a bit worried over it.'

She boggled at him. 'Smallpox? Calum? What do you mean?'

He grinned. 'Just that. Want me to spell it for you, nurse? For his overseas trip.'

More boggling. 'But he wouldn't want that for Australia. It's just a hop across the pond. And anyway, he went on a sudden whim, dying to see Victoria.'

The doctor banged his cup down, looked dismayed. 'Oh, lord, I forgot! Now I've put my foot in it. Calum asked me to say nothing to anyone. It had gone completely out of my mind. But even so I thought he only meant to all and sundry – I was sure the Strathallan folk would know.' He hesitated then said, 'I've gone too far not to tell you now. Look, his mother wrote and told him to be prepared to fly across to her at a moment's notice if she thought she needed him. Something to do with Blair. He said he didn't want it to come to Victoria's ears in Sydney. But if she's still in Australia, I can't see that it will. But of course say nothing at Strathallan, or to Victoria's mother. But perhaps he changed his mind – or his mother found she didn't need him – so he just flew off to Vicky to tell her about it. His smallpox injection played up. The others didn't. He had the lot in case he came back by a different route. Though he thought it would be a very brief trip because of his commitments on the farm.'

Anna said, 'I'll tell no one, so don't worry about it. It's Calum's business and his alone. I wonder if that's why Victoria is staying on in Sydney, to cover up his absence, if they don't want the trip to England talked about. Mrs. Doig may not have wanted to worry her husband – he has some pretty stiff worries at the Hydro at the moment – and yet she may have needed a man's advice. He probably rang Victoria and told her to do that. If she'd come back alone, the secret would have been out.'

Two nights after that, Anna answered the phone in the lounge. Gilbert switched the TV off. The operator's voice said, 'This is a person-to-person International call. Mr.

Calum Doig is calling Miss Anna Drummond from Buenos Aires. Is she available, please?'

Anna gasped. 'Buenos Aires? Oh, yes, she's available. I mean, I am. Anna Drummond speaking. Put him on, please.' Over the receiver she saw Grandy and Gran stand up, their eyes looking startled and apprehensive. She put a hand over the mouthpiece. 'It's all right, my darlings. It's not Rosita, or her agent. It's Calum, though what *he's* doing there, I can't imagine.'

There was a little jiggling, some strange voices, then, blessedly, Calum's, as clear as if he wasn't thousands of miles away.

He said, 'Anna, is that you? It's Calum here, but you'll know that. Are Kitty and Gilbert with you?'

'Yes, right beside me.'

His voice was clear and strong and happy. 'Then tell them right away all is well, there's nothing to fear. Alexo isn't their grandson. Everything is all right. He's not even Alexo, he's Alonso. I found that out before I even contacted them. I quizzed the neighbours with an interpreter. They were trying it on. Go to it, Anna, don't worry about the cost, tell them now.'

She steadied her voice, told them almost word for word. Then back to the phone. 'Calum, how did you get there? I mean, what—'

'Well, of course I didn't go to Sydney. I flew here. I'd made up my mind there was something so fishy it would take months of correspondence straightening it out and I thought that while I was so doing, it would nearly kill Kit and Gilbert, it wouldn't be fair at their age. Stornway knew, in case anyone had to get in touch with me.

'Now I must put you in the picture. As I tell you each bit you can repeat it briefly, not to keep them in suspense. Then I'll speak to them both when I finish. You can fill in the gaps later. Ready? Rosita is married to a husband of her own nationality, has been for over twenty years. Alonso is *his* son. He was born before the records show Alex reached South America. You were right about the age, he's nearly twenty, so he must have been born before your father left Fiji. You said you were six then, didn't you? They run a sleazy boarding-house. Alex just stayed there two nights. But the affair of the mine got a bit of publicity and Rosita's brother is that agent, no less. He's a private eye, specializing in divorce cases – a shady character. They thought they might get something out of an old couple. Right, let them know the bones of that. . . .

'I've seen to it that the authorities will keep an eye on him in future and I scared hell out of Rosita and her husband. But – and this is wonderful news, Anna – I went further inland to this little mining village, tucked away in the mountains. Oh, the poverty there! I found out that during his last two years, Alex was a reformed character. Not just a case of them whitewashing someone who had become a local hero – he really had turned over a new leaf. I'm bringing back proof of that. He had identified with these poor people to such an extent, improving their lot, fighting legal battles for them, that when he died, with the ones he hadn't managed to bring out, although he wasn't a Roman Catholic, special arrangements were made, and he was buried in consecrated ground with the bodies of those who perished with him. That's all you need to tell them, Anna. . . .'

Then he went on, 'Victoria co-operated so they'd think I was staying in Sydney. Tell Kitty and Gilbert that, will you? I should be home on Wednesday. Now I'll speak to Kit and Gilbert.' He paused, added, 'Take care of yourself, won't you? Goodnight, Anna.'

She heard in his voice all the things he mustn't say. Oh, Calum, Calum! She managed to reply: 'The same to you, of course. You're the one in a foreign country. Take no chances, Calum. Goodnight.'

When her grandparents finally turned from the phone, their happiness had to be seen to be believed, but they were both in tears. They all three sat on the couch and rejoiced with each other.

'It's just as if he had come home,' said Kitty, 'as indeed he has, in a very real way. I've never been one who believed anyone was eternally lost – that would be crediting God with less love than human parents – who sometimes grieve more over the lost ones than any, but how wonderful to think that he redeemed himself, paid back the debt he owed to life for a childhood that knew no want. I remember reading during World War Two something the Queen Mother had said – she was the Queen then, of course. That our work is the rent we pay for our room on the earth. So if Alex was able to do just that, in striving for those poor people in his last two years, then he'd feel square with himself ... and I need no longer grieve.'

She was silent for a moment, then said, 'When first we knew he was gone, I wished I could have known in time to have him cremated and his ashes flown here to go beside his forebears' remains in the Crannog kirkyard, but now I'm glad we didn't. It's fitting that his bones should rest in the village of the people he gave his life for.'

Anna slipped out to make them some coffee. Later she would write and tell Mother. Mother had always sorrowed over that seemingly wasted life. She would be glad about this.

The shadow that had lain over Strathallan these past weeks was gone. Calum would come back and perhaps next year he would wed Victoria. Don't, Anna Drummond, shrink from that thought. Don't you remember what Mother said about *her* lonely years when you asked how she'd endured them? 'By taking a day at a time, Anna. You can bear anything for a day at a time. You can't if you think: this will last for ever at this height of pain.'

Victoria, who had collaborated in this with Calum, would probably make rendezvous with him in Auckland or Christchurch, and come back with him. When they arrived there must be no hint of reserve in her gladness at what, together, they had achieved, to give her grandparents peace of mind.

It seemed as if Wednesday would never come. However hopeless the situation as far as her own ultimate happiness seemed, Anna would know joy and relief when Calum was safe home again. So much could happen in these days of lawlessness, of senselessly indiscriminate bombing ... it would be enough to know he was home, and his mission accomplished.

They'd all forgotten to ask what time he would arrive. They worked out that it would probably be about the time of the evening meal. It was a glorious day, but oh, how long to wait! The weeping willow in the lower garden trailed green fingers in the chattering brook waters, ferns sprang crisply from every crevice of its mossy banks, a thousand roses scented the air, lavender added its pungency, sweet peas fluttered like butterflies on the trellises, gypsophila flung bridal mist in the corners, and delphiniums and lark-spur lifted blue spires heavenward.

Anna thought the kitchen garden was a poem in itself. In the frames apple cucumbers were swelling, strawberries offering ambrosial sweetness. Little turf paths ran between the raspberry canes for easy picking, black and redcurrants too hard to pick yet in early December glowed like rubies and jet among the branches, but promised abundance later. Runner beans twisted round rough-barked supports and garlanded them with scarlet flowers. Grandfather spent hours earthing up his leeks and celery, planting out lettuces almost every week for regular succession, kept taking Anna out to see his golden pumpkin flowers, chuckling because they were trying to climb up the ribbonwood trees, bringing in the first of the peas, trying to resist digging the new potatoes.

'Far too early,' said Kitty admonishingly. 'You'd think when a man's lived almost a lifetime in the one place he'd know it was too early. But there's never been a year since we were wed that I've not had to scrub taties as small as marbles, so he can say to his cronies in Crannog, "We lifted the first of our potatoes today." I notice he's never game to ask any of them out to stample the first! They'd laugh him to shame.'

Oh, yes, Gran and Grandy were back to normal, rejoicing in all the small joys of daily living at Strathallan.

They were both weeding in the kitchen garden when the phone rang. Anna flew to it. What if Calum had landed in New Zealand and was phoning to say when to expect him? But it was Victoria's mother. She said, 'Calum will be home today,' and paused, as if she wanted Anna to comment.

Anna said cheerfully, 'Yes, tell me, is Victoria coming back with him?'

A pause. 'Anna, haven't you got a bit addled again? You don't fly to New Zealand from South America via Australia.'

'No, I know. But I thought perhaps Victoria would meet him in Christchurch and fly on down with him.'

'I see. No, she's not coming home yet. I expect you're dying to see Calum, all of you, and get the full story from him. Oh, how glad I am for the Drummonds! Theirs has been the most cruel grief of all. And I hope it has made your mother happy too.'

'Oh, thank you, Mrs. Sherborne. I appreciate that. Yes, it's made us all happy. I'm glad I'm not working today, Wednesdays are my days off. It will be wonderful to hear about my father, how he rehabilitated himself. Not just the spurt of bravery at the end, but real service to people in need. I want to hear it from Calum as he tells it first, to the three of us.'

'That'll be why he made it Wednesday to return.'

'Oh, I think it'd be pure chance. Plus the fact that the earliest he could make connections probably made it a Wednesday arrival here. He's going to be terribly tired after travelling all that distance, especially with time changes and so on. So hard to adjust to.'

Grace said, 'I think he'll have had such a boost in morale to know he's freed Kitty and Gilbert from anxiety that he'll be on top of the world.' She seemed to hesitate, then said with firmness, 'And Anna, when Calum gets home and tells you *everything*, don't allow yourself to retain a single vestige of doubt. It's been a trying time for you, my dear. And I just want to say we all love you for the way you came to Strathallan and made those two dear people there live again. So remember that whatever Calum tells you, I'm with him all the way. Please don't ask me anything about that right now, just remember it when the time comes.'

'Th – thank you, Mrs. Sherborne.' Anna was really bewildered by now. What could she mean? Grace caught the tone and laughed and said, 'Dear Anna, you must think me crazy. Don't ask me what I mean. You'll soon know. Give my love to Kitty and Gilbert.'

She said nothing to her grandparents about this odd behaviour. Kitty had taken a turkey out of the deep freeze, and now, in the afternoon, it was sizzling in the oven. Grandfather was podding the peas, sitting on the step, sheer happiness in his every glance round the smiling garden. Kitty had earlier instructed Anna how to make Calum's favourite pudding with the last bag of redcurrants in the freezer, from last summer. It was quite a complicated one. You lined a greased mould with the thinnest of bread and butter. It took ages to get it to stick perfectly. Then you filled it with stewed currants drained and whipped through an egg custard, capped with more strips of bread, symmetrically arranged, and chilled till stiff, when it had to be carefully unmoulded and served with icecream and whipped cream. He was certainly getting five-star service!

The fatted calf, in fact. Only the prodigal in this story hadn't come home. He had stayed in the far country, and Calum was the messenger bringing the news of the lost one to the ones who had stayed home and longed for his return.

Kitty said happily, 'We must dress up. This is an occasion. I'm sorry Ian and Betty won't be here, but Betty was adamant. She said we'd be able to talk more freely without little ears pricked up, which is true. I shall wear my new blue crimplene.'

'Oh, do, Gran, it's so beautiful with your white hair and blue eyes and pink cheeks. And the little touches of lavender and purple in it make you look like a herbaceous border.'

Kitty's resultant peal of laughter reached her Gilbert's ears on the back step. He smiled to himself. He'd not heard Kitty laugh quite like that since . . . since Alex was a stripling.

Kitty said, 'Anna, wear your white and gold and brown dress. I do love it. And Calum's never seen you in that. You've only started to wear it since the weather got really hot.'

Anna dropped her eyes swiftly. Dress up for Calum? Who was she to do that? But she would, Kitty wanted to make this an occasion.

The shower was cool against her skin. She picked up a shaker of sandalwood talcum. It suited this dress somehow. She dabbed skin perfume to match at her ears, her wrists, and brushed out the gold layers of her hair till it shone like spun gossamer, gilded by some alchemist.

She stepped carefully into the cream dress, ran downstairs to have Gran zip it up. It was sleeveless with a plain round neck and had a dropped waistline, with box pleats forming a tiny skirt. Printed tricel in big splashes of gold and orange and brown formed patch pockets above that hipline, and epaulettes at the shoulder, fastened with gold buttons. Over it she dropped a fijian necklace of shells in all shades of brown, and clasped a bulky copper bracelet about her tanned wrist. She was so brown now, one could see a faint golden down on her arms bleached by the sun.

Gilbert was bringing in the peas. He caught her to him, kissed her. 'Eh, lass, but you're like summer itself. What a season for Strathallan, my Anna!'

She kissed him back, her strong young arms hugging him. He added: 'The mail's come at last. I saw dust at the end of the drive as he took off. I'll away down for it.'

'Oh, I'll go. You go and put your best duds on too, Grandy. I'd love a walk, it will fill in the time.'

Kitty and Gilbert watched her go, then turned to smile at each other.

Anna sauntered, delighting in the feel of the grass on the verge, cool against her toes in the thonged sandals she was wearing. The hawthorn blossom had long since faded. If you looked very closely you could see the tiny beginnings of the berries that would redden the avenue all next autumn and winter.

Beyond her and above her the hills were clothed in the tussocky-gold of Central Otago Decembers. Above her a lark sang in the sky, symbol of summer happiness, so high it couldn't be seen, yet its song trilled over all Strathallan and beyond.

This was *her* land, born and bred in her; that skyline, that horizon, that intersecting of trees and streams, the flocks that grazed, were her heritage through a father who had redeemed himself and paid his debt to the world he had lived in. It had to be enough. How could she ask for more?

She drew out the mail. Lots of window envelopes, no doubt receipts for the cheques Grandy had posted off recently. There was a letter for Calum, and the name on the back meant it was from Doug Fenton, who'd given them that blue-and-gold day at the sea all those weeks ago. That one day that had been all hers, to remember always.

Two letters for her, from friends in Suva, one from Auntie Edna, and ... why, this one bore a London postmark. The writing was vaguely familiar. But she knew no one in London. She turned it over and stared, grew still. *It was from Victoria.*

She didn't know why she began to shake. She looked round, saw the octagonal seat round the third hawthorn along and went across to it. She put the other letters down, carefully weighted them against the breeze, with a stone, then slowly began to prise the envelope open. How could a letter from Victoria bear a Heathrow postmark?

The address was merely the name of the jumbo jet in which she was flying from Los Angeles to Heathrow.

'Dearest Anna,

I know you'll be surprised to hear from me away up in the clouds, unless the situation has been too much for my lady mother and she's rushed over to Strathallan to tell you. I was speaking to her by phone before I left Sydney. I'm spending the hours I cannot bear to sleep up here, in writing you. Otherwise I'm going to be so consumed with impatience to get to my journey's end I'll be a wreck when I get there, and if ever I want to be at my best, it's then.

'Anna, I broke it off with Calum, by letter, from Sydney, some time ago I'd been trying to do it for ages, but knowing how I'd felt when Blair jilted me, I couldn't bring myself to do that to Calum. Long before you came to Strathallan, I was trying to screw up my courage. He and I just drifted into that engagement. He took me round out of sheer compassion after Blair went away – did it for years. I think I clung to him because I could see Blair in him, which was hardly fair to Calum.

'Maybe some people can settle for second-best, but not me. I'm an all-or-nothing person. Nobody else had ever got Calum going ... I had it borne in on me more and more than I was cheating him too. That he ought to have the chance to find out if there was someone, somewhere, he could *really* love.

'I was away when you arrived at Strathallan, much longer than I needed to be. I'd wanted to think things out, to come to a decision. And of course, as always when I was with Calum, I felt I couldn't do it to him. But that night, when you in some way brought Philip and Sophy together, I saw Calum look at you. And something in his voice as you two laughed and teased each other filled me with hope. I thought if I waited just a little, Calum might by then know his own heart more – would realize that ours had been a very milk-and-water affair.

'But I still couldn't find the courage to break it off. It's so hard to do these things face to face. The other one interrupts all the time. I'd a pretty strong feeling by then that he'd only be glad, but a chap can't show relief to a girl. He'd feel caddish. So I did it by letter, from Sydney. Oh, Anna, I'm so glad Calum didn't tell me, when he first knew, that Blair was a widower. If he had, I wouldn't have had the courage to break it off. It would have seemed as if I was doing it so I could be free to marry his brother.

'When Calum got my letter, he rang me – from Alexandra Post Office, so no one would know – and told me about Blair. And he was so generous – told me that his mother had written him to ask if he would go across there to see her, but to say nothing to me. She wanted to ask him face-to-face if he really loved me as one ought to love a wife-to-be. She'd always thought he didn't. But the main reason was this: When she asked Blair why on earth he hadn't told them about Yvette, he told her that he'd wanted to let a year elapse before he told *me*. During that year he wanted to prove he *could* manage as a solo parent so I could never think he'd asked me to marry him for a mother for his children.

'He had the letter half written to me to tell me and to ask me to come to him in England when he heard Calum and I had become engaged. So, Anna, I'm on my way to my true destiny. Blair's found his niche in life. I'll stay in England with him. I can probably do a bit of my own work round there. It would help financially. But mostly I just want to look after Blair and small Beth and Michael.

'But I've been so afraid you might wonder all sorts of things. I told Calum (he confessed he loved you) not to ask you too quickly, in case you thought he'd proposed to you on the rebound. That wouldn't be true. I do so hope that you get this before he gets back from the Argentine. I'm a great believer . . . or hoper . . . in journeys ending in lovers' meetings. That it will be that way for me and Blair, and for you and Calum. Knowing Calum, I'm quite sure that he'd never let a glimmer of his feeling for you escape him while he was still engaged to me, but he told me on the phone that when he met you, he *knew*. So *please*, Anna, don't let any thoughts of his prior engagement cloud any of the happiness you so richly deserve. Oh, how happy your grandparents will be! And Anna, may we remain the best of friends? Please write to me, always.

'The dawn is coming up over Ireland, all rosy-pink and pearly with mist . . . the clouds have parted now. My seat-mate has just told me that the lough below is Killarney. Now we're across the Welsh hills. Isn't air travel wonderful? . . . I'm looking south, and somewhere there, in the beech woods that Blair's mother has described, Blair is waiting. Oh, you and Calum must have a trip over here, bringing Kitty and Gilbert with you, and stay with us. I'm as sure as that. But pray for me, Anna, that it *is* like that. Oh, the patchwork of fields, the silver glimmer of rivers that till now have just been names in a geography book! Anna, I'll stick this down now. I'll post it at Heathrow. May it speed to you on the wings of prayer. Love, and God bless you both,

Victoria.'

Anna sat gazing into space, dazed. You are dazed when happiness has just been handed to you in a sealed envelope. She looked down at that envelope, touched it caressingly. Calum hadn't needed to go to England to sort things out, after all. But he'd been prepared, would have had his immunizations, his passport. He'd only have needed to get a South American visa, once he'd decided to go to the Argentine.

This, then, was what Victoria's mother must have meant. Victoria must have rung her before setting off. Oh, what dear, dear people. The vagueness departed and other memories crystalized. Victoria's mother saying both her children were tarred with the one brush, like their father, 'Once they love, they love for keeps.' Not only Philip, but Victoria too. Now she could look back on things with joy, not with a faint feeling of guilt . . . the sunrise-to-sunset day Calum had given her; the way he had washed her feet that night to warm them; the way he had taken her chin in his hands after that involuntary kiss when she was looking for the divorce papers, and had looked his fill in a renunciatory farewell to all that might have been and couldn't be, because of Victoria.

She was still smiling over the memories when a car swept round the bend, up to, and across the cattle-stops, before it came to a squealing stop at the third hawthorn. She was on her feet, the pages of the letter falling unheeded to the grass.

It was like a miracle. He was leaping out, tall, craggy, broad, smiling ... how could she ever have thought him forbidding?

The sunlight was in those Highland blue eyes, she saw a white flash in his tanned face as his smile broadened, took in the scattered pages ... he said, 'I like a woman who smiles to herself when she thinks she's alone ... Oh, Anna, Anna, dare I hope that letter is from Victoria?'

'Yes, oh yes, Calum. I've just read it, my darling. Oh, Calum, Calum, Calum!'

Just as well this wasn't a main road, because any passer-by might have been forgiven for imagining he was watching something on a television screen, not on a country road in Central Otago. They kissed and kissed again, drew apart, then closed together again, touched each other's faces, all quite incredulously.

Then Calum laughed. 'My love, we'd better pick these pages up. That breeze is blowing them about. Imagine if some busybody came along and picked them up! Or would it matter? Come to think of it, we're going to have some explaining to do before we dare announce our engagement in the *Central Otago News*. How on earth can we do it without telling it over and over? Oh, I have it. We'll go over to see Mrs. de Paget tomorrow. Bridie would love to be the first outside the family to know it. Before the end of the week all Crannog, Roxburgh and Alexandra will know.'

Anna said reproachfully, 'Why didn't you tell me before you went flying off to South America, Calum?

He laughed. 'Sweetheart, did you really think I could bear to squash a proposal into half an hour before I had to pack? Besides, I wasn't sure I could even convince you that Victoria had done this of her own free will. You're such an addled-Anna at times. I thought if I had to rush explanations you'd have all sorts of doubts while I was away ... you'd think I'd somehow let Victoria see I loved *you*. And I just couldn't bear to put six thousand miles of ocean between us if we'd been at cross-purposes. Apart from that, I'd so much on my mind, with this business about your father. Anna, I've the best present in the world for your grandparents here.'

She still had hold of his arm as if she were frightened her happiness might dissolve in a cloud and disappear. She said, 'What is it? A photo of the memorial they'd put up to Dad, recording his bravery?'

'No, at least I have, but this other is far, far better. It will be poignant for them, but I hope it will also give them great joy. I want them to go away quite by themselves to read it. It's a letter your father wrote them, the day he was killed. He tells them about his rehabilitation in it, that when first he came to himself, and began thinking of others, he felt he had to make good before he got in touch with them. He didn't want them to think this was just another wild enthusiasm that he'd take up and drop. And by the time he'd spent two years there, trying to improve the lot of these very poor people in Latin America – and succeeding in much of it – he knew this was his destiny.

'He mentioned that he'd deserted a wife and child, that she had divorced him and he hoped she had found happiness again, and if so, he would never disturb her, but he asked his parents' pardon for all the grief he'd caused them, and hoped they would forgive him. He would come home for a visit, when he could leave these people. He finished it, but had only got as far as 'Mr. and Mrs. Gilbert—' on the envelope, when he must have been called out to the disaster in the mine.

'He'd lodged with a dear old lady in the village. But she had only the few words of English he had taught her, and didn't realize this letter was for his parents. She took the Gilbert for a surname, and didn't know what to do with it. She put it inside his Bible, and put it beside her little statue of the Virgin Mary on a little shrine she had in her home. It had a candle each side. She thought that someday, if it was the will of the Lord, someone would come seeking it. She said she prayed for that every day. Let's go and take it to them now, Anna. Perhaps we will tell them this, before our news, what do you think?'

'Yes, Calum, because they will weep a little, naturally, then it will make them very happy when they realize that you and I will be living at—' She stopped, looked almost indignant, said, 'Calum Doig! You said you didn't think half an hour before you left for South America was time for a proposal. Well, my lad, let me remind you, you haven't proposed yet! How am I to know you were meaning marriage?'

He gave a great burst of laughter, scooped her up, said, 'You're just shameless, then, talking about living with me before I've had a chance to tell you I love you and want to marry you. Oh, Anna, you've got me addled too. But I'm damned if I'll ask you now. What an anti-climax that'd be! Besides, how stupid, when I've already bought my wedding present for you.'

Her lips parted, she stared, 'You – you've bought my wedding present before you – oh, I suppose you saw some jewellery in South America and thought you'd never have the chance to buy that sort of thing again and—'

'Jewellery nothing! I bought it at Momona Airport before I left New Zealand.'

'Momona? But what have they got except a few paperbacks and postcards?'

'I bought it by phone. I got it from Doug Fenton. It has four walls and a verandah from which you can see sunrise and noon and sunset. It faces the open sea ... it now has welcome written on the mat for you, for our children ... they're all bound to love the sea. We're going to honeymoon there ... Anna, can't you guess?'

She looked as a child might look beholding a Christmas tree for the first time. 'Calum, you can't mean – you mean you've bought Captain Bluenose's darling house for us? Oh, Calum, how wonderful, but can you afford it? It's like a dream ... Strathallan to live in, the Captain's house for holidays. Oh, there's a letter for you here from Doug. But—'

'But me no buts. It's not all ours yet. I've paid a good deposit on it, that's all. We'll have to hope wool prices hold – the last few years they've gone up and down like a seesaw – I heard some time ago that Doug was getting a transfer to Auckland. He's bought a residence in one of the bays up there. He'd rather sell to me than to anyone, he said, because he knows I love it and that way any time they want a holiday down south, they can have the loan of it. Anna, did you hear what I said? We're going to honeymoon in it. Before long, too – February. We don't do much harvesting, so we'll be able to get away then. Philip and Sophy are having theirs in January. Sophy can marry us when they get back, and Philip and Ian can manage on their own here in February. Your mother and stepfather must come over for the wedding. We'll ring them tonight. *And* we'll ring Mother and Blair and Victoria.'

Anna was laughing helplessly. 'Calum, you're sweeping me along! We'll never get that beach-house paid off if you keep ringing all over the world.'

'Oh, what matter? This is a once-in-a-lifetime occasion. Of course we'll ring them. My lady mother has been in mental turmoil for too long, torn between the separate happinesses of her two sons. Oh, lord, I forgot. Perhaps a letter would explain it better to your mother and Magnus. How could we possible explain that Victoria and I have broken up, and we've got engaged, all in the one call?'

Now it was Anna's turn to reassure. 'Oh, that part wouldn't matter. I never did tell them you were engaged to Victoria. In fact,' the dimples showed, 'I hardly mentioned you at all beyond saying if you got married, we'd retire to the Annexe. I was afraid to say much about you in case Mother read between the lines.'

Calum was mightily relieved. 'We'll just tell them when they come for the wedding. Now for Kit and Gilbert. Don't forget, we'll tell them about Alex first, then I'll feel the best comes last. After we do that I'll ring Dad and get him to come over.'

They were therefore astonished as they got out at the terrace steps and looked up to the front door, to find Kitty and Gilbert standing there, hand-in-hand, knowledge in their smiling eyes.

As Calum and Anna reached them they burst out laughing. 'Made it at last, have you, Calum?' said Gilbert Drummond. 'Well, you two have sure taken a long time to get *your* wires uncrossed.'

It wasn't often Calum Doig looked winded. Then he managed, 'But how could you know?'

Kitty, her eyes blue as forget-me-nots above her blue dress, said softly, 'Grace Sherborne came over here one day Anna was on duty. She was so happy for you, Anna, for Victoria and Blair, and for your mother, Calum. Victoria had written her. We thought you'd never come home from Australia, Calum, but instead of that, you were in South

America, restoring Alex to us, in pride and love. . . .'

It was much later. Alex's letter had been read, wept over, rejoiced over. Plans had been made. Kitty had whisked Anna upstairs to find with joy that her own wedding-dress, carefully packed away, fitted her; the calls had been put through to Hong Kong, to Haslemere. There had been a gathering of the clans at Strathallan for after-dinner coffee and congratulations.

Calum's father had arrived, beaming, whispered into Anna's ear, 'You're certainly the girl I'd have picked for Calum,' and had joined in the lengthy international call to his wife, his son, his grandchildren, and to Victoria, his new daughter-in-law-to-be. Grace and Henry Sherborne had spoken to them all too. Gilbert had said, 'Spare no expense. This is all on me. What a night for Strathallan!'

Lois and Magnus, because they had known nothing of the undercurrents of pain that had underlain this betrothal, were wholeheartedly excited and assured them nothing would stop them from coming over in February for the wedding.

Maggie didn't wait to be asked to be a junior bridesmaid. She just announced that she'd rather be that than a flower-girl. 'That's kid's stuff,' she said firmly. Betty began to protest it was manners to wait till you were asked, but Anna silenced her. 'It will be quite novel to have mother and daughter for bridal attendants.'

Betty gasped. 'Me? Matron of honour? Why, I thought I was past all that.'

Ian looked at her fondly. 'You don't look a day older than when I married you.'

Betty said, laughing, but flushed with pleasure, 'I've a feeling that marriage turns men into practised liars. But I like it.'

Bill and Mac hurriedly said to leave them out of it. They wouldn't be page-boys for anything. Anna said, finally, to the others. 'Stop teasing them. No self-respecting tough hombres like these two could possibly fancy being pages!'

Bill beamed on her, then said anxiously, 'It won't change you, will it, Anna?'

'What won't change me?'

'Marrying him.' He indicated his uncle with scant respect.

Mac explained, 'We're scared you won't let her go climbing trees again and turning cartwheels and things.'

186

'I'll still let her,' promised Calum gravely, 'though her prowess in some things still surprises me. I've never seen her turning cartwheels. I'm constantly learning.'

Gilbert chuckled. 'You always will. That's me with Kitty. It hasn't stopped yet. Never a dull moment with Anna of Strathallan as your wife, I'll warrant.'

'I think that too,' said Calum softly, looking at Anna.

Ian said, 'Look, I've got to ask this or I'll die of curiosity *When* did you propose, Calum? We saw the dust of your car, heard you come over the cattle-stops, and just half an hour later Kitty was on the phone to us with the news. I mean, the night I asked Betty to marry me, it took me two and a half hours to screw up my courage to do it and then she had the nerve to tell me she thought I was never going to get round to it!'

They all laughed, and then Anna said indignantly, 'Ian, he hasn't done it yet! Talk about being taken for granted!' The pansy-brown eyes above the cream and gold and brown of her dress were alight with laughter, belying the rueful sound of that declaration.

Calum said, 'I think I'll have to rectify this or I'll have it cast up to me for the rest of my life. There's a crescent moon outside. It will be shining down on Blue Spur and reflecting in Crannog Dam. Ideal pleace for a proposal, if proposal she must have. I'm sorry the daffodils and lily-of-the-valley are over, Anna. You'll have to put up with buttercups. There's a sheet of them in that field now.'

Philip looked wicked, nudged Sophy. 'Better watch it, Anna, there's a heavy dew tonight. Don't I remember the fact you don't like getting your feet wet! Better propose on the terrace, Calum.'

'Ah, bah!' said Anna, getting up and holding out a hand to Calum, 'when there's a moon over Crannog, who cares for wet feet?'

A silence fell over the entire company as they heard their footsteps fading down the path.

Calum's father raised his glass again. 'The last toast of all,' he said, 'even if they aren't here to share it.' He smiled at Kitty and Gilbert Drummond as they sat, hand in hand, on the couch.

'To Strathallan . . . to generations yet unborn . . . and may they never again, Anna and Calum, have to gang warily.

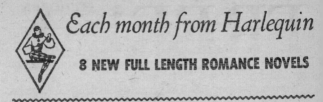

Each month from Harlequin

8 NEW FULL LENGTH ROMANCE NOVELS

Listed below are the last three months' releases:

1897 WESTHAMPTON ROYAL, Sheila Douglas
1898 FIREBIRD, Rebecca Stratton
1899 WINDS FROM THE SEA, Margaret Pargeter
1900 MOONRISE OVER THE MOUNTAINS, Lilian Peake
1901 THE BLUE JACARANDA, Elizabeth Hoy
1902 THE MAN AT THE HELM, Henrietta Reid
1903 COUNTRY OF THE VINE, Mary Wibberley
1904 THE CORNISH HEARTH, Isobel Chace
1905 TABITHA IN MOONLIGHT, Betty Neels
1906 TAKE BACK YOUR LOVE, Katrina Britt
1907 ENCHANTMENT IN BLUE, Flora Kidd
1908 A TOUCH OF HONEY, Lucy Gillen
1909 THE SHIFTING SANDS, Kay Thorpe
1910 CANE MUSIC, Joyce Dingwell
1911 STORMY HARVEST, Janice Gray
1912 THE SPANISH INHERITANCE, Elizabeth Hunter
1913 THE FLIGHT OF THE HAWK, Rebecca Stratton
1914 FLOWERS IN STONY PLACES, Marjorie Lewty
1915 EAST TO BARRYVALE, Yvonne Whittal
1916 WHEELS OF CONFLICT, Sue Peters
1917 ANNA OF STRATHALLAN, Essie Summers
1918 THE PLAYER KING, Elizabeth Ashton
1919 JUST A NICE GIRL, Mary Burchell
1920 HARBOUR OF DECEIT, Roumelia Lane

PLEASE NOTE: All Harlequin Romances from #1857 onwards are 75c. Books prior to that number, **where available** are priced at 60c through Harlequin Reader Service until December 31st, 1975.

These titles are available at your local bookseller, or through the Harlequin Reader Service, M.P.O. Box 707, Niagara Falls, N.Y. 14302; Canadian address 649 Ontario St., Stratford, Ont. N5A 6W4.

U

FREE! Harlequin Romance Catalogue

Here is a wonderful opportunity to read many of the Harlequin Romances you may have missed.

The HARLEQUIN ROMANCE CATALOGUE lists hundreds of titles that may possibly no longer be available at your local bookseller. To receive your copy, just fill out the coupon below, mail it to us, and we'll rush your catalogue to you!

Following this page you'll find a sampling of a few of the Harlequin Romances listed in the catalogue. Should you wish to order any of these immediately, kindly check the titles desired and mail with coupon.

PLEASE NOTE: Harlequin Romance Catalogue of available titles is revised every three months.

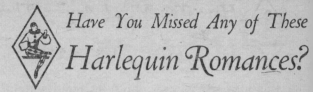

Have You Missed Any of These
Harlequin Romances?

- [ ] 427 NURSE BROOKES
  Kate Norway
- [ ] 438 MASTER OF SURGERY
  Alex Stuart
- [ ] 446 TO PLEASE THE DOCTOR
  Marjorie Moore
- [ ] 458 NEXT PATIENT, DOCTOR
  ANNE, Elizabeth Gilzean
- [ ] 468 SURGEON OF DISTINCTION
  Mary Burchell
- [ ] 469 MAGGY, Sara Seale
- [ ] 486 NURSE CARIL'S NEW POST
  Caroline Trench
- [ ] 487 THE HAPPY ENTERPRISE
  Eleanor Farnes
- [ ] 491 NURSE TENNANT
  Elizabeth Hoy
- [ ] 494 LOVE IS MY REASON
  Mary Burchell
- [ ] 495 NURSE WITH A DREAM
  Norrey Ford
- [ ] 503 NURSE IN CHARGE
  Elizabeth Gilzean
- [ ] 504 PETER RAYNAL, SURGEON
  Marjorie Moore
- [ ] 584 VILLAGE HOSPITAL
  Margaret Malcolm
- [ ] 599 RUN AWAY FROM LOVE
  Jean S. Macleod
  (Original Harlequin title
  "Nurse Companion")
- [ ] 631 DOCTOR'S HOUSE
  Dorothy Rivers
- [ ] 647 JUNGLE HOSPITAL
  Juliet Shore
- [ ] 672 GREGOR LOTHIAN, SURGEON
  Joan Blair
- [ ] 683 DESIRE FOR THE STAR
  Averill Ives
  (Original Harlequin title
  "Doctor's Desire")
- [ ] 744 VERENA FAYRE, PROBA-
  TIONER, Valerie K. Nelson
- [ ] 745 TENDER NURSE, Hilda Nickson
- [ ] 757 THE PALM-THATCHED
  HOSPITAL, Juliet Shore
- [ ] 758 HELPING DOCTOR MEDWAY
  Jan Haye
- [ ] 764 NURSE ANN WOOD
  Valerie K. Nelson
- [ ] 771 NURSE PRUE IN CEYLON
  Gladys Fullbrook
- [ ] 772 CHLOE WILDE, STUDENT
  NURSE, Joan Turner
- [ ] 787 THE TWO FACES OF NURSE
  ROBERTS, Nora Sanderson
- [ ] 790 SOUTH TO THE SUN
  Betty Beaty
- [ ] 794 SURGEON'S RETURN
  Hilda Nickson
- [ ] 812 FACTORY NURSE   Hilary Neal
- [ ] 825 MAKE UP YOUR MIND NURSE
  Phyllis Matthewman
- [ ] 841 TRUANT HEART
  Patricia Fenwick
  (Original Harlequin title
  "Doctor in Brazil")
- [ ] 858 MY SURGEON NEIGHBOUR
  Jane Arbor
- [ ] 873 NURSE JULIE OF WARD
  THREE   Joan Callender
- [ ] 878 THIS KIND OF LOVE
  Kathryn Blair
- [ ] 890 TWO SISTERS
  Valerie K. Nelson
- [ ] 897 NURSE HILARY'S HOLIDAY
  TASK, Jan Haye
- [ ] 900 THERE CAME A SURGEON
  Hilda Pressley
- [ ] 901 HOPE FOR TOMORROW
  Anne Weale
- [ ] 902 MOUNTAIN OF DREAMS
  Barbara Rowan
- [ ] 903 SO LOVED AND SO FAR
  Elizabeth Hoy
- [ ] 907 HOMECOMING HEART
  Joan Blair
  (Original Harlequin title
  "Two for the Doctor")
- [ ] 909 DESERT DOORWAY
  Pamela Kent
- [ ] 911 RETURN OF SIMON
  Celine Conway
- [ ] 912 THE DREAM AND THE
  DANCER, Eleanor Farnes
- [ ] 919 DEAR INTRUDER
  Jane Arbor
- [ ] 936 TIGER HALL
  Esther Wyndham

PLEASE NOTE: All Harlequin Romances from #1857 onwards are 75c. Books prior to that number, **where available** are priced at 60c through Harlequin Reader Service until December 31st, 1975.

AAA

Have You Missed Any of These
Harlequin Romances?

Have You Missed Any of These
Harlequin Romances?

CCC